Moontide

Also by Stella Cameron in Large Print:

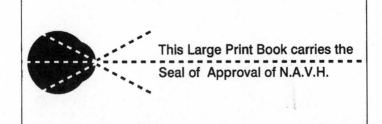

This Large Print Book carries the
Seal of Approval of N.A.V.H.

Moontide

Stella Cameron

WHEELER
PUBLISHING

Published in 2005 by arrangement with Harlequin Books S.A.

Wheeler Large Print Romance.

The text of this Large Print edition is unabridged.
Other aspects of the book may vary from the original edition.

Set in 16 pt. Plantin by Elena Picard.

Printed in the United States on permanent paper.

Library of Congress Cataloging-in-Publication Data

Cameron, Stella.
    Moontide / by Stella Cameron.
      p. cm. — (Wheeler publishing large print romance)
    ISBN 1-58724-948-0 (lg. print : hc : alk. paper)
    1. Loss (Psychology) — Fiction. 2. Physicians — Fiction.
  3. England — Fiction. 4. Large type books. I. Title.
  II. Wheeler large print romance series.
  PS3553.A4345M66 2005
    813′.54—dc22   2005000379

Moontide

As the Founder/CEO of NAVH, the only national health agency solely devoted to those who, although not totally blind, have an eye disease which could lead to serious visual impairment, I am pleased to recognize Thorndike Press* as one of the leading publishers in the large print field.

Founded in 1954 in San Francisco to prepare large print textbooks for partially seeing children, NAVH became the pioneer and standard setting agency in the preparation of large type.

Today, those publishers who meet our standards carry the prestigious "Seal of Approval" indicating high quality large print. We are delighted that Thorndike Press is one of the publishers whose titles meet these standards. We are also pleased to recognize the significant contribution Thorndike Press is making in this important and growing field.

Lorraine H. Marchi, L.H.D.
Founder/CEO
NAVH

* Thorndike Press encompasses the following imprints: Thorndike, Wheeler, Walker and Large Print Press.

Prologue

Blue light pulsed across the darkened corridor from windows high in the wall. The
wailing siren slurred to an echo and died.
Andrew stood still for a moment and rubbed
his eyes. God, he was tired. Emergency must
be busy tonight. Summer always brought
visitors streaming from the industrial re-
gions of England to the south coast. With
them came an increased rash of accidents.
He'd heard the familiar sounds of controlled
drama again and again while he worked on
the Beckett baby.

Why? The question swirled in his head.
Damn it all, why hadn't he been able to
save her? For three weeks the tiny child
had hung on, and just when he thought
success was only a matter of time, she gave
up. Andrew sat on the edge of a chair just
inside the double doors leading out of the
premature-infant unit.

The usual response to learning he was a

pediatrician often ran along the lines of "It must be fun dealing with kids. I don't think I could stand all the misery of older people and dying every day." He slid back and rested his head against the wall. Did they think one had to be old to die? Or was it supposed to be easier to watch eyes close for the last time if they had never seen much? Once he had thought there could be only joy in helping children, and it was true, except when he failed.

It was almost midnight. Greer Beckett would be asleep by now. Andrew pressed his lips together and felt the muscles in his jaw quiver. Hadn't it been enough for a twenty-four-year-old to watch her husband die in a car crash that had also left her with a smashed hip? A few hours after the accident Greer went into labor and her condition demanded immediate cesarean section. Any fetus delivered two months prematurely was a high risk. But this one had been a fighter, and she had almost made it.

Earlier in the day he had visited the young American woman to give a good report on little Colleen. He flinched. When Greer said what name she'd chosen for her daughter, even the blasé nurse in the room sniffled. Colin had been the husband's name. Now Andrew supposed Colleen would be buried close to her father in an English churchyard, thousands of miles from the Becketts' Seattle home.

Andrew wanted to see Greer. Unfamiliar smarting in his eyes made him blink. All the study and training, the years of practice, hadn't been able to stop him from losing Greer Beckett's child. It was no one's fault, yet he felt responsible.

You care about the woman. Andrew stood and swept through the doors. The impact of metal pressure plates against his thrusting wrists stung. *You wish this was another time and place, and that you were in it with her. The rule, Monthaven, remember the golden rule — never become personally involved with a patient.*

He turned the corner and punched a button on the elevator panel. Exhaustion was making him rummy. Greer Beckett was alone in a foreign country. It was natural for him to feel sympathetic and drawn to her. The elevator doors slid open and he stepped inside. Glaring white light made him squint. Andrew didn't remember why the Becketts were in Dorset County. Must simply have been on vacation. Each one's passport had borne the other's name as an emergency contact. Greer insisted that neither had any family to be notified. She said she did have a younger sister in the States, but wouldn't allow the hospital to call her. "Casey would try to come. We'll manage. By the time we get back the worst will be over." "We" had meant she and the baby.

Greer had written one letter that Andrew offered to mail. She commented that it was business. Sent to a Josh Field, the envelope showed no return address. She was strong, determined to get through this ordeal alone. He prayed silently that she would prove strong enough after tonight.

The elevator ground slightly before it jolted to a stop on the third floor of the Dorchester Medical Center. Andrew headed for the nurses' station, then hesitated, staring at a sign on the desk that read Surgical Unit. She was bound to be asleep. Better wait until tomorrow.

"Hello, Dr. Monthaven. You're off your beaten track tonight."

Andrew stared. "Yes." He fingered the stethoscope that still hung around his neck and smiled back at a student nurse whose face he didn't recall. Just a kid. Bright. All pink and white and optimistic.

The girl tucked a wisp of blond hair behind her ear. "Dr. Monthaven . . . ?" A puzzled frown clouded earnest blue eyes.

"It's okay, nurse. Carry on. I don't need

any assistance." He strode purposefully past, catching her bemused expression. During her next coffee break, "that dishy Dr. Monthaven" would be the main topic. Andrew grimaced. At some point, being eligible, single and, as he knew he was frequently described by the female staff, a dish had lost appeal. Tonight he felt closer to a hundred than thirty-three. And the only woman he wished would look at him with even a spark of interest was recovering from surgery in one of the rooms ahead. *Was he losing his mind?*

Certainly his behavior was irrational. Coming up here in the middle of the night proved that. What did he intend to do? Leave a note beside her while she slept? *Dear Mrs. Beckett. I didn't want to wake you, but I thought you'd like to know that your little girl died at 11:07 p.m.* We did our best. Very sorry —

Andrew halted. He tried to take a breath and felt it lodge at the top of his lungs. Down the hall, a pale wedge of light painted the tiled floor outside her door. Greer must be awake.

In the seconds that followed he felt his blood drain away, then rush back to pound in his ears. This *was* personal, and he knew it. He'd been in practice too long, watched people die too often, to react so passionately for any other reason.

The first time he saw Greer Beckett he'd been struck by her smallness. He was accustomed to towering over most women, and many men, and Greer had been lying down. But when he came to talk to her about Colleen, a few hours after delivery, the almost boyish figure outlined through the sheets had made him feel like a giant. A tangle of dark red curls tumbled over the pillow, and huge blue eyes contrasted brilliantly with her pallid, bruised face. And despite the contusions and the anguish in those lovely eyes, something about her had touched Andrew in a way he had never thought possible. He had wished she was his, that Colleen was his and that he could insulate them both from any more pain.

That had been three weeks ago. Three weeks that almost made him forget what his world was like before Greer Beckett became part of it. He had invented reasons to visit her frequently. And every moment they spent together intensified his protective urge. Her strength seemed to keep pace with her baby's valiant fight for survival, as if they unknowingly spurred each other on toward life.

He walked forward slowly, concentrating

on his own footfalls. The fleeting temptation to turn back came and went. There would never be a good time to do what must be done. The tenth step brought him into the slice of light from Greer's room. Andrew grasped the doorknob in one broad hand and looked into the room.

Rather than being in bed as he expected, she sat in a chair by the window, gazing into the blackness outside. Her right leg stretched out, she balanced most of her slight weight on her left hip. For several days she had been walking with the aid of crutches but she still tired quickly. The surgeon whose care Greer was under had mentioned how determined she was, but that he would prefer her not to push too hard.

She raised her head and Andrew saw her jump. He glanced up at the window and realized she had seen his reflection in the glass.

"Didn't mean to startle you, Mrs. Beckett." He thought of her as Greer, but had never spoken her first name aloud.

She turned her head. "Hi. Fellow insomniac, or are you so dedicated you never go home?" Her gentle smile revealed even white teeth. Americans always seemed to have marvelous teeth, he thought irrelevantly.

"Neither," he said, "just busy." That wasn't what he should have said. It wouldn't help to fence.

"Up here?"

"No. I came to see you. I just got off duty."

She cleared her throat and smiled again. "You've been very good to me, Dr. Monthaven. Come and sit down."

He went to stand in front of her. His every nerve, every muscle was tightly coiled. Suddenly he felt so awake that the air seemed to sing about him. Andrew couldn't sit. He studied Greer, ignoring the question in her glistening eyes.

Her russet hair was no longer matted, but brushed into glossy waves and curls that reached her shoulders. Color had returned to her perfect, softly bowed mouth, and her skin was creamy, dotted with a fine sprinkling of freckles across her cheeks and nose. Livid suture marks emphasized a small scar above her right eyebrow, but the bruising below the eye had faded, and all the swelling had disappeared. She wore only a hospital gown and her small firm breasts rose and fell beneath the thin fabric. Her right leg and hip were immobilized in a walking cast but the left leg, which was amply revealed, confirmed she was indeed slender and finely boned.

Tinkling music snapped his mind into sharp focus. She held the music box he'd given her for Colleen, and must have turned the base unconsciously as she waited for him to speak. "Brahms Lullaby." Flowers would have been too obvious. The Hummel box had been a perfect solution, apparently intended for the mother to wind up for her child: secretly designed to be touched by the woman and, perhaps, to remind her of the giver.

Andrew drove his long fingers into his dark hair and kept them there. He pivoted away sharply. "I've got to tell you this."

"Yes." The single word was almost inaudible.

"Colleen." Andrew faced Greer and for a ghastly instant he thought he might cry before he could finish. "She didn't make it. Her heart just stopped. We tried to start it again for over an hour, but . . ." He paused, horrified by the slow transformation in the woman's features. Then he rushed on. "This happens sometimes, and we're never a hundred percent sure why. The lungs are bound to be immature, and the circulatory system. But she'd been off support for over a week — totally on her own. Everything looked so good. Seven months is the most critical time where the respiratory system's concerned. And the strain can catch up with the baby's heart, even when you think you're home free." Andrew only had to look at Greer to know nothing he could say would help now.

Her pupils had dilated and the skin on her face had stretched taut and shiny over the bones. With exaggerated care she set the music box on the windowsill and started to push herself upright.

"Sit still. Please." Andrew went to touch her but she instantly rejected him. "Please," he repeated, crossing his arms to restrain the urge to hold her.

She dragged and shoved until she stood, the top of her head not even level with his shoulders. Then she met his eyes. "You said she was fine." Her voice was as stretched taut as the rest of her. "This afternoon, you told me Colleen was thriving. You said that."

"She was, Greer, she was. I can't explain what happened, but it's always a possibility, even when the child seems to be gaining strength. She didn't suffer — just slipped away. You'll have other children." The platitudes, like her first name, rolled out thoughtlessly.

"And that will put everything right? Will

I find another man to replace Colin, too? Well, for your information Dr. . . . Monthaven, I don't want anyone else. I want to be where they are. I want to die."

Before Andrew could react, she lunged at the bedside table, sweeping a water carafe to the floor. The glass exploded, fragments and clear liquid sparkling like a million tears. Greer's hand closed convulsively around a small vase of yellow carnations. He expected her to throw it. Instead she squeezed it tightly, and crumpled the flowers in her fist.

"Greer, please."

She jerked to face him and overbalanced. Her short fingernails scratched the skin at the open neck of his shirt and dragged at the hair. The stethoscope dug into his flesh before it slithered down among the glass. He supported her waist, felt how his fingers almost met around her. For an instant they stood there, Greer's breathing coming in short gasps before the last of her frail energy ebbed and she sagged, clutching the lapels of his white jacket.

Andrew wrapped his arms around her, his hands touching satiny flesh where the gown gaped at the back. Trembling shook her body in violent waves and all he could do was hold on, crooning meaningless words into her hair. She smelled like the roses in his own gardens when the breeze off the ocean moved their lush petals. Each tiny move she made, deepened his awakened longing for her. But she would never be his — the fragile hope he'd nurtured had dissolved in the past five minutes.

Effortlessly he lifted her, carefully cradled her right hip and leg until he could lay her on the bed. He pulled the gown around her, covering bare skin, although she appeared oblivious to her near nakedness.

Greer closed her eyes, but Andrew knew she didn't sleep. He waited.

"Give me the music box," she said clearly, without looking at him.

Andrew did as she asked.

With one twist of the base, familiar, soft notes filled the room. And as they faded to a last, few, punctuated sounds, silence seemed to expand around Andrew. The mid-August night was humid and sweat coursed between his shoulder blades.

"Here." Greer held the music box toward him. "I don't need this. I'll be going home to my sister soon and I like to travel light."

"Of course." She was already thinking of getting away from England. Why wouldn't she? It had been her hell on earth. "Sleep now. I'll sit with you until you do, if you like."

"That won't be necessary."

"I want to. Then I'll come back tomorrow."

"No, no. Thank you. I'd prefer it if you didn't. I'll be fine. I'm not your patient and I'm sure you've got plenty to do."

"Greer, Mrs. Beckett. Won't you let me do something for you?"

She rolled her head toward him. All light had left her eyes. "You've done enough, Dr. Monthaven. Allowing my baby to die was quite enough."

Two days later Andrew stood beside a tiny grave at the base of a much larger but still fresh mound of earth. He was the only mourner for Colleen Beckett, daughter of Colin and Greer Beckett.

"Colleen will rest close to her father," the minister said in a reedy monotone. He clutched a closed Bible to his chest and stared skyward.

Andrew only half heard the rest of the odd little eulogy, about a human who had barely existed. It was delivered solely for his benefit, and he wondered if it would have been spoken at all had he not come. A single grave digger had retreated to pour tea from a Thermos and drag on a skinny cigarette that he'd rolled himself.

When the minister finished his homily, he held out his hand. "So sad. So very sad," he said.

Andrew shook the man's thin fingers. "So pointless," he replied. Then he knelt and filled one hand with earth. Slowly he let the hardened clumps fall.

Before the last hollow drum of soil on white wood sounded, he stood and walked briskly toward the green metal gate leading out of the churchyard. As he climbed into his car he wondered again why Greer had chosen to bury her family in an obscure village like Ferndale. If she didn't want to fly them to the States, it would have seemed more logical to use a cemetery in Dorchester, close to the hospital. He'd thought about it when a staff member told him that Colin Beckett had been interred in Ferndale. But Greer hadn't mentioned the subject, and there had never been an appropriate time to ask her the reason.

The accident happened late on the night when she and her husband arrived in Dorset. They'd driven from London and, as far as Andrew knew, could never have visited the isolated hamlet. Ferndale *was* a peaceful spot. Perhaps one of the nurses had suggested it. He dismissed the question.

Three more weeks passed before Greer Beckett was discharged. The days and nights became a tormented blur for Andrew while he battled his desire to go to her. He ached to see her, but knew he was part of a nightmare she must long to forget.

On the evening of September 28, he broke a late-blooming rose from a trellis on the grounds of his house. The night air was intoxicating, and Andrew wasn't tired. He walked down a double flight of stone steps leading to the cliff path, and moved on until he stood above the ocean.

Could it have been four days since he watched from a hospital window as Greer was helped into a taxi? She had glanced over her shoulder at the medical center just once, before disappearing into the back seat. His last thought as the cab rounded the corner was that she was wrong to blame him for the baby's death, but in the same instant he knew he could never be angry because she did.

One day, when the pain faded, she'd stop hating him. Eventually another man would help her forget what she had lost. Andrew frowned. It made no sense to be jealous of someone he would never know — but he was.

Andrew rested the rose against his lips and looked out over the sea. The tide was coming in. Across the water a full moon spread a silvered path that transformed obsidian into burnished indigo: the color and quality of Greer Beckett's eyes when she'd first seen him on the night Colleen died. For a few minutes they'd been as vibrantly alive and welcoming as this moontide.

Chapter 1

Greer Beckett breathed deeply, filling her lungs with the same air that caressed her upturned face. Indian summer. She had once heard Seattle's weather described as "perpetual drizzle interrupted by occasional rain." The remark was fairly accurate much of the time, but she doubted if any city could be more spectacular on a balmy, mid-September day like this.

She glanced at her adoptive sister who sat beside her on a bench. A breeze ruffled Casey Wyatt's short, blond curls. Her pert features were arranged into a distant expression.

"What are you thinking about, Case?"

Casey stirred. "How much I like being here, with you. I've been very lucky."

"Not half as lucky as me," Greer replied. She touched Casey's hand lightly and concentrated on the familiar scene around them. "I'm still grateful I managed to salvage enough out of the business to open Britmania. I've also never regretted deciding to have the shop down here. This place always feels so alive."

Pioneer Square was crammed with its usual assortment of humanity. Tourists and local workers rubbed shoulders with shambling street people amid a jumble of small, offbeat shops and restaurants bordering the cobblestone plaza. The city hugged the square on three sides. Towering modern buildings in the central business district loomed immediately north, like a painted backdrop against a cerulean sky. To the west a warren of narrow streets led beneath a viaduct to Elliot Bay and the awesome vista of Puget Sound and the snowcapped Olympic mountains beyond.

On a bench across from Casey and Greer, an old man lay outstretched, his bare ankles pale between ragged polyester pants and the tops of new army boots. A yellowed newspaper shaded his face from the early afternoon sun, and his crossed hands rose and fell atop a protruding belly that jiggled with each breath. Greer eyed the brown paper sack wedged between his body and the back of the bench, noting that the wine was probably the only possession he had in the world. She began to wonder where the man came from and who missed him. Dozens of transients roamed the area day and night, but she could never think of them as faceless and forgotten. Everyone had a past.

Casey had hooked her elbows over the seat back and crossed her long legs. Her pink T-shirt, which read, Seattleites Don't Tan, They Rust, was hiked up to show an inch of smooth midriff.

"Sis," she said, peering sideways at Greer. "Let's be irresponsible."

"What did you have in mind?" Greer asked cautiously.

Casey's eyes closed like a lazy cat. "Taking the afternoon off."

Greer chuckled and brushed sandwich crumbs from the lap of her beige cotton jump suit. "Lunch break's over for me. Time to get back to the grind. You can fritter away the rest of the day if you want to. But if we're going to keep on paying the rent and covering my expensive whims, someone had better tend the shop."

"Don't start that again." Casey put an arm around Greer's shoulders and squeezed. "This trip back to England isn't a whim. It's something you've got to do. And it'll be good for the store, too. Where better to dredge up some oddball British memorabilia?" She tugged her hair theatrically, stopping with her elbows pointing to the sky. "The mind boggles. I can see the newspapers. 'Glamorous proprietor of Seattle's trendiest shop does it again. Import store becomes the only American establishment to stock genuine imitation crown jewels. Orders are being taken at Britmania by —' "

Greer placed a finger to Casey's lips. "You're wonderful. I love you. But you talk too much. Stay and soak up the sun for a while. I'll start back." She stood, threw the remnants of her lunch into a garbage can and adjusted the corded belt around her tiny waist.

"Okay, slave driver. You win." In one smooth motion Casey was beside her sister. "I was only trying to make you take it easy for once. You push yourself too hard. Remember what the doctor said? It hasn't been two months since the hysterectomy and he told you to give yourself at least three before returning to full activity."

"I don't want to discuss that."

"Why?" Casey shook her head impatiently at a grizzled man who approached from a doorway, his hand held out. "Why don't you want to discuss it, Greer? It's unnatural for you to avoid something so traumatic as if it never happened."

While Casey marched ahead Greer dug in her purse for some coins. "Here, Charlie," she said to the white-haired man, who gave a courtly, slightly wobbly bow. "Something to eat this time, okay?" She handed him the money. He closed his grimy fingers around the money and displayed a mouthful of stained teeth.

"I wish you wouldn't do that," Casey said when Greer caught up to her. "You shouldn't encourage these people. They know you're a soft touch."

Greer shrugged, grateful for the change of subject. "It doesn't hurt anything. And I've seen you do the same thing. Want to go to Takara for dinner tonight?"

"Maybe. Is it four weeks or five before you leave?"

"Five. October 21."

"I worry about you going alone. Why don't we hire someone to run the shop and I'll come with you?"

Familiar threads of anxiety started to wind through Greer. "No. Even if we could afford it. This is one thing I want to do by myself. And there's nothing to worry about. Anyone listening to you would think you were the one who was four years older instead of me. I know what's best for me."

"Josh would help us out . . ."

"No!" Greer snapped. Somehow she must make Casey understand without hurting her. Josh Field had been Colin's partner and, since she became a widow, Greer's close friend — too close for Greer. Lately she sensed his growing impatience for more than a platonic attachment. She wanted to gently discourage the relationship, not encourage it.

Casey caught Greer's elbow and pulled her to a halt. "Look at me," she said. "Your behavior isn't normal."

Two couples passed, glancing curiously at the women. "This isn't the time or place for this," Greer muttered, feeling her color rise.

"There never is a time or place. But at least out in the open, you can't hide. Please, Greer, don't stay clammed up like this. I've waited weeks for you to let your feelings out."

"I don't feel anything," Greer insisted. At five-foot-one, Greer had to crane her neck to meet her tall sister's eyes. "What difference does a hysterectomy make to me now? We're late."

"Fine," Casey said as she released Greer's arm. "Keep on pretending you don't give a damn. When you said you were going back to England, I thought you'd decided to stop pretending you don't care about all that's happened to you. You're only twenty-six. And you're gorgeous. You ought to marry again and we both know who'd be only too happy to oblige."

Greer walked faster, but Casey hardly lengthened her stride to stay alongside. They crossed Occidental Square and headed for Post Street where they had rented space in the basement of a renovated building.

"Listen, Greer," Casey began, before having to dodge a wild-eyed teenager in a headset who practiced a dance that took up the width of the sidewalk. "Listen," she repeated as they fell into step again.

A panicky sensation invaded Greer's stomach. She smiled, knowing the effort was obviously phony. "If you're still planning to palm me off on poor Josh Field, forget it. Just because he used to be Colin's partner, and he's been good to me, it doesn't mean he wants to get permanently saddled with a cripple."

"Give me a break," Casey exploded. "You limp a bit. Since when did that make you a cripple? And if you're worried about not being able to have children, big deal.

Mom and dad adopted you. They felt exactly the same about both of us, and if you adopted kids you'd love them, too. Anyway, I don't think Josh even likes children that much. You'd be perfect for each other."

The panicky sensation spread to Greer's legs. Why would Casey choose now to bring all this up? There was nothing to say that hadn't already been said a hundred times. She slowed down, forcing herself to take deep breaths. "Don't get mad, Case. Let's drop it," she managed to say.

A garish poster flapped away from a wall as they passed and Casey batted it with a fist. "I'm not mad, just frustrated. Josh isn't good to you, as you put it. The guy's crazy about you and all he gets is the runaround."

"That's not true."

"It is, sis. He wants you to be his wife."

They reached the flight of stairs leading down to Britmania. "I've been a wife. And I had the best husband in the world. That's enough, more than most women ever have," she said, favoring her right leg slightly as she walked down.

Casey's backless sandals slapped the concrete when she loped past, taking two steps at a time. She fumbled in her jeans' pocket and produced a key. "Colin was a good man. But he wasn't a saint." She unlocked the door and went inside. Quickly she flipped the sign on the door to read *open.* "I understood that the main reason for you going to England again was to make another attempt to find your biological family. And I thought that was great. But I'm beginning to suspect the real reason. What you want to do most is be where you last were with Colin, isn't it? You're going to his and Colleen's graves, aren't you?"

"Yes," Greer muttered. She took a comb from her purse and started to drag it through her hair. "Is that so strange?"

"I suppose not," Casey said. China wine decanters — each shaped like one of the wives of Henry VIII — clattered as she pushed them to the end of a shelf. "Maybe there you'll finally cry the tears that must be waterlogging your brain by now. Put the ghosts to rest and get on with your life." She twisted a ceramic head sharply on its cork neck.

"Look, Casey," Greer said laying the comb on the counter. "I'm not falling apart. When I first got back here I was pretty broken up. Destroyed would be a better description, but who wouldn't be? If I didn't cry then it was because I was too numb, and later there wasn't time."

"Greer . . ."

"No, Case. You wanted me to spill all this, so let me finish."

Taking several deliberate steps, Greer reached the door, locked it and turned the sign around to read *closed*. She paced in front of her sister. "I want to trace my original family very much. And I do intend to search for them. But I never faced up to Colin and Colleen dying. They say you have to go through a bunch of phases to grieve properly, and I missed just about all of them. I thought about it a lot while I was in the hospital for the hysterectomy and decided I'd like to try and catch up. Does that make sense?"

"Yes. I'm glad. You know I didn't mean to criticize you, don't you, sis?" Casey inquired gently.

"Yes, I know, but it's important to get things straight between us," Greer answered just as gently. "Before the accident, Josh had already signed the papers to buy Colin out. I took what money was left after — after everything — and made it work for me. You make it sound as if I've sat around for two years feeling sorry for myself."

"I never said that . . ."

"Pretty close. I know Colin would approve, of Britmania and of what I've done. He'd be proud of me. And I thought you enjoyed all this — this crazy stuff we deal in. It works, and it uses my only real talent — imagination. I love selling ash-trays with coats of arms to people named Smith. It's a kick to watch customers cart away bits of the white cliffs of Dover in plastic bags or key rings with Wimbledon locker-room numbers. Oh, sure, they pre-tend the whole thing's a big spoof but they enjoy every minute of it. And we make a good living. As far as I'm concerned that's success, and I made it." Greer paused. Her blood pumped hard and it felt good.

Casey massaged her temples. "Every word you say is true. You've done marvel-ously well. I love being a part of it all, and you know that. But I still say you're avoiding the point."

"I don't know what you mean."

"You do." The younger woman grasped Greer's shoulders and backed her to a chair. "Sit there and listen. All you're talking about is the business. There's no question that it's a success. But I'm wor-ried about you — Greer Beckett, the woman. If Josh twists your arm you go out to dinner or the theater. By eleven you're home and he's fortunate if you allow him in for coffee. The guy wants you. If you gave him one little word of encouragement he'd whisk you down the aisle so fast our heads would spin."

To her horror Greer felt moisture well in her eyes. She tipped her head back, but the tears sprang free and coursed down her cheeks. "Do you think I don't know that?" she whispered. "And feel like a creep about it?"

Casey dropped to her knees, cradling Greer's head against her shoulder. "I don't know how you feel. You never tell me."

"I don't want to marry Josh. I don't want to marry anyone. If I live to be a hundred I'll always miss Colin. I haven't cried because I'm afraid that if I do I'll never stop." She felt herself begin to tremble and took a deep, controlling breath. "If you just relax Casey, everything will be fine. Josh will find someone else and, hopefully, still be my friend. I have all I want. Forget the idea I'm yearning for new beginnings."

"Oh, Greer," Casey said in a wobbly voice, "I want you to be happy."

"I am. Please let it go at that."

Casey sat back on her heels and sniffed. "Okay. I guess I'll have to — for now. Need a tissue?"

Greer swiped her cheeks with the backs

of her hands. "Yup. But I'll get it. Turn that sign over, kid. I'm going to unpack the stuff that was delivered this morning. Then I'll make us some coffee." Before she went through the door to the storeroom she looked over her shoulder. Casey was still on her knees, staring through the window. "You didn't say yes or no to Takara's for dinner," Greer said, deftly smoothing over the awkward moment. "Sushi's healthy, you know. Then we could go upstairs to the ice-cream place and have seven-layer mocha cake — just to keep up our energy."

"You're on," Casey said, not turning around. Her voice was muffled.

Greer went into the sloping space under the stairs of the business behind Britmania. A naked electric bulb hung from a long wire that could be looped over various hooks in the wall, depending on where light was needed. How could she explain feelings that were a mystery even to her? Greer started the coffee maker and went to work opening boxes.

"Hey, Greer," Casey said as she stuck her head around the door. "Josh just called. He sounded lonely, so I invited him to come with us for dinner. You don't mind, do you?"

Yes, I mind. I mind. "Of course not."

"Great. I told him to meet us here at six."

The door closed and Greer stared hard at it. Maybe if she stayed in England long enough, Josh would lose interest or meet someone else. He was handsome, charming and well-off. Too bad he wasn't ten years younger so she could encourage a liaison with Casey — maybe she still should. She wrinkled her nose. Josh wasn't Casey's type. He was basically a quiet man, with brown hair and liquid hazel eyes. Casey went for the flamboyant Nordic types, just as Greer had . . .

Greer attacked the boxes with fresh ardor. After weeks of not really thinking about him, the familiar picture of Colin sprang to mind. It was always the same. He was asleep beside her, his sun-streaked hair tousled against the pillow, his slender tanned face turned toward her. Then he opened eyes so blue they seemed to burn and smiled as he reached for her.

Sweat broke out on Greer's upper lip. She filled her arms with crackly packages but they kept slipping. The second she straightened, the mental picture of Colin changed. A lattice of blood wove across his forehead, staining the pillow, his eyes became dull and puzzled. Greer squeezed her eyelids shut and leaned against the wall. The scene had always faded there, but this time it only blurred.

Musical notes tapped like ice spicules across her brain. Colin's image dimmed, to be replaced by the stricken features of a tall, dark man whose honey-colored eyes stared pleadingly into hers. The music persisted. Greer twisted her head, pressing it against the cool brick. She heard the man's deep voice from a long way off, unclear. Then his lips formed a single word and she knew what he said, "Colleen."

Greer felt hollow. She'd made Andrew Monthaven the target of all her hate. No one could know for sure why her baby had died — or if it was anyone's fault. Yet she had blamed him and still did in the times when it hurt, and she ached for what she could never have. But he had been kind — he cared. If she'd just said Thank-you, it might have helped them both. Please let her have the courage to go to him and say those two words.

Greer opened her eyes, but the music still played.

"Brahms Lullaby."

Chapter 2

☾

What a fantastic evening, Andrew Monthaven thought. October in Dorset. Perfect.
Too bad everything else in his life wasn't
equally satisfying. He stood at the edge of a
bluff behind his house with his friend, Bob
Wilson, staring toward the English Channel.
Below them, fog bumped in soft heaps
against sheer chalk cliffs. Where the va-
porous mass thinned, steely water glistened
in the dusk like fine pewter.

The sound of Bob's impatient intake of
breath came as an intrusion. Andrew bent
to pick up a limestone pebble. Asking
Bob's opinion had been a mistake. If one
sought advice, one should be prepared to
listen. But Andrew's mind was already
made up.

He faced Bob and the two men ex-
changed a long look. Both an inch or so
taller than six feet, any physical similarity
ended there. Bob was husky and blond,

with a studied stylishness, Andrew dark, lean, unconsciously elegant.

"What do you want me to say?" Bob said at last.

"Nothing." Andrew leaned back and shied the rock high into the air, then listened, hand outstretched, until it plopped into veiled waters. He faced Bob. "I shouldn't have laid this on you. It was wrong to involve you in my problems. But we've known each other so long it's instinctive to ask your advice."

Bob began to pace slowly. He stopped, puffed out his cheeks, then let air slip past his teeth in a hissing whistle. "You're not thinking, Andy. Only reacting. Drop this thing with Coover. If you don't, he'll have your head on a platter."

It took three sharp tugs for Andrew to loosen his burgundy silk tie. "Winston Coover is senior pediatric consultant for Dorset County, and he's my boss," he said. "But his incompetence caused the death of one of my patients and I'm going to prove it."

"The only thing you'll prove is that you can't fight the system." Bob's light blue eyes shifted slightly. "Coover's powerful. He's got everyone who counts in his hip pocket. They'll crucify you."

Moisture had made Andrew's sable hair curl over his forehead. He raked it back. "So toe the line, right? Michael Drake's dead and there's no point in causing trouble now. It'll probably never happen again. Come on, Bob. You know me better than that. I can't take the risk."

Bob patted the pockets of his tan suit until he located a pack of cigarettes. "Your conscience is admirable," he muttered, cupping his lighter to protect its flame from the breeze. For a moment he dragged thoughtfully on a cigarette. "It's also going to ruin you," he continued. "The bottom line is that you can't win. The surgeon who operated on young Drake will back Coover and so will the pathologist. They already have."

"There's no record of blood work in Michael's files," Andrew said. "If nothing else, with his symptoms, a white-cell count should have been routine."

"What if they say you removed the lab sheets?" Bob challenged him.

Resolve glittered in Andrew's golden-brown eyes. "Hell, I don't know. But that boy was my patient, and he was something special. Sensitive. He was fifteen, Bob. Remember when you and I were fifteen? We were dreamers and planners and nothing

40

was ever going to stop us. Michael was like that."

"You knew him pretty well, didn't you?"

"He'd been my patient since I first took the job in Dorchester. Six years. One of those intense kids who run into a lot of abdominal pain. I checked him out for appendicitis several times. If he hadn't chosen my weekend off to pull the real thing, he'd be alive now."

The tip of Bob's cigarette glowed briefly. "You were in London, weren't you?"

"Yes. You know I usually go up when I get a couple of free days. It's a good idea to keep the flat lived in as much as possible."

Bob bit a thumbnail, then examined it closely. "Were you alone again?"

"Yes — what about it?" Andrew spread his hands on his hips beneath the jacket of his navy suit. "Why should you care how I spend my spare time — or who I spend it with?"

"Forget it. I worry about you, that's all. You're alone too much. Some steady female company would do you good."

"Somehow we got from Michael Drake to my love life. What's the connection?"

Bob turned up his collar. "Coover's bound to be looking for something to nail you with."

Irritation mounted in Andrew. "Great. And I repeat. What point are you making?"

"How long is it since you took a woman to bed?"

Andrew dropped his hands to his sides. "I didn't hear what I just thought I heard, did I?"

Ruddy streaks blazed across Bob's flat cheekbones, but Andrew sensed something other than embarrassment was the cause. He felt his scalp tighten as an invisible screen seemed to separate him from the man who had been closer than a brother since they were children.

"Bob," Andrew persisted. "What is this?"

"Okay. You might as well hear it from me as from a disciplinary board." Bob threw down the cigarette and ground it underfoot. "You're thirty-five and unmarried. You may not be filthy rich, but you're not a pauper, either. There isn't an unattached nurse on the staff of the medical center who hasn't made a play for you, but you don't even seem to notice."

Andrew began to laugh. "Who's keeping track?" Bob wasn't making any sense.

"This isn't funny," Bob said. "Damn it, Andy. Do I have to spell it out word for word? I haven't been keeping track. But someone has. And when one or two comments were dropped, I couldn't defend you because I had nothing to defend you with."

"Defend me?" Andrew turned back toward the sea and tried to concentrate on the fuzzy panorama. "I don't understand."

When Bob answered, his tone held a softness that was menacing. "The last time I remember you with a woman was when you and Lauren and I went to Stratford to see a play. You took Chris Hardy — nice and safe — one of the girls we both knew from medical school. That was over two years ago — two years last July to be precise. Since then, apart from occasional dinners at our house, when you come alone, your private life has been just that — totally private. Andy, are you gay?"

Disbelief seeped into Andrew's brain, followed almost immediately by rage. He grabbed Bob's sleeve, then let go as if it burned. "This is madness. Gay? Is that what Coover and his cronies are going to suggest. Are they spreading nasty little rumors to muddy up my reputation and hoping that'll be enough to keep me quiet?"

"Something like that. Yes."

"And you couldn't defend me? Bob Wilson who grew up on one of my father's

43

farms right here in Dorset? The kid who spent as much time at my home as he did at his own? You listened to that obvious fabrication and didn't stand up for me?" Andrew said, wanting to retch.

"It wasn't like that." With one fist Bob slowly pounded his other palm. "I listened so that I could tell you what was in the wind. Then I thought it through and realized they might be able to make their accusations stick. The only thing to do now is back off and hope things die down," he concluded.

"By that you mean that if I shut up, I won't be dragged before a board on a charge of possible misconduct. What am I supposed to do? Start carving a notch on my stethoscope for every nurse I take to bed?"

Bob kicked loose gravel over the edge of the cliff. "You're being irrational," he snapped. "It wasn't easy to tell you any of this. I probably shouldn't have." He started up the path.

"Wait. Good Lord, man, wait." Andrew caught up. "This is too much to take in. I wouldn't have been surprised if you'd said Coover might make a thing out of my opening Ringstead Hall to the public." He nodded toward his Jacobian mansion atop a rise of smooth lawn. "It struck me that he could suggest I was after his job because I was short of money. But homosexality? You floored me."

"I'm not surprised. It didn't do much for my equilibrium when I heard the rumor."

Bob's lapse into a hint of a Dorset accent alerted Andrew to the depth of his friend's agitation. He squinted at the driveway beside his house. A straggling line of visitors steadily disappeared aboard an orange-and-white bus that already belched a murky cloud from its exhaust pipe.

"Monday's last load of eager sightseers appears about to depart," he said. "Join me for a drink?"

Bob's expression was enigmatic. "Thanks, but Lauren will have dinner ready. Pick you up in the morning?"

"Pass, Bob. I'm going in late tomorrow — and Wednesday."

"To avoid me?"

"Of course not. My morning clinics have been canceled this week. Not enough patients." Andrew blew into his cupped hands, then rubbed them together. "Maybe my reputation's already catching up with me," he said lightly even though he could not smile.

"And maybe you'd be wise to take this very seriously," Bob replied quietly. "You're important to me, Andy. That's why I'm so worried." He hurried toward a flight of crumbling steps that led to the back of the house. A cobalt sky silhouetted the impressive, gray stone structure on its grassy knoll.

"Bob," Andrew called out to the other man. "Trust me. Whatever happens, I'll make sure it doesn't touch you."

When he faced Andrew, Bob's expression was unreadable. "You may not be able to."

Andrew flinched. "What exactly does that mean?" he asked tightly.

"That's something I don't think I have to explain." Bob said. "See you sometime tomorrow. In the meantime . . . think."

Chapter 3

☾

The tea in the bottom of her cup was tepid. Greer took another swallow and grimaced at the bitter taste. Tea as the English obviously preferred it — strong enough to stand a spoon in — would never take the place of her beloved black coffee.

She should be more tired than she felt. Less than forty-eight hours ago she'd still been in Seattle. Excitement had made sleep impossible both the night before she left and on the plane. The long flight to London and then a three-hour train journey had brought her to Weymouth in Dorset County the previous evening. The seaside town would be headquarters for her stay. She'd settled gratefully into her ocean-front boardinghouse but had again been too wound up to relax. After a restless night she was up at five, watching a gray dawn, impatient to explore the town that had been her home when she was too young to remember. Armed with a map, she'd set off on foot immediately after breakfast.

Greer looked around the tiny second-floor tea shop. It was lunch time and every table was occupied — mostly by fresh-faced women engrossed in animated conversation. Their voices all seemed to have a similar high, clear quality, and the speed with which they drank tea and ordered more told Greer they wouldn't appreciate her opinion of England's national brew.

Bumble's. The name of the shop had caught her attention from the other side of the street. The ground floor was a charmingly cluttered retail showroom that reminded Greer of Britmania. Every shelf was jammed with locally made pottery, unusual kitchen tools, beaten copper jewelry and a profusion of wooden bowls and ornaments. Racks displayed greeting cards and gift wrappings. Boxes of chocolates were stacked on the counter amid piles of partially unpacked merchandise. Greer had browsed, noting one or two possible ideas for her own stock, before climbing a short flight of stairs to the restaurant. Small original paintings of local scenes dotted the walls on her way up. The pictures were for sale and she immediately thought of approaching the artist to see if he'd be interested in exporting some of his work.

The spinach quiche she'd ordered was excellent, but too much. She speared a forkful and pushed it around her plate. It was time to take her next step. To make peace with her past she must return to the unfinished business of two years ago. And Dr. Andrew Monthaven was the first loose end to be tied.

She had looked for his name in the telephone book as soon as her suitcases were unpacked. She'd found only one listing: "A. Monthaven, M.D., Ringstead Hall." Twice she dialed the number and listened to the grinding rings, so different from those she was accustomed to. An hour later she again inserted coins in the hallway phone. Still no answer. Then she lost her nerve. She should have tried the Dorchester Medical Center as she had planned, but even the idea of making contact with that place had wrapped ribbons of tension around her heart.

Dorchester was only eight miles northeast of Weymouth. It would be easy to catch a bus or train and go to see him.

At breakfast her landlady had hovered while Greer spread marmalade on toast. "Not much to see here but hills and a lot of wild seas at this time of year," the woman had said, crossing her arms over a wraparound floral apron. "If you like old places, there's Thomas Hardy's cottage — muddy to get to. Or Athelhampton Hall in Puddletown. They say parts of the house are more than five hundred years old. Crumbling and drafty I'd call it — probably — never been there. Then there's Ringstead Hall. Some of my people have liked that. You could go to Lawrence of Arabia's house . . ."

Ringstead Hall — Andrew Monthaven's home? Greer had only half heard the rest of the woman's words. "Ringstead?" Mrs. Findlay had sniffed at her interest. "It's open to the public for tours twice a week. Mondays and Tuesdays. I'm not much for that sort of thing myself, but foreigners seem to like it."

Tomorrow would be Tuesday. Impulsively Greer had decided to visit the tour offices in the center of Weymouth and make a reservation. She'd already made up her mind to see Andrew as soon as possible, say what she should have said years ago, then put the episode behind her. If Ringstead Hall was his house, she might be lucky enough to run into him. Not likely, but possible. One way or another she must get the meeting with Andrew Monthaven over. Glancing around Bumble's once more, her only regret was she couldn't stay here forever. Maybe she'd just have one more cup of tea before she went to make a reservation.

What had she expected? Andrew Monthaven playing the gracious host to a bevy of tourists? And if he had appeared, what would she have said to him in front of several dozen strangers?

Good grief, her feet hurt. Greer hung back until she was the last of her sightseeing group in the room, then slumped into a stiffly upholstered chair. This was the ninth bedroom she had been ushered through, each one crammed with what the tour guide pompously described as "priceless pieces." Stuffy was the only adjective that came to Greer's mind. She smiled a little wistfully. Colin would have loved every inch of Ringstead Hall. European antiques had been his passion and his area of expertise. Too bad she'd never been interested enough to learn more from him.

The guide's voice came from the corridor, "Ringstead Hall is one of the best examples of Jacobean architecture in the country. Very early sixteen hundreds.

Please don't touch the wall hangings." His words gradually ebbed beneath the sound of many clumping feet on the stairs.

Greer unzipped her boots and slid them off. She wiggled her toes. The guide had promised "a quick peek" at the wine cellars before they left and she ought to hurry or everyone else would get too far ahead. But how her feet ached. She yawned. Delayed jet lag had her in its grip.

The house reminded her of a museum. All spectacular, but remote. The information pamphlet confirmed that the owner was still in residence, but Greer saw no sign of life. And any occupant of such a house should be Lord or Sir something, not an unassuming young doctor.

There must be two Andrew Monthavens in southern Dorset. The one she knew was surely married with a gaggle of happy children. His home would be tasteful, yet comfortable, not a repository for curios. But she had found only one listing for Monthaven in the telephone directory.

She'd better move. If the guide noticed she was missing, he would come searching for her and she'd feel like a fool. She tugged on her rust suede boots with difficulty. Why did feet always choose the most inconvenient times to swell?

Greer left the bedroom and made her way along a narrow hallway lined with grim portraits — mostly of men in armor or elaborate, military uniforms. Expressions were dour; long, austere features, carefully posed to convey the serious nature of each subject. She slowed down. Scattered between the men were likenesses of a few women, heavy jewels prominent on curved bosoms, soft hands folded around a small book, a flower, a delicate piece of needlework. Greer began to wonder about the people in the pictures. What had the young girl with pale ringlets and luminous gray eyes thought a century earlier? Next to the shy-looking girl was a painting of a young man dressed in dark green velvet with a froth of white lace at neck and cuff.

Slowly she backed away, studying each plane and angle of the face intently. The features were finely chiseled, yet intensely masculine. Dark brows arched above the golden-brown eyes that held a flicker of mirth in their depths. The bridge of the straight nose was narrow, balanced perfectly by high cheekbones and an angular jaw. Unlike most of his silent companions he wore no hat, and his curly black hair appeared damp. Greer found herself smiling as if the man who had sat for the artist so long ago was inviting her to share his own secret joke.

It was him. The smile slipped from Greer's lips. Not really Andrew Monthaven, of course, but a man so like him that he could have been Andrew dressed in the clothing of another era.

The distant sound of a large engine bursting to life broke into her thoughts. The bus couldn't be leaving, not without her. She had no idea how she would get back to Weymouth if it did. She ran to the top of the stairs and started down before she saw the vehicle bumping away. Distorted through the stained-glass windows of the great entry hall, the bus moved steadily out of sight. When the guide had said "a quick peek" at the wine cellars, he must have meant exactly that.

For several seconds Greer stood immobile, then she sank onto a step and cupped her chin in both hands. What a nitwit. She tried to remember how far they had traveled from the main road, down a winding lane to the driveway of Ringstead Hall. Greer had never thumbed a ride in her life, but there was a first time for everything, and if she could reach a thoroughfare she'd take whatever help she could get.

Uncertainty crowded in. It was already getting dark. She would probably have to walk a couple of miles over rough ground — far more stress than she had put on her hip since the injury. There must be a telephone somewhere. Of course there was. She'd found the number herself, yesterday.

Deepening gloom at the foot of the stairs intimidated her. Greer retraced her path along the upper hallway, peering hopefully into alcoves, but finding only an endless array of marble statues.

Not sure what to do next, she hesitated. Then she realized she was a few feet from the portrait that resembled Andrew Monthaven. She went to stand in front of it once more. This time, so close, she could make out brush strokes, cracked with age.

Tentatively she touched a shaded area beneath one cheekbone, followed it to the hint of a groove beside the mouth. A beautiful mouth. Andrew's had been like that, wide and mobile. How strange that she only realized how handsome he was in retrospect.

With the tip of one forefinger she outlined the sharply defined lips in the painting. Would Andrew want to see her again after the way she had treated him?

Perhaps he'd forgotten about her and she should leave the past alone. She shook her head impatiently. *Looking for an easy out again.* Tomorrow she'd call him in Dorchester.

At the sound of a door clicking shut to her left, Greer froze, her finger still resting on the portrait. The footsteps that approached so slowly were soft. She looked over her shoulder and clutched the rolled neck of her raincoat. Her heart soared upward to jam in her throat.

The man who approached was in shadow, until he stopped a few feet away, in the light from the bedroom where Greer had lingered too long. "Good Lord," he said. "Greer Beckett? It can't be."

Greer couldn't answer. Her heart plummeted like a runaway elevator. Andrew Monthaven looked so much like the portrait that she felt suddenly disoriented. Instead of green velvet, he wore a brown terry robe, loosely tied at the waist. But his hair *was* wet. It glistened dark and curly about his forehead and ears, and on his muscular chest where the robe gaped. Greer glanced downward. His bare feet accounted for the muffled footsteps.

He came closer until she could see the soft gold of his eyes, and the expression of shocked disbelief she saw there made her knees weak.

"What are you doing here?" he asked quietly.

"I looked you up —" Greer's voice broke and she cleared her throat. For some inexplicable reason she felt like crying. The sensation that engulfed her at the sight of him threatened to destroy every shred of her composure, but she held herself erect. No way was she going to fall apart. He'd pity her again — something she didn't need — from anyone.

"How? I mean . . ." Andrew took another step, then stopped and ran his fingers through the hair at his temples.

The way he did that night, Greer thought. She'd hurt him then and now all she could possibly do was remind them both of those terrible moments. Fool.

His lips moved, but he made no sound. Finally he raised his chin and Greer saw him swallow. "I don't understand any of this."

"Your address was in the phone book," she said, keeping her voice level. "Then I found out about the house tours. I came on a bus."

"The bus left."

She hooked a thumb into each pocket. "I

know. This is a wonderful house. I got too interested in one of the rooms and didn't realize everyone else was gone." At least she didn't sound as garbled as she felt.

"You were hoping you'd see me? That's why you came?"

He wouldn't have to be very bright to figure that out. Greer turned to face the painting. "Yes — no. I'm not sure why I came now." *I'm babbling like an idiot.*

She felt him move close to her shoulder, felt his height and breadth overpower her. He smelled of soap and fresh air.

"Why didn't you call me?" he asked. "Instead of coming on a tour bus, for pity's sake?"

"I did call. You weren't in." Heat suffused Greer's cheeks. What else could she say that would make sense? "I like this painting. It reminds me of you . . ." Her voice faded.

"He was Giles Monthaven, my great-great-grandfather. A bit of a rake I'm told." An almost palpable tension underlay Andrew's words.

Greer couldn't get enough oxygen. "He was a very handsome man," she blurted. Why had she said that?

They both became silent, but Greer was acutely aware of the man behind her.

"Your hair's longer," Andrew said at last. "It always reminded me of autumn oak leaves."

Greer heard a soft breath escape his lungs and then felt his fingertips pass lightly over her hair from crown to the curling ends at her shoulder blades. The contact made her throat squeeze and her brain refuse to operate.

"How are you, Greer?"

"Fine," she said, vaguely surprised at the steadiness of her voice. "Never better."

"And your sister? I don't remember her name."

"Casey. She's terrific." Greer wanted to bolt. This was miserable — for both of them.

Andrew touched her shoulder. "Look at me. I keep expecting you to disappear."

She faced him and found herself close enough to see the rapid pulse in his neck. "This was a bad idea, Dr. Monthaven," she began, avoiding his eyes. "I'm sorry for barging in on you. I didn't want to visit the area without at least saying hi . . . you were very good to me and I was rotten." She finished in a rush.

"It's been two years," Andrew said extremely quietly. "Two years exactly. If you knew how often I've thought of you and wondered how you were. I almost wrote a couple of times. But I knew how you felt." He waited until she met his gaze.

"I almost wrote, too. I should have." Greer took a step backward and her heel scraped the wall. *He had thought of her.* "Anyway. You're probably tired. I'm sorry I disturbed you."

His hand on her elbow stopped her retreat. "You aren't disturbing me. Could you manage to call me Andrew?"

The unmistakable tingling in Greer's belly frightened her. "Andrew," she said. "It was great to see you again. But I'd better go."

He continued to hold her arm. "Where are you staying?"

The man was magnetic. "In Weymouth. A boardinghouse in St. John's Terrace. It's near an old church, by the ocean." She was bound to be affected by him, but so strongly?

"I know St. John's Terrace. I hope you have a view of the bay from your room," he said, studying her intently. When he ran two fingers along the scar above her eyebrow, Greer almost jumped. "This has healed beautifully," he said. "Have you had any trouble with the hip?"

The quivering in her belly made it difficult to speak. "It's a bit weak, that's all," she answered. She pushed her hair behind one shoulder. There was no way he wouldn't notice her nervousness.

"Maybe you don't exercise enough." Andrew was absorbed in thought. "You can't be giving it what it needs or you'd be able to do anything by now."

"I do what I want to do, Andrew." In her agitation, she'd pulled the house-tour pamphlet from her pocket. When she tried to stuff it back, it slipped through her fingers.

Andrew dropped to one knee to retrieve the paper, then sat back on his heels and looked up at her. "Sorry," he said, grinning, deepening the grooves beside his mouth. "I didn't mean to lecture. Habit, I suppose. Did I ever tell you that you have the bluest eyes I've ever seen?"

"No," Greer muttered. And she wished he wouldn't now.

"With that hair they ought to be green, but blue is definitely more interesting on you. I'd forgotten those marvelous freckles."

He was too close, too masculine. His robe fell away from one thigh, revealing a well-toned muscle, finely covered with dark hair. Beneath the carefully belted terry cloth he must be naked. The realization jolted Greer. "It was good to see you. But I really must run," she said once again, painfully aware she was beginning to sound like a recording.

Andrew stood immediately. "Come and have a drink while I dress. Then I'll drive you back."

Greer straightened her shoulders. What was it that made everyone she met want to take care of her? "No," she said quickly. "Thanks anyway. I'll manage." There had to be public transportation, even in such a remote spot. She lowered her eyes and ducked around Andrew to head for the stairs.

"It's dark. And I don't think you'll be able to —"

"Don't worry," she said, cutting him off. "I'll catch one of those green buses, or something." What the "or something" might be she had no idea, but the sensation Andrew Monthaven aroused in her was an element she did not want to deal with.

Her booted feet thudded rapidly on the wide, curving staircase to the ground floor. At least he wasn't following. Powerful attraction had come Greer's way once before in the person of Colin Beckett. The result had been to love him with all that she had, only to lose him. It was outrageous to compare anything about her marriage with the encounter she'd just experienced. Nevertheless, she had felt the same kind of sexual attraction to Andrew as she had to Colin, and it upset her. That element in her response to men must be cut off, had been since Colin died. And nothing could be allowed to change that.

She tried to visualize Colin, but for the first time couldn't see his face in her mind. When they met, Greer was only eighteen and they married before her nineteenth birthday. Colin was eleven years older, an odd mixture of sophistication and boyishness that had swept Greer's heart and soul away. He had made her feel safe and special, and she wished he were with her now.

The empty hallway echoed as she crossed to the double front doors. She turned one heavy, brass knob and pulled, grateful for the rush of cool breeze, accompanied by the heady scent of autumn roses and sea salt. There had been a suggestion of the ocean's pungent fragrance about Andrew . . .

Greer closed the door behind her with more force than she intended to, and her right leg gave out. She stumbled, then regained her balance. That hadn't happened

63

for ages. She must have done too much in the past few days. Or had seeing Andrew Monthaven upset her even more than she realized?

She didn't go far. Rough stone steps led down to a gravel drive that wound between a tunnel of yews toward the main gate. With no moon the darkness was complete, and the whispering grove of trees seemed to swallow her. A white wrought-iron bench glowed a few feet ahead, and she hurried to reach it and sit until she could decide what to do next.

No public transportation came out there. Why should it? There were no houses but this one. Andrew had been trying to tell her as much when she interrupted him, and now he was assuredly waiting for her to come back and ask for help. *Damn it.*

Greer wrapped her black raincoat more tightly around her slim body. This mess was the result of her own foolishness. She should have stuck to her original intention and made an appointment with Andrew. Their interview would have been brief and dignified, the misunderstandings of two years before neatly straightened out. As it was, she felt unsettled and defensive.

More reluctant than ever to return to the

plainly aristocratic owner of Ringstead Hall, Greer sank farther into her collar. He knew who he was, where he came from; there were no holes in his family tree. He had probably never experienced an insecure moment in his life.

It wasn't important to see her great-grandfathers' pedigrees — or portraits. Simply discovering the story of the first two years of her own life would be enough. And somewhere among Dorset's gentle hills, contrasted by its wild shores and fickle weather, she intended to find that story.

Tom and Dianne Wyatt adopted Greer out of a foster home in Weymouth when she was two years old. The American couple were on a work exchange with a British aircraft company. When Greer was four, a year after their return to the States, Casey was born — the child the Wyatts could supposedly never conceive.

Greer grew up surrounded by love and security, and hid a curiosity about her shadowy beginnings that made her feel traitorous, even now. But although Tom and Dianne were open with her, Greer always felt there were bits and pieces of her past that they knew, but didn't divulge. She and Colin had discussed the possibility that, if this was true, it was probably more for her sake than theirs. Greer resolved to ask them the questions that plagued her, but never did. They both died the year before her visit to England with Colin.

It had been Colin's idea that they make the trip. He often attended European antique auctions as a buyer. But his short absences were confined to well-publicized offerings, usually in London or Paris. This time, he said, he'd stay a month and look for the unexpected finds that sometimes surfaced in private estate sales far from major cities. Colin planned to concentrate his efforts on the south of England, particularly Dorset, so that Greer could look for her original family while he worked.

Almost seven months pregnant at the time, Greer was reluctant at first, but her enthusiasm grew with Colin's persuasive arguments, "The doctor says it's fine for you to travel. You've never stopped wondering about your past. If you decide you don't want to pursue it once you get started — then stop. But I want you with me, especially now." He'd stroked her expanding belly possessively and kissed her. And Greer had acquiesced.

The crash occurred three days after they

left Seattle. If only she hadn't agreed to go. Colin had wanted to please her because he loved her. His love had killed him and it was her fault.

She blinked and tilted her head up. The motives for being here again had become distorted. Casey had guessed correctly that Greer wanted to return to the last place she and Colin had been together, to visit his grave — and Colleen's. But she would also never rest unless she at least tried to find out something of her ancestry. Then there was the opportunity to come up with new ideas for Britmania. And Andrew Monthaven . . .

Gnarled branches scraped together above her head and goose bumps raced across Greer's skin. The temperature was dropping steadily and she wasn't dressed warmly enough. There was no choice. She would have to take Andrew up on his offer of a ride to Weymouth. Even if it was possible to call a taxi out here, she certainly didn't have enough cash to pay for one. A cabbie was likely to frown on traveler's checks, particularly in large denominations.

Greer started back slowly. By the time she cleared the trees, she discerned the open front door and the silhouette of a tall man with dim light behind him. Andrew must have thrown on some clothes and come downstairs to wait for her. He stood with feet apart, hands in his pockets as he stared into the night. In her dark clothing she was probably invisible to him.

"Hi," she called in a falsely cheerful voice, wondering uncomfortably what he thought of her. Empty-headed or flighty no doubt. Unflattering and untrue, but he couldn't know what she was really like. And he never would. How could she have been careless enough to miss the bus? "Hi," she repeated, drawing closer. "This is awful. I'm a pest and I know it. But there's obviously no way for me to get to Weymouth under my own steam — unless I walk. And I wouldn't know where to start." She still chattered as she mounted the steps. Why didn't he say something?

Greer didn't look at his face until she felt his hand under her elbow. Andrew's smile wasn't patronizing. His expression showed no annoyance, only what she thought for a moment might be relief. She was crazy, of course. He had to wish she'd never come, but she returned his smile with a great deal of gratitude.

"I almost came after you," he said casually. "But I was afraid of giving you a shock in the dark. You were so determined to leave, I didn't have the heart to embarrass you by saying you were marooned here." He shut the front doors and led her upstairs.

You are so gentle, she wanted to say. *Confident enough of your own masculinity to be comfortable displaying sensitivity. Forgive me for the way I treated you before.* But the words remained locked in her heart.

Andrew steered Greer to the upper passageway and through the door at the end. "Come and get warm, then I'll run you in to Weymouth." His hand found her waist. "Don't feel badly. You've brightened up a lonely man's dull evening. By the way, although I love every inch of this house, I only live in a very small part of it. The rest I share with the National Trust. This is my wing."

Greer moved with him, conscious of his proximity, the virility he so subtly exuded. She couldn't believe that the handsome Andrew was ever lonely unless he chose to be. But why shouldn't she enjoy his charming company, just for a little while? Wasn't that what she'd hoped for, without admitting it until this moment?

"You must think me naïve," she said in a thin voice. "It was silly to take the tour at all. I should have kept calling until I reached you. I really did start a letter once, but I've never been good at putting my thoughts on paper. And there are things I ought to . . . I should have . . ." She couldn't finish.

Andrew seemed not to notice the uncompleted sentence. "In here." He showed her into a room that appeared untidy at first glance. "Give me your coat."

Greer allowed him to help her out of the black raincoat with its rust knitted collar. She hoped her simple dress, of matching knit fabric, didn't look the way it felt — baggy and rumpled.

A fire crackled in the fireplace. "This is lovely," she said more brightly than she felt. "Was it a music room once?"

The impression of untidiness was created by piles of books, folders, papers and magazines heaped on every available space, jammed in floor-to-ceiling bookcases and stacked on the floor. But it was an ornate cornice above the bookcase that had prompted Greer's question. Cherubs, trailing wisps of fabric, cavorted among harps, cellos and other less recognizable instruments.

Andrew glanced from Greer to the molded cornice she studied. "Not in my family's time." He waved her into an enormous brown leather chair and turned to poke the fire to brighter life. "We've only had the house for two hundred years, but the original owners may have planned this as a small music salon. In fact I think I was once told as much by my father. I'm surprised you noticed or made the connection."

Greer tried not to be irritated. He did think she was empty-headed. "European antiques were my husband's business. I know very little on the subject, but I went through some of his books occasionally. I remember reading that ceiling decoration often suggested the original purpose of the room. Several examples were shown and one was a bit like this."

"Interesting," he said, punctuating his comment with a smile. Greer lost interest in the ceiling. "Now. A drink, or would you prefer coffee?"

"I think I'd like a glass of dry vermouth. If you have it," she said as her mind focused on something more important. Surely he didn't live here alone.

Andrew went to a desk in the recess of a bay window and sorted among some bottles on a silver tray. He selected one, uncapped it and poured vermouth into a tall glass. "Probably not cold enough for your taste," he said, handing it to her. "But it'll relax you. Shall I get you some ice?"

Greer shook her head and took a sip. He wore a ring on his left hand but it was on the little finger. Not that it mattered to her whether or not he was single. She glanced at her own platinum wedding band that had never been removed since her wedding day.

"Tell me what's been happening to you," Andrew said as he fixed his own drink. "What made you decide to come back? Seems an odd time of year for a holiday. Particularly in a place like this. England can be pretty grim once winter sets in."

The invisible doors started to close inside Greer. "I'm here on business," she said, more shortly than she intended.

He wasn't deterred. "What sort of business?"

"Buying." Please let him leave it alone. Go back to the weather. The English are supposed to love discussing their climate.

Andrew settled himself in a wing chair facing her own. He wore a V-neck black sweater over well-worn jeans that hugged every line of his lean hips and powerful legs. Absently switching his glass from hand to hand, he pushed up his sleeves, revealing muscular forearms covered in the same sprinkling of dark hair she had noticed on his thigh. The unwelcome heavy warmth invaded Greer's body again.

For a few seconds he was silent. Firelight glinted on strands of silver at his temple that hadn't been there when she last saw him. The planes beneath his high cheekbones were accented, as was the hollow under his full lower lip and the slight cleft of his chin. Two years had only made him more attractive. She riveted her attention on the strong hands that slowly rolled a stubby goblet of glowing, amber liquid back and forth. A thin, white scar showed from the base of his left thumb to a point beneath his black watchband.

Greer crossed and uncrossed her legs. He must be searching as frantically as she for a way to bring up the past. They both knew she wouldn't be in his house for any other reason.

He leaned forward to throw another log on the fire, and the sweater tightened over his broad shoulders. "How complicated is importing?" he asked suddenly.

She swallowed too much vermouth and smothered a cough. "Not complicated on the scale we do it. In fact importing, or even buying, is stretching it a bit. I probably should have said I was fishing for ideas rather than buying." Greer met his eyes squarely. Bending the truth had never been her strong suit. If Andrew Monthaven was less impressed when he found out exactly what her business was — too bad.

" 'Curiouser and curiouser,' as Alice in Wonderland said." Again his brilliant grin worked its magic.

"Not really. I run a small store. We specialize in the unusual. Everything has a British flavor, although not everything is actually made here. Americans tend to deny it, but they have a tremendous interest in Britain." She hesitated, running a fingernail around the rim of her glass. "A lot of us have roots here. Most people are drawn to their original homelands. Have you noticed that?"

"I suppose so," he said noncommittally. "Who's minding the shop while you're away?"

"My sister. Casey works with me." Greer drank some more vermouth. She felt foolish. How could she expect him to relate to what she was talking about? Andrew Monthaven may have been born in the same country as Greer Beckett, but their worlds were as different as the moon and the earth.

"When you say that you deal in the unusual, what do you mean? Seems you'd run out of unusual British products fairly quickly."

"The shop's called Britmania," she said, as if that might somehow answer his question without her having to elaborate.

"Britmania? Catchy. Sounds like a disease."

Greer became immediately defensive. Regardless of what she sold, Britmania was a success, and it was hers. She'd salvaged her life with it and helped Casey in the process.

"Greer? Are you all right? You're pale."

"I'm just fine, thanks. Fine. When I chose the name of the store it was intended to suggest a disease as you put it. An addiction to anything British," she said, pausing to breathe deeply. "We sell a lot of heraldic stuff. Coats of arms on transfers for windows or car doors. Plaques, ashtrays, glasses and so on."

One of Andrew's long fingers rubbed at the area between his raised brows. "Doormats, too, I suppose."

He was laughing at her. "Absolutely," she said a little too eagerly. "Doormats are big. Nothing like having people wipe their feet on one's family emblem. But we have something for everyone. This year kits have been very successful. Assemble your own Tower of London or Buckingham Palace. All to scale, of course. Complete with lifelike figures of beefeaters, or the royal family, depending upon the kit."

Andrew sank back into his chair and stared at her with what appeared to be fascinated disbelief.

Greer felt shaky but defiant. "We've also had luck with spittoons, cuspidors I think you call them here," she added, unable to stop herself.

"I know what a spittoon is," Andrew assured her.

"Ours are shaped like the royal coach and come complete with a bag of barroom sawdust to use inside."

"I hope it's genuine sawdust. Nothing that's been cleaned up," he teased.

"We guarantee that it's been used in a London pub," she said seriously.

Andrew began to laugh. He set his glass on the hearth and covered his face with both hands.

Greer waited, trying to keep a serious face, but she wanted to laugh, too. Not because she found her business amusing, but because it would be a relief.

A snort punctuated Andrew's attempt to

control himself. Finally he straightened and laced his fingers behind his head. "You're marvelous. You turn up in my house like a specter and scare me half to death. Then you barrel out into the night while I can only wait for you to come back. Now you sit in an Englishman's study, telling him that you make a living by apparently poking fun at anything British. And I thought this was going to be another run-of-the-mill evening at Ringstead Hall, the disgustingly ostentatious little manor I call home."

The flush that crept from beneath Greer's collar swept over her cheeks, dull and throbbing. She'd overdone it. He thought she was deliberately trying to insult him. "Sorry," she muttered.

"Why should you be? I've been highly entertained. Now I'd better get you home so you can rest that active brain of yours. Tomorrow's another day. Who knows what new and lucrative ideas you'll come up with once you get started?"

Greer felt she had been dismissed. He was a busy man and must have other things to do. Perhaps he had a date. As she put on the coat Andrew held for her, Greer struggled with an irrational sense of disappointment.

This time they left through a side door and walked behind the house to a ramshackle outbuilding. She waited silently while he backed a car from its unlighted shelter.

The decrepit appearance of the tiny vehicle appalled her. It was an Austin Mini and resembled a chipped, black bread box with strategically placed dents. Her own secondhand Chevy was elegant by comparison.

"You were expecting a Rolls?" Andrew said, startling Greer.

He had slipped from the car and come to open the passenger door without breaking her reverie. "What makes you think you can second-guess my thoughts?" she asked, amused.

He laughed. "It doesn't take much effort. They're written all over that gorgeous face of yours. Wait," he said as if he'd just been struck with a dazzling insight. "I've got it. You can sell me a couple of your car decals — something classy. They'll improve the image no end."

"Touché. I asked for that," Greer answered as she moved quietly past him and got into the car. He didn't see her smiling in the dark.

They took the coast road leading southwest to Weymouth. Andrew insisted it was more interesting, particularly since the moon had decided to appear and paint a wide swath of unpolished silver over an inky English Channel. As Greer looked at the glittering path it seemed encrusted with shifting sapphire flecks.

"Have you planned every minute of your stay?" Andrew asked, just when she thought the silence would split her head.

He's as uncomfortable as I am, she thought. "Tomorrow morning I'm going to a market in Dorchester. My landlady told me it's a good one."

"I'm not sure what it's like now," Andrew answered. "That market's been held every Wednesday for as long as I remember. I used to go with my father. He enjoyed the animals. But it'll be the stalls you want to see. Maybe you can buy a supply of miniature chamber pots from some local concern. Perfectly authentic, just a little undersized. People could use them as planters."

"Wonderful," Greer said, determined not to be baited. "I'll remember the idea. Silk flowers might look good in them."

"Then what?"

"After the market, you mean?"

Andrew changed gears to go up a steep

hill. "Yes. It's all over by early afternoon." They crested the rise and the lights of Weymouth spread before them. The curve of the bay was outlined by a continuous, looped strand of brilliant lights along the promenade.

"I'm going to the village of Ferndale. There's a church I want to visit." Greer hadn't intended to mention Ferndale. She held her breath, expecting a question from Andrew, but surprisingly he made no comment.

It was time to close one segment of her life and try to open another. Ferndale was more than a burial place for her husband and child. Tomorrow she'd see their graves for the first, and maybe the last time. But she also hoped to begin her quest for the family she had never known.

One of the details she had gotten from Tom and Dianne Wyatt was that Ruby Timmons, Greer's biological mother, came from Ferndale. An address in the village was on her own birth certificate, although the Wyatts also mentioned that her mother moved away shortly after her birth. The certificate didn't give her father's name.

As the car swept down toward the town, Andrew remained silent until they neared St. John's Terrace. Then he only inquired in which boardinghouse she was staying.

Ocean Vista was a grandiose name for the narrow, terraced establishment where Greer had rented a bed-sitting room, with breakfast. When they pulled up outside she tried to concentrate on the comforting thought of the nightly hot water bottle Mrs. Findlay had promised.

She forced herself to wait for Andrew to get out and come to her side of the car. They hadn't mentioned what she knew was as much on his mind as hers. But maybe it wasn't necessary. She had botched their conversation, but surely he sensed that she no longer blamed him for her baby's death.

"Thank you very much for being so kind," she said. He had cupped her elbow as they walked to the steps. "And again, I am sorry for being a nuisance." Why did she wish that he would hold her, that he wasn't about to walk back out of her life?

He opened the unlocked front door and pushed it wide. "You aren't a nuisance. Except when you keep apologizing."

An impulse made Greer turn around before going inside. "I'll send those decals."

Andrew was striding around the car. "Thanks," he said, and without pause continued on. "I'll pick you up in the morning. Is nine too early? All the best bargains go first and we wouldn't want to miss any."

"What do you mean?"

"The market. We should be there early. Wear comfortable shoes."

Greer realized her mouth was open. "Andrew," she started to protest.

But the car door slammed. The engine sputtered, then turned over before the little black vehicle circled toward the coast road and Ringstead Hall.

Chapter 4

When Andrew got home, he didn't bother to put the Mini away. He strode through the side door and upstairs to his rooms.

Greer had come back. All the way from Weymouth he had silently repeated the phrase. At the top of the lane leading to his gates, he'd rolled down the window, cut the engine and coasted. Wind tore through hedgerows almost bare of foliage, to carry an earthy aroma of gorse into the car. Instead of distracting him, the scents, the sounds, the cold snap around his ears, had made Greer's lovely image more pervasive.

In his study, he threw the car keys on his desk and splashed a shot of whiskey into a glass. He flopped into the chair Greer had used and flexed the cramped muscles in his long legs. The only problem with the Mini was that it didn't fit him.

Andrew stood abruptly and swallowed the Scotch. With the fire out, a draft stole down the chimney, cooling the room. The casement rattled and he smiled. His favorite kind of night. Only holding Greer secure in his arms until dawn would make it more perfect. His fist clenched around the empty glass. He must take one slow step at a time, or he'd lose her before ever having her. Another shower sounded good. That's where he did some of his clearest thinking.

The bedroom was colder than the study. As Andrew stripped, his skin tightened. He liked the invigorating sensation, but someone who wasn't used to it might not. Installing central heating in a house like this would be costly and difficult: as soon as possible he would look into it, though.

Naked, he crossed the hall to the bathroom and jerked a yellowing shower curtain around the tub. Made of enameled metal, the bath stood on high legs and claw feet. Bluish traces of iron showed through where the coating had thinned.

He rotated the faucets and waited, shivering. It took a while for the water to heat. As a boy he had learned to gauge the right moment to enter this same tub by the amount of steam on the black-and-white tiled walls. Rivulets formed on the shiny surface and Andrew climbed behind the billowing shower curtain. Something about the way air slid beneath the door and along the floor always made the rubberized sheet flap against his body.

Greer was accustomed to the modern-istic life-style he had experienced when he visited the States. She probably preferred it, and who could blame her? It wasn't out of the question that he'd choose to move there himself one day. He had good contacts and the career opportunities appealed to him. Perhaps, with Greer . . . he was fantasizing again. He had been thinking of updating his own part of Ringstead, anyway. This would just speed the process. Maybe she would enjoy helping him make decisions, choose styles and colors — she certainly had plenty of ingenuity. He laughed and allowed the water to beat on his face. Her eyes had glittered when she told him about her shop, challenging him, testing. As he knew very well, Greer was a strong, independent woman, but she cared what he thought of her.

He soaped his skin vigorously. Logical planning was essential. There was a lot of ground to cover, old wounds to heal. And he couldn't be certain of her feelings to-ward him, not yet. But she came back, dammit. And she had engineered a way to see him. Unanswered questions swarmed in his mind, but one fact remained certain: she wouldn't have sought him out simply to say hi, as she put it.

They had avoided mentioning her husband and child. Tomorrow she planned to visit Ferndale. Andrew's thoughts raced and he scrubbed harder. Any normal man or woman would do the same thing. In the morning he'd tell her he knew why she was going to the village and offer to take her. Make everything open between them. Suffering could push people apart, but it could also bring them together. Greer's loss had already done both. The next move should be his.

He had been the one to suggest taking her back to Weymouth. What would she have said if he'd asked her to stay with him tonight? Would she have agreed? The intense rush of desire that spread through his loins made him arch his back and grit his teeth.

Greer was beautiful. Fragile, like a titian-haired, porcelain doll — so totally feminine that she aroused an overwhelming combination of sensuality and protectiveness. No other woman had reached him in the same way. He wanted her. But it was too soon to make love to her, despite his countless dreams of doing so since he last saw her. In the seething dark of many nights he had mentally undressed and carried her to bed. He imagined her softness beneath him, around him, her blue eyes glazed with passion as he entered her. Each time the fantasy ended, he awoke bathed in sweat. And always as his eyes closed again, he felt her lying in the hollow of his shoulder, her hair spread across his chest. Then, while she slept, he kissed her eyelids, her pliant lips, and bent his head to her breast . . .

His legs were rubbery. Andrew turned off the water, then dropped his head forward and pressed his palms against the tile to support his weight. He didn't even know how long she intended to stay in Dorset. Their exchanges had been awkward, general, avoiding anything too personal. But it didn't matter. It took time to wear down barriers and he hadn't begun to work at them.

If there were another permanent man in her life she wouldn't be using the name Beckett or wearing the same wedding band he remembered. The only rival he had to contend with was dead, Andrew was sure of that. He was sorry that Colin Beckett had died a violent, senseless death, but there was no reason for Greer to remain a widow indefinitely. She was ready to love again, ready for him.

Andrew stepped onto the linoleum floor and reached for a towel. He hadn't lived the celibate existence his peers apparently suspected, but his liaisons had become infrequent, bringing only fleeting, physical satisfaction. All the time, the woman he hopelessly desired lingered, partially hidden in his subconscious. Two years ago there had been no choice but to let her go. Now there could be no question of losing her again.

Distant ringing jarred his concentration. The phone. Immediately he made a mental check of his hospitalized patients. Francine Stevens was still in the guarded phase with meningitis. Everyone else should be comfortable.

Hitching the towel around his waist, he went to grab the phone in his bedroom. "Monthaven," he said sharply. A steady buzzing told him the caller had hung up.

Andrew depressed the cradle and started to dial the medical-center number, then changed his mind and softly replaced the receiver. It could have been Greer. When he failed to answer, she would assume he'd gone somewhere other than home after he left her. He could get the boardinghouse number and call her. No, he couldn't. All those houses had one phone — in the hallway. He'd disturb everyone and embarrass Greer. Please, he thought, let her call back. He lay on the bed and stared at the ceiling.

When the phone rang again he almost knocked it off the bedside table in his hurry to answer. "Hello — Greer?"

There was a short silence before Bob Wilson asked, "Who's Greer?"

Andrew felt himself redden. "It's late, Bob. Problems?"

"You didn't answer my question, Andy. Who's Greer?"

"A friend. No one you know."

"I'm glad your friend is female. You may need her."

Andrew bit back a sharp retort before answering. "I thought we'd covered that topic. If Coover's looking for a way to shut me up, he's going to have to come up with something better than a question about my sexual preference." He paused, but Bob made no comment. "I'm beat, Bob. Is this important?"

When the other man finally spoke, Andrew had to strain to hear. "Neil called."

"You mean Neil Jones?" Andrew said, frowning.

"Yes, Neil Jones. He said you two had dinner in London a couple of weeks ago."

"So what?" Andrew was getting irritated. "I was eating alone at Simpsons. He asked if he could join me. What could I say? He called to tell you that?" he said, sitting up.

"The man's homosexual," Bob said flatly.

A sliver of cold worked its way up Andrew's spine. "I know what Neil is. It was never a secret, even in school."

Bob's voice dropped to an angry rasp. "Last night he had a visitor, you fool. Lewis Kingsly. He practices dermatology in Harley Street and uses Neil's supply house. His excuse for dropping by Neil's was thin — they only know each other professionally. But Kinglsy's one of Coover's buddies and he asked questions about you. He found out you shared rooms with Neil at Oxford."

"A lot of people know where I lived in Oxford — and with whom. I've never attempted to hide it," Andrew answered.

He heard the familiar sound of Bob inhaling on a cigarette. "Andy. I care what happens to you. We've been friends too long for me to allow you to destroy yourself over a point of — of — you know, I'm not even sure what is making you persist with this — vendetta. Honor, I suppose. Honor won't pay the bills, friend. Or stop you from dying inside if they take your license away. You've got too much to lose. Please, see Coover personally, tomorrow. Say whatever it takes to stop this thing. Tell him you were too hasty about the Michael Drake case and you'll call off the inquiry."

"Like hell I will," Andrew exploded. "I've got nothing to hide." The moisture on his skin had turned icy. "Sure, I lived in a house with Neil, the same as you did," he said sharply. "But that's all. He wasn't my type any more than he was yours. Still isn't. I just can't bring myself to ignore the guy when I see him. He's lonely. It can't be easy for him and it isn't up to you, or me or anyone to judge him." Andrew paused to gain control. "And I'm not launching a vendetta. Simply trying to protect potential victims from Winston Coover."

"Okay," Bob said stiffly as he tapped his fingernail against the mouthpiece. "All true. All admirable sentiments. But. Neil told Kingsly what good friends the three of us still are. Stories are easily distorted. If someone wants to embellish the facts it won't be hard," he warned.

"Bob." Andrew gripped the telephone cord between his fingers. "No one could make an accusation like that stick. It won't wash. Thanks for the concern, but stop worrying."

Muffled laughter skittered across the line. The Wilsons had company. "I've got to go," Bob said shortly. "Contact Winston Coover and stay away from Neil. Believe me, he can do plenty of damage."

Andrew continued to stare at the receiver in his hand long after Bob hung up.

Chapter 5

"He said, 'You won't get anything like it, anywhere else, for less than twice the price.' Roughly," Andrew explained. "Or something pretty close to that. Sometimes I wonder if even a cockney understands what another cockney says."

Greer and Andrew stood in the middle of a throng surrounding open doors at the back of a truck. A thickset man, balanced on the tailgate of the vehicle, held high a red enameled saucepan. He turned it slowly, displaying the utensil as if it was an exquisitely delicate piece of crystal. His sudden loud guffaw at a comment from an onlooker brought an answering ripple of laughter. Then he lowered his head to rub his bulbous nose on a grubby woolen sleeve.

"I love the way he sounds," Greer shouted to make herself heard above the market's cacophony. "Do many people come down from London to sell here?"

Andrew nodded. "Loads. Every week. They make a circuit of markets like this all over the country."

"Now what's going on?" Greer asked. "Is it an auction?" She watched Andrew's profile. His chin was lifted, accenting the sharp angle of his jaw. She noticed the way his hair curled forward behind his ears, and the gold of forgotten summers tipped his thick eyelashes.

He glanced down at her and put a hand on the back of her neck as she was jostled against him. "It's not really an auction. It's a sort of ritual. The seller throws out an inflated price. Then the crowd collectively forces it down to just about what the item's worth. A dozen or so customers buy identical *bargains,* and everyone concerned thinks it's a personal coup. Perfect."

His hand on her neck had been an unconscious gesture. But when their eyes met Greer was sure they both felt drawn together in ways other than totally physical. Carefully, still gazing into her eyes, he rubbed his fingertips up and down, tangling them in her hair. Greer wanted to slip an arm around his waist, to lean against him. Instead she looked away and stood on tiptoe, pretending to be engrossed in the sale until he dropped his hand.

"We'd better move on," he said evenly. "The *collectors'* stalls are on the far side of the yard."

Greer followed in the path he made through straining bodies. A part of her wished she could break free of the reservations that kept her captive. That errant scrap of romantic longing that refused to be snuffed out wanted him to touch her again. Fortunately, he was bound to be more reticent in the future. Although her withdrawal had been subtle, she was sure he'd understood her unspoken message. *Don't come too near.* Her own reactions unsettled Greer. It was as if she'd known him well for a long time. There was a kind of familiarity with him, a closeness. He was gentle, yet masculine in a way that made her guarded femininity come alive. And most disturbing of all, she found him incredibly sexy. The various effects he had on her were threatening, too potent for comfort.

Gravel scrunched under their feet. Spicy scents mingled with the aroma of coffee and warm sugary buns coming from a food vendor's van. Over all hung the earthy smell of farm animals. Myriad rows of clothing dangled from poles wherever Greer looked. She smiled and shook her head each time a garment was held toward her.

"Come on, love. Takes a redhead to wear this color green," a squat man in a checked wool cap cajoled.

Andrew broke his determined stride and turned back to meet her grin. His answering smile did something strange to her insides. They examined the proffered sweater together.

"It would look good on you," Andrew said. Then to the salesman he added, "We'll take it."

"*I'll* take it," Greer corrected firmly, when he reached inside his tweed jacket for his wallet. She shouldn't buy anything she didn't need, but neither could she accept a gift from Andrew.

It was a mistake to be with him again. She should have followed her first instinct this morning and told the landlady that she didn't want to be disturbed — by anyone. But he wouldn't really come, she had assured herself, while she tried to ignore the flicker of hope that he might. The doorbell had rung at exactly nine o'clock and she'd barely stopped herself from grabbing her coat and running to meet him.

While Greer paid for the sweater, she heard Andrew's soft whistle. A tune she'd heard on the radio and liked. Now it grated on her nerves. She received her change and waited for her package to be wrapped. The process took too long. And all the time Andrew whistled. This was pointless. He didn't really want to be here, and she wouldn't be able to concentrate on the merchandise as long as he was.

"Andrew —" she began.

"I know," he said, cutting her off as he tucked the parcel under his arm. "You're sorry. And again, don't be. I'm a man you hardly know and you'd probably be too in-dependent to accept a gift from me if we'd been friends for years. Am I right?" he said, flashing her his winning smile.

I wish you wouldn't smile at me like that. "Yes. Only I couldn't have said it so well. Anyway, I wanted to say something else," she hedged.

"Shoot." He ducked under an empty rack and started away.

Greer fell into step beside him. "It was nice of you to bring me here. I appreciate your kindness. But you must be bored sick and knowing you are embarrasses me." She pressed her lips together and stared ahead with fierce concentration.

They walked in silence for endless moments before Andrew stopped and pushed the parcel into her arms. She almost dropped it.

"Are you trying to tell me to get lost?" he asked bluntly.

Blood rushed to Greer's cheeks. Ugly blushes — the curse of having pale skin. "No," she said, hating the wobble in her voice. "I just know you're a busy man with a job to do. You can't be getting anything out of this, and I don't want you to feel you have to guide me around. You wouldn't spend a morning here by choice. You're being polite. Of course, I think that's very nice, but I also think it's time we both got on with what we should be doing."

A battery of expressions crossed Andrew's features, ending with a smile that made a mockery of Greer's speech.

"Have you finished?" he inquired softly. "Polite. What a laugh. I don't spend time anywhere I don't choose to be just as you didn't come to Ringstead Hall yesterday because you wanted to admire antiques. Greer, you were looking for me, whether you admit it or not. You and I have a past to confront. Before you left England you were hurting too badly to see straight, and

I didn't have what it would have taken to help you. The feelings I had for you then were confused. I still don't entirely understand them. But I know I've never forgotten you. And once you started to recover from — once you recovered you remembered me, too . . ."

"Please . . ."

Andrew grasped her left wrist. "Admit it."

"You're very sure of yourself," Greer answered evasively. Her nerves felt raw.

People bustled around them but Andrew seemed oblivious. "Not as sure as I'd like to be," he said.

"We shouldn't be having this conversation — not like this. All I wanted was to face up to the things I can't change, then let them go. I needed to apologize to you — and to say thank-you for everything you did for Colleen."

"It wasn't enough." His mouth closed in a bitter line. "And I'm still sorry about that."

"I think we should both try to forget it all," Greer said shakily.

He slid his fingers to her wedding band. "Colin's ring, right? You didn't marry again?"

"No."

"If you're trying to make a fresh start, isn't it time you took this thing off?"

She shook her head. "I never thought about it." *I can't cope with this.*

"You aren't in love with someone else?"

"No!" *Too emphatic.* Her temples throbbed.

"Then why are you so standoffish? Is there something about me that you don't like? If so, tell me and I will get lost." Andrew's voice dropped a fraction.

Greer was disgusted to feel tears well in her eyes. She squinted at an overcast sky. "I'm . . ."

"*Don't* — say you're sorry."

She tapped the toe of her suede boot against the gravel. Obviously, he would not take no for an answer. The only thing to do was confront him. "I think you're attractive," she began. "Much too attractive. But I can't stay in England indefinitely and I have a lot to accomplish. I don't have time to — to waste." *Or to fall in love.* The air about her took on a crystalline quality. Was she allowing this man to awaken her sexually and emotionally? Had she unknowingly wanted him even when he was merely a memory, separated from her by five thousand miles and a mountain of bitterness? The idea was incredible — out of the question.

A hint of satisfaction in Andrew's eyes irritated her. He'd been pleased rather than angered by her response — gratified by the confusion her face must have betrayed. He retrieved the parcel from her unresisting grasp. "What's the hurry to get back to the States?" he said easily.

"I didn't say there was a hurry. But I do have a business to run. That's how I make a living and I can't afford to be away too long."

Englishmen of Andrew's class were never supposed to discuss money, particularly the lack of it. Greer watched defiantly for his reaction. His expression revealed nothing.

"I understand," he said, sweeping his free hand in a wide gesture. "But all this definitely counts as attending to business. Let's get a cup of coffee and one of those fattening buns. Then we'll track down chamber pots, or whatever other treasures we can find."

At first, Greer's reaction was total frustration. This man was impossible! Ruffling Andrew Monthaven for more than an instant would never be easy. It seemed the only thing to do was to give in gracefully. Summoning a smile, she decided to throw caution to the wind — temporarily, of course. "I'd love some coffee," she enthused. "But hold the bun or I'll lose my girlish figure."

Immediately she regretted the last comment. Her coat was draped around her shoulders. Andrew surveyed the thin, peach silk blouse and camel gabardine skirt she wore, and there was no mistaking his approval.

"Risk the bun," he teased her. "I don't see any reason why you shouldn't."

The glow of pleasure Greer experienced remained while she took the coffee Andrew bought her. She bit into a doughy round cake that sent a shower of powdered sugar down her front. They both laughed as she tried to balance the sticky confection in the same hand as her Styrofoam cup, while she brushed at her skirt.

Andrew's "Messy, messy" was met by Greer's disdainfully raised brows. "Allow me," he said as he dropped to one knee and flicked away the last grains of sugar with his napkin.

The sight of his dark bent head and the clean hair touching his shirt collar tilted her heart. "There," he said, standing and straightening his sleeves at the wrist. "Good as new."

Greer stared at his wrist, suddenly fascinated by the sinew running along the back of his hand. She had never been so totally aware of a man. Not true. There had been Colin. Her attraction to Andrew could be easily explained by the fact that she was so vulnerable right now. But what about Andrew? What was drawing him to her? She drained the last of her coffee, keeping her lashes lowered. He was attracted to her. He'd as good as said so and she could feel it.

"You're very quiet," he said. "Something wrong?"

Greer blinked rapidly and met Andrew's questioning eyes. He was more than attractive. All man, in an elegantly powerful way. Tall and broad, but not clumsy as some big men were. A mental image of him naked shocked her and she looked away. But she'd pictured him anyway — finely toned muscle, slender waist and hips, the strong legs and arms she'd already glimpsed. Thank goodness he couldn't read her mind. The sooner she put distance between them, the better. No point torturing herself with ideas she could do nothing about. Even if she wanted to get involved, a man like Andrew would never be interested in a woman who was no longer whole.

"Greer?"

She tossed her empty cup into a garbage can. "Just taking everything in. It's all so purposeful — and cheerful. People with missions they expect to accomplish. No doubts," she said emphatically. *Don't think aloud. He's astute and he'll make the right connections if you're not careful. He'll figure out how insecure you are.* Quickly Greer covered her thoughts. "It's amazing how the stall owners can say the same things over and over, then keep laughing with all that gusto," she pointed out.

Andrew paused before replying. "They're a unique breed. Doing the best they can with what has to be done. We could all take a lesson from them," he said seriously. He watched her closely for a second longer then threw his empty coffee cup away with both of their napkins stuffed inside.

When he took her hand and tucked it into the crook of his elbow, Greer stiffened. Then she made a deliberate effort to relax, to stroll nonchalantly beside him. The heat of his body made her acutely conscious of her skin that seemed to consist of a million exposed and vibrating nerves.

"Well —" Andrew exclaimed suddenly. He grinned and swerved away from her.

Before Greer could follow, a small girl

shot from a crowd in front of a vegetable stand and launched herself into Andrew's outstretched arms. Greer heard the child's high-pitched, "Andy, Andy," then he scooped her up and swung her around.

Unable to help herself, Greer approached slowly, like a moth drawn to a flame. The man and child were the flame, she was the moth. Simply watching them could bruise her newfound wings, but she couldn't resist the urge to see clearly.

"Why aren't you in school, young lady?" Andrew was saying. "And where's your mother?"

The girl was about five or six, thin, with spindly, blond pigtails and bright blue eyes behind pink-rimmed glasses. "Got a cold," she sputtered, swiping at her nose with the back of a tiny hand. "Mummy's buying cabbage. Yuck. Can't you tell her it's bad for kids with colds to eat cabbage? Ple-a-se, Uncle Andy?"

Small and blond. Greer's build, Colin's coloring. Suddenly so cold that goose bumps chased up the backs of her arms, Greer stood a few feet from them. Her legs seemed like concrete. Colleen might have looked . . . not now, she mustn't do this now. It was time she ought to be able to get within touching distance of a child without coming unglued. *Stay calm.*

Andrew felt his heart expand to see the trust in Simonne Wilson's bright eyes. He hugged her to his neck. "Little girls should eat what their mothers tell them to eat." When Simonne began to object, he said, "No — don't try soft-soaping me." Her small body was angular, her clutching fingers bony. A waft of licorice met his nostrils and he pulled gently on a pigtail to look at her face. A telltale black rim outlined her bowed mouth. "I see kids with colds can still eat their favorite candy." And she laughed. As always, he was struck by the girl's fragility. Bob and Lauren's child should have been a great, muscular specimen, not this delicate will-o'-the-wisp.

Greer. He held Simonne closer and stood still, smiling at Greer. Her clear blue gaze froze his blood. What was she thinking? A couple passed between them, momentarily obscuring her from him. Then he saw her face again, unchanged, a waxen mold. Simonne twisted to sit more comfortably. He studied her face briefly, kissed the end of her pink nose, then took a step toward the beautiful red-haired woman who suddenly seemed totally removed from him.

"Come and meet my friend Simonne

Wilson," he called to Greer.

Why was she making no attempt to move or respond? *Colin and Colleen.* She was looking at a man who bore no resemblance to her dead husband with a child years older than her own ever became, yet he knew she was reminded of them both. Tears pricked at his eyes. She wasn't over any of it. The certainty shook him. So he hadn't imagined her confusion when he'd touched her. For two years she'd kept her emotions on hold. Somehow Greer had managed to avoid coming close to anything — anyone who might peel off the thin veneer she'd drawn over the gaping wound of her loss. He could help her if she'd let him. She needed him as much as he wanted her. She should have another baby — and soon. Her catharsis was long overdue. A baby could be that for her; together with a man who would love her. Simonne wriggled and he set her down, shrugging tense muscles in his shoulders.

Greer felt them coming. She looked into the distance and took a deep breath. Of course he loved children, was wonderful with them. That's why he'd become a pediatrician. Her eyes met Andrew's, then the child's. Something was irresistible about the sight of a strong man's tenderness toward little ones. He should have his own children — something she could no longer give any man. Andrew would marry and have a family. It shouldn't freshen her sense of emptiness to recognize that or make her feel — what — jealous? No, no.

"Simonne, this is my American friend, Greer Beckett. She likes markets — and cabbage," Andrew said, giving Greer a knowing look.

He hadn't noticed her hesitation. "Hi, Simonne. It's nice to meet you," Greer said easily. Her face felt stiff, but no one else could know that.

"Hello," Simonne said. Her pointed chin showed above a gray woolen scarf wound several times around her neck. "My friend Stacey's mother went to America. To Phila— Phila— well anyway, she went there."

"Philadelphia." Greer laughed despite herself. "That's in the state of Pennsylvania. Just as hard to say, and more difficult to spell. I come from the other side of the country."

Simonne grunted thoughtfully. Her glasses gave her a wise-elf appearance and made her nose resemble a slightly squished cherry. Greer held her smile in place. Without thinking she brushed away a

108

strand of hair caught in the girl's mouth, then took an involuntary step backward. Soft little face, innocent eyes. This was exactly why she always avoided getting too near children — easier on the heart.

"Hi, Andy. What brings you here?" A pretty blond woman, carrying a shopping bag, joined them. "Don't tell me you've taken up buying your veggies with the rest of us ordinary mortals," she teased.

Andrew snorted. "Hello, Lauren. How are you? Meet Greer Beckett. Does this child have a fever?" he said all in one breath. His hand lay along Simonne's cheek and neck.

"It was up a point this morning. That's why I kept her out of school," Lauren explained impatiently. "Could you stop being a doctor long enough to make proper introductions, please?" Lauren gave Greer an exasperated nod.

"Why is she dressed like an Eskimo? You'll drive her temperature up," Andrew said, unwinding the scarf from Simonne's neck. The child sighed in relief, sending her wispy bangs off her forehead.

"Thank you, Andrew," Lauren said. "What would I do without you and Bob to tell me how to be a good mum?" The woman was an older, rounder version of her daughter, with the same piercing blue eyes. And her pleasant face was showing signs of irritation.

Andrew reached to pull Greer to his side. "Lauren Wilson. This is Greer Beckett —"

"From America," Simonne interrupted.

"Right." He pretended displeasure by scowling at the girl. "Greer, Lauren Wilson is a friend of mine. Her husband, Bob, and I grew up together. They're also my closest neighbors — three miles east."

Lauren Wilson's appraisal was frankly curious but cheerful. "Pleased to meet you. This is dreadful," she said turning to Andrew, "but I've got to run. I didn't expect to take so long and Bob will fillet me if I get another parking fine. It costs a fortune if you run over the time limit now, and they won't even let you argue. I think the town keeps running on money extracted from harassed drivers. How about dinner tomorrow night?" she said, taking Simonne's hand. "Bring Greer so I can get to know her," she added.

"Will do," Andrew called after Lauren's retreating figure. Simonne, trotting to keep up with her mother, swung back once to wave.

Left alone, Greer and Andrew avoided direct eye contact.

"Do you usually accept dinner invitations on another person's behalf?" Greer asked finally. "I can't go anyway."

"What did you think of them?"

Greer pivoted to face Andrew, only to find him comfortably slouched against the side of an animal pen scratching the ears of a liquid-eyed calf.

"Don't try to buffalo me with avoidance tactics," she said sharply.

He swatted at flies on the animal's head. "This will grow into a cow, not a buffalo. Actually, it'll only grow as far as it takes to become veal, poor little devil."

She wasn't amused, or distracted. "Give my regrets to Lauren. It was nice of her to include a stranger in her invitation, but I've got a couple of busy days ahead. Thanks for the lift."

Before she'd taken two steps, Andrew blocked her path. Greer moved to go around him and the wretched hip locked. She faltered, and immediately his hand was under her forearm, supporting her. His touch provoked a series of reactions. To be held, desired by a man she might be able to care for — the idea sent her into turmoil — but perhaps this attention sprang from pity or the professional concern that must come so naturally to him.

111

Flights of fancy were a dangerous luxury she should avoid.

"I'm fine, Andrew," she said, but his grip only tightened.

A deep line formed between his fine brows. "I'm not sure you are. But that's something we can discuss later," he said, forcing Greer to look into his eyes. "I wasn't being overbearing when I accepted Lauren's invitation for both of us. She was in a hurry and it was a reflex action. Will you come with me, please? They're nice people — the best. I think you'd have a good time."

He was irresistible when his honey eyes darkened like that. She eased her arm free of his fingers.

"Come on, Greer," Andrew said, unwilling to give up. "Get me off the hook. Lauren will make sure I never hear the last of it if you don't show."

"I shouldn't," she said, sighing. "But — okay. Write down their address and I'll meet you there."

"Don't be ridiculous," he scoffed. "How? On horseback? They live miles from anywhere just as I do. I'll pick you up."

Greer opened her mouth to argue, then shut it with a snap. Petty squabbles weren't her style. And he was right. "Thank you," she said perfunctorily. "What time?"

"I'll find out and let you know." There was a gruffness in his tone. "Greer, we have to talk — you know that?"

I can't. "We will — before I go home."

Andrew studied Greer's averted face. Waiting for her to approach him again would be futile. He straightened the parcel beneath his arm, placed a hand at her waist and propelled her toward the exit. "I think it should be now," he said. "We shouldn't hedge about Colin or the baby any longer."

She didn't answer. It wasn't going to be easy, but he'd wear her down. Little invisible thorns protruded from her, trying to put him off every time he approached. But he wasn't about to be deterred. Not when he wanted something, or someone, the way he wanted Greer Beckett.

Twice she stared at him over her shoulder, a wary glimmer in her wonderful deep blue eyes. Her lashes had to be the thickest and darkest he'd ever seen. All last night, while he tried to sleep, he remembered different things about her. The way those lashes formed shadows on her cheeks when she looked down, the way the loose russet curls swished about her shoulders as she tossed them back. And her mouth, full and soft. How would it feel . . .

Just what he needed while he was trying to cope with impending disaster in his professional life. The return of the one woman with the ability to knock him flat.

A few large drops of rain started to fall. "Wait." He guided Greer beneath a green-and-white-striped awning. "Put your coat on properly or you'll get soaked," he told her. He held the coat while she slid her arms into the sleeves. The temptation to pull her against him made him feel almost disoriented. "Let's make a run for it."

With one arm around her shoulders, he held her close at his side, and they hurried down the steps and out of the market yard. The rain wasn't heavy, but it gave him an excuse to get near her. At the curb the lights changed and they had to wait before they could cross to South Walks Road. He knew every inch of the little town. Dorchester was only eight miles north of Ringstead Hall, about the same as its distance from Weymouth to the southwest. The medical center was also in Dorchester. Damn — the medical center — he was due there before noon. If, as he suspected, she wanted to get away, that would make it easy for her. Unless he could persuade her to wait for him.

Andrew checked his watch. Eleven-thirty. He glanced down at Greer. She felt insubstantial under his arm and he slid it lower across her back. To appear uncertain could be fatal. Understanding but firm should be a good approach. "How hungry are you?" he inquired.

Her face came up — even paler than usual. "Not very," she said, dropping her head.

A gust of wind whipped her hair across his chest. Several strands flew against his face and he closed his eyes. He couldn't let her slip away from him again. "Do you feel like talking?" he asked tentatively.

"If you want to." Her voice was muffled.

"I want to," he said firmly. "We'll have lunch. But first I have to stop in at — at the medical center. You could scout out the town for an hour. The museum's interesting —" The stiffening of her body alerted him. "You don't like museums?" he said.

Something pinched his back. It was her fingers closing on his skin. "Take me with you," she said. She kept walking although his own pace had slowed. "Then we'll have lunch."

He felt slightly sick. "You'd be bored in the visitors' room. Nothing to do but read old magazines."

"Andrew." Abruptly she pulled up and looked directly into his eyes. "The main reason for coming to England was to confront the things I've avoided. If you'll let me, I'll come to the center with you."

The artificially cheerful voice that said, "Nothing I'd like better," didn't sound like his own.

Chapter 6

C

Greer leaned her head against the Mini's cool window. Where had it all begun? Was it back in Seattle, when she and Colin had planned to come here? She supposed that could be the real start of her journey to this point. But it wasn't. Her adoption by Tom and Dianne Wyatt was. Now she must discover her true beginnings in this place. A nerve twitched at the corner of her right eye. Work through the stages, then get on with life.

Small shops slid by. On the left they passed a Tudor building, now a restaurant. *Judge Jeffrey's* was the name painted on a swinging sign above the leaded windows. Across the street black metal railings guarded the gray statue of an unsmiling man. Next she saw a museum. Must be the one Andrew had mentioned. Soon they'd be at the medical center. She didn't feel apprehensive. Odd. As soon as she'd made the decision to go, it had seemed inevitable. Later, after lunch, she'd leave Andrew and go to Ferndale.

"Are you sure you want to do this?" he asked quietly. His fingers were outstretched as he shifted gears with the palm.

"Of course. Apart from anything else, it makes more sense than wandering around in the cold," she said. For the rest of whatever time they spent together, she would prove she wasn't an emotional wreck.

Andrew smiled faintly, his eyes on the road. "That's what I like. Practicality. Unfortunately, you may not find the waiting room much warmer than it is out here. But I won't be long," he assured her.

He swung right onto a narrow street lined with terraced houses and Greer sat straighter. She remembered this. Identical bay windows, one above the other, sporting lace curtains. Only drainpipes, painted in different colors to match the trim, separated and distinguished one building from the next. The taxi had brought her past these homes on her way back to Seattle. Greer looked ahead. Titian ribbons wound along the pavement where many wheels had passed over fallen leaves.

After a left turn, then a right, she saw the medical center. Greer's stomach contracted sharply. The same building, the tall gates she'd seen before, and the wide crescent-shaped steps to the front entrance. Why did she feel as if this was the first time she'd been here?

"Here we are," Andrew said, pulling the decrepit Mini in between a Jaguar and a silver Mercedes sports. "Hang on while I get my stuff."

He got out and tipped his seat forward to reach a black leather medical bag. It was scuffed at the corners, scratched around the latches. The man didn't care about things — only people. So special. Greer watched him gather a pile of folders and tuck them under his arm before slamming his door. She glanced at her hands, deliberately relaxing the fists she'd unconsciously made.

A blast of chilly air blew her hair forward when Andrew opened her door. Immediately she tossed her head and swung her feet out. *Hurry, now. This is easy — just one tiny step forward. There's nothing to be afraid of.*

"Okay?" Andrew held the back of her arm while he slammed the door with an elbow.

Greer smiled up at him. "Mmm. This place hasn't changed much. Looks as thoroughly uninviting as I remember. Not travel-brochure material." She sounded bright. The thought gave her confidence.

"I suppose I've never really looked at it," he said, wrinkling his straight nose. "But you're right. It is a bit grim. I'd better get in so we can have that lunch. I'm starving."

Food didn't interest Greer. She concentrated on the sound of their footsteps crunching gravel. The rain had stopped and there was a smell of damp earth. Andrew walked slightly behind her to the steps, his height and bulk a solid reassurance. They started up and she glanced back. Even a step above him, the top of her head was only level with his chin.

He stopped abruptly and Greer sought his eyes, but he wasn't looking at her. "What is it?" she asked. "Did you forget something?"

Andrew didn't answer. The corners of his mouth turned down, then his features became still, graven. She followed his gaze and saw only two men, deep in conversation outside the doors. After a few seconds he moved slowly on, propelling her up with him, although Greer felt he had forgotten her presence.

At the entrance Andrew paused. The men stood to one side and both saw him at the same time.

"Monthaven." The older man acknowledged shortly. His thin white hair was combed from a low part across his pink, domed scalp.

"Coover." Andrew nodded dismissively before turning to a handsome, blond man about his own age. "Hello, Bob," he said casually. "Just ran into Lauren and Simonne at the market. We're invited for dinner tomorrow."

Pale blue eyes slid to meet Greer's before making a swift inventory of the rest of her. "Great. And who's this?"

Greer heard Andrew introduce her and made the appropriate polite noises. This was Bob Wilson, Lauren's husband — the man Andrew had referred to as his friend since childhood. There was a reserve in his response to her, a speculative glimmer in his expression. A sensation of being judged bothered her. She took the hand he offered and felt power in his brief handshake.

"You're an American, Miss — ah — or is it Mrs. Beckett?" the man Andrew had addressed as Coover broke in.

She touched her ring automatically, then shook his pudgy hand. "Mrs. Yes. I'm visiting from Seattle."

"Well," Andrew said with a tightness she doubted anyone missed. "We must get on.

Duty calls, y'know."

Coover set his own shiny medical bag down with a thump. "Nonsense, Andrew. It isn't often an old man gets to meet a beautiful American redhead. The least you can do is share her a moment longer." He turned his shoulder, giving her his full attention. "How long have you been here, my dear?"

Fine hairs on the back of Greer's neck prickled. "A few days," she said briefly, hoping to discourage conversation. There was an undercurrent in the atmosphere she wanted no part of.

"You and Dr. Monthaven just met?"

She hesitated for an instant, feeling Andrew's eyes on her. "No, Dr. Coover. Andrew and I are old friends. We met on my first visit to England."

"I see. Is your husband with you?"

Greer flinched and noticed Bob's face at the same time. He frowned from behind Coover, not at Greer but at Andrew. "My husband's dead," she said flatly, the muscles along her spine so tense they hurt. Glancing quickly at Bob, she could see he was intent on sending some silent message to Andrew. He must think she was too engrossed to notice.

"I'm sorry," Coover said. "Has it been long?"

"Two years," Greer replied.

The fabric of his check worsted suit had a fine sheen. Expensive. Everything about Coover, from the striped silk tie he fingered over his large belly, to the satiny finish on his brown, tasseled shoes, testified to accustomed affluence. His dark eyes had the sharp intensity of a much younger man. Greer waited silently. His flaccid jowls wobbled at the edge of her vision, but she deliberately held his gaze with her own eyes and forced a smile. Bob was still transmitting his wordless message to Andrew and she was sure, without knowing why, that it was important — to Andrew.

Coover gave her a serious nod before his head jerked up. The sympathetic expression on his face altered to something unreadable. Greer couldn't stop a shiver.

"Did you intend to see me, Monthaven?"

Pressure at her elbow surprised her. Andrew pushing her on. Bob lifted his head, mouthing a silent, yes.

"No, thanks, Coover. I've got rounds to make," Andrew answered brusquely.

Bob shook his head slowly. Greer wanted to see Andrew's face but willed herself not to turn around. She trained her eyes on a brass bell set in the wall.

"Have you given any more thought to what we talked about?" Coover closed the top button of his jacket. His nails shone, the tips very white. Soft hands, Greer thought, professionally manicured. There was no reason to dislike him, but she did. The long gaps in what seemed like a coded exchange were wearing her composure thin.

"I left a message on your service," Coover prodded. "Somehow I expected to hear from you before now."

"Andy's been backed up, Winston." The sudden intrusion of Bob's deep voice startled Greer.

"Yes," Winston Coover murmured. "I'm sure he has. But you didn't answer my question, Monthaven. Have you thought about our — ah — little discussion?"

"Certainly," Andrew said evenly. "Constantly. I rarely think of anything else. I'm sure everything will shape up nicely."

She had to look at him. The sarcastic note in his voice was unmistakable and completely new to Greer. The darkly intense fire in his eyes was also new. There was no doubt what she felt emanating from Andrew was hatred and it shocked her.

Coover's restless shifting suggested he

felt it, too. "Meaning?" The word was steady but barely audible.

"Exactly what I say. I don't see any benefit from further discussion now. There'll be an appropriate time and place for that." Andrew was barely civil.

"I see." Coover's purplish lips flattened. "The hearing. I'd hoped you'd come around to my point of view —"

"Never," Andrew interrupted, a dull flush spreading over his cheeks.

"You . . ." The older man's eyes narrowed on Greer and she saw him struggle for self-control. "Andrew. My main concern is for the department — and you, of course. You know how highly I regard you professionally. If I hadn't thought you were talented I wouldn't have hired you."

"That's good of you — sir. The department's reputation must always be of paramount importance, I agree, to say nothing of that of the head of the department."

"Quite. And with that in mind, I think we should find a way around this hearing. For your sake."

Andrew's breath escaped in a hiss. "I'm grateful for your concern. I think it's unfounded — on my behalf. You, on the other hand . . ."

"Andy," Bob said loudly. "I'm driving

Winston to the Antelope for lunch. Why don't you join us?"

"Afraid not. Thanks anyway. I already have a luncheon date — after rounds. Now, if you'll excuse us . . . ?"

Bob's swift move blocked the door. "With Mrs. Beckett — Greer?"

Andrew grunted. He hooked the pile of folders higher beneath his left arm and placed the other hand at Greer's waist.

"Have you been to the Antelope yet, Greer?" Bob stood his ground, turning the full force of a charming smile on her. "It's not to be missed. One of the oldest pubs in the area. Terrific bar food."

Before she could reply, Andrew let her go and reached around Bob to push wide the door. "Greer will get to the Antelope," he said. "But we have other plans today. We wouldn't want to bore her to death with shoptalk anyway, would we? See you later, Bob. Simonne's got the start of something — let me know if you want me to check her over." His failure to look at Winston Coover again was an obvious insult.

The pressure of Andrew's hand at her back, and the purposeful speed with which he entered the building, forced Greer to trot. The door swung shut with a click.

"There's an office for visiting physicians.

You can wait there," Andrew said stiffly.

Everyone had another side. Greer hadn't expected Andrew to be any different. But this thinly disguised fury — the overpowering sensation that he was infused with contempt? He was rigid, a stranger.

There was no time to take in the foyer before he whisked her past a glassed-in reception room where a switchboard operator pushed and pulled the leads on an ancient contraption. The first room off a dismal green corridor proved to be the office Andrew intended her to use.

"Andrew," Greer began, facing him deliberately. "If you need to be with your colleagues for lunch, I understand. I don't want to be a nuisance."

He rotated his shoulders almost imperceptibly. "That sounds suspiciously like another apology." His smile was lopsided, an obvious attempt at lightening the mood. "I assure you, lunch with you is what I need — today of all days."

She wanted to ask him what was wrong, why he was angry. *None of your business, Greer. Probably all your imagination, anyway.* "I'll be here. Don't hurry."

He turned and was gone, leaving her with a clear picture of his preoccupied expression. If she hadn't been with him, would there have been an open argument? Greer crossed her arms, hugging herself tightly. Last night she'd felt defensive because he seemed so secure and untroubled. She'd been wrong. Andrew Monthaven had his own problems. But they didn't concern her. The only reason for her being in this hospital was to chase away a few of the shadows she'd harbored too long.

At one side of the room the central bar of a gas fire glowed orange. It gave off little heat, just occasionally hissed and sputtered. A writing desk stood against the wall beneath a high window that rattled incessantly. Greer wandered to sit in a leather armchair that spilled yellow stuffing from its torn cover. She should feel something stronger, some sense of treading on old and unpleasant ground. But all she could respond to was the memory of three men facing each other on the hospital steps and Andrew's subsequent animosity. She wished she could take away the rage, shield him from whatever threatened him. Once he had comforted her, given his support when there was no one else, and now she felt he was as alone as she had been then. Her eyelids sank wearily, then snapped open. She cared for him — whether she wanted to or not.

A grandfather clock ticked loudly in the corner. On its face was a sun, a moon and a cloud that slipped to and fro. Colin had bought a clock like that on one of his buying trips. When he'd seen her admiring it, he'd wanted to give it to her. Greer smiled wistfully. Perhaps, after the next few weeks, she'd be able to think of all those sweet moments without wanting to cry.

The old magazines Andrew had promised were arranged on a circular rosewood table. She knelt to examine them, smelling a hint of lavender polish from the wood. All the publications were medical or surgical. Greer turned enough pages to decide she would rather not look at the photographs and that she didn't understand much of what was written, then retreated to the chair once more.

Sitting alone with nothing but the old room's percussive noises for distraction made her edgy. She went to the door and peered down the corridor. There must be a coffee machine somewhere. A hot drink would warm her up. If Andrew returned before she did, he'd wait.

Closed oak doors lined the hallway. Greer walked quickly past them and turned the corner to find an identical passage stretching ahead. Shiny paint, chipped and peeling in places, reflected overhead strip lighting. This part of the building seemed unfamiliar — the whole building seemed unfamiliar.

Greer reached an elevator just as the doors squeaked open. Two nurses in purple-and-white-striped uniforms got out. Starched white aprons, cinched tight at the waist and pinned to their bodices, swished with each step.

The same uniform. Greer stared and remembered a voice, *"Mrs. Beckett. Mrs. Beckett. Can you hear me? Don't move your head — you've had a bit of a bang. It's all right."* The woman's tone had been soft, her face blurry. When Greer's brain unfogged, the first thing she had seen clearly was the round gold pin fastened to an apron. Then the pain in her hip had struck down her thigh and the circle of gold faded again.

"You look lost. Where did you want to go?"

Greer's head snapped up. She swallowed, meeting one nurse's kind questioning eyes. For a moment she felt bemused, past and present merging.

"Are you a visitor?" the other nurse asked. They looked at each other, then back at Greer.

She smiled vaguely. "I was hoping to find a coffee machine somewhere. Can you point me in the right direction?"

"One floor up," they spoke in unison and laughed, holding the doors until Greer stepped inside. She heard their cheerful voices recede as she pressed the button for the second floor and stared at the illuminated panel above.

A vibrating bump came a few seconds later. Exiting the elevator, she found herself in a square anteroom flanked on one side by three vending machines, on the other by a row of orange plastic chairs.

Her hand closed around the wallet in her pocket at the same time as a watery sensation invaded her legs. Greer glanced around and took an instinctive step toward the closed elevator. Sweat broke out on her temples and upper lip. Had she been in this room before? *Easy. All the rooms in this place look the same.* Impatiently, she went to study the instructions on the coffee machine and searched for the appropriate coins. She made her selection and watched a cup plop down, wiggle, then settle under the weight of pouring liquid.

The waxed cup rested against her lower lip, steam rising to mist her vision, when the elevator opened again to reveal a young woman in a wheelchair, accompanied by an orderly. Greer gulped coffee, burning her tongue and throat. She coughed, then covered her mouth, but not her tearing eyes.

"They said I could hold him today," the patient said breathlessly. "I can hardly wait. It's only been two days but it feels like forever."

If the orderly replied, Greer didn't hear him. He pushed his charge through double doors that swung gently against each other before closing tightly.

For the first time she noticed a sign on the wall next to the doors. Premature Infant Unit. No Admittance Without Permission.

Chapter 7

C

Hot coffee splashed her fingers. Greer shook her head and bent to set the cup on a chair, never taking her eyes from the sign. Why hadn't she seen it immediately?

The room had seemed familiar because she, too, had passed through it by wheelchair — several times. Invisible bonds with those other visits, propelled her on. Slowly she pressed a palm on each door and walked into the dimly lighted area beyond.

Windows, high in one wall, filtered in little of the gray midday outside. Several more orange plastic chairs stood against the opposite wall. Institutionally laundered supplies, antiseptic solution and warm dust from old exposed radiators formed a suffocating cocktail of scents. Greer remembered it all now. A wall of glass faced her, the moving shapes on the other side indistinct from a distance. *Go back. What will it prove? You managed to forget all this. You wiped it out.*

She had suppressed everything. Abruptly Greer sat on the closest chair and clamped her hands together between her knees. All those times when Casey asked her to talk about what had happened in England, and she insisted she couldn't — there had been no deliberate attempt to avoid the truth. A shell had formed around the events that took place in the weeks here, walling them off where she couldn't find them. When she'd made up her mind to come back, the locked part of her mind must have been asking to be opened. Would the openness set her free or simply destroy the fragile peace she'd made with life?

Greer heard voices and shrank back in the chair. If someone saw her and asked what she was doing here, she'd have to leave. She didn't want to stay, but she couldn't go, not yet.

There was a loud clatter followed by the squeak of rubber wheels, then silence. When she'd visited Colleen for the last time, in the early morning of the day she died, Greer had felt Colin's presence all around them. In the nursery the baby had been taken from the incubator and nestled in her arms. So tiny. A rapid pulse had beat through almost transparent skin, and beneath tightly closed lids, Greer saw the side to side movement of sleeping eyes. Legs no bigger around than a man's thumb had wiggled free of their pale blanket to reveal the brilliant plaid diaper each premature infant wore. The jerky, splayed fingers had been tapered and slender, like Colin's.

She stood and turned resolutely toward the glass. The cesarean section had been performed shortly after her admission. It took two days of begging for Colin before she learned he had been killed. From that moment every ounce of her will had turned to Colleen. At least they would have each other. Greer would tell their daughter about the father who had wanted his baby so desperately and, in watching the child, she herself would never completely lose the man who'd been everything to her.

Then Colleen died. That seemed like the last day in this hospital now because the weeks that followed were still a faded series of dawns and dusks with endless hours between.

She lifted her chin and walked on. It had been hell to return to Seattle alone, to face a house where she half expected to see Colin everywhere she looked. For months Casey and Josh Field had cast worried glances at each other whenever they thought she wouldn't notice. Moving into a condominium was supposed to help. It simply increased her pain, made her more aware of the chasm widening from her married existence. Then there'd been the hassle over business; made easier by Josh but still exhausting and unwelcome. But she'd made it through. And she would keep on making it, dammit. She was a survivor.

Seven babies. Greer counted the swathed bundles inside their clear plastic cocoons. She huddled into the corner. From there she could see clearly without being easily noticed by anyone who was engrossed in a task, as all the staff appeared to be. The woman in the wheelchair was talking to a nurse who stood beside an open incubator, swabbing a baby's eyes. Greer looked away to concentrate on two infants immediately in front of her.

With their temperature controlled, they wore only diapers and cotton stocking caps. When Greer had asked about the cap on Colleen, the nurse explained that most heat was lost through the cranium. The hats were hand-embroidered, by the hospital auxiliary, the woman had said. Trains for boys, rosebuds for girls. A band of yellow roses for Colleen's . . .

Greer shut her eyes and took several measured breaths. She gritted her teeth and looked again. These babies would live. They *must* live. Science and the skilled people who applied it could pull these minuscule humans through. Miracles happened here every day. The same kind of miracle that had almost saved Colleen.

For a moment she thought something moved inside her belly. Both hands moved of their own volition, settling on her stomach. Empty. There would be no more babies. The part of her where Colleen had grown was gone.

While she sat staring, someone came to work on the closest infant. Gloved hands unsnapped the plastic porthole covers to enter the incubator access sleeves. Greer couldn't move. Fingers covered the baby's quivering chest and abdomen, confidently palpating, testing. Blood pumped in her ears, and she gripped a narrow sill beneath the window.

Sterile.

She would always be sterile. Why did it hurt so much to say, even in her head, when she'd known as much for months? Why did it matter anymore?

The hands were rapidly withdrawn from

the incubator, and Greer looked up to meet concerned eyes above a green mask. Andrew.

He bent his elbows, holding his hands with palms turned in, as she'd seen him do before in the same room. His gown was too small and pulled across the shoulders. Surgical green also covered his hair, an almost perfect disguise except for the troubled golden eyes she'd know anywhere.

She smiled, but the effort tipped free tears she hadn't known were there. Her throat closed. Andrew nodded toward the nursery door, made a move in that direction, then stopped, staring at her face. Greer shook her head, said "It's okay," although he couldn't hear her. It was okay, or it would be in a little while. With a wave and a broader smile, she backed away, turned and walked blindly out of the unit.

The weather had brightened. Grubby clouds still scudded over a wind-brushed sky but patches of blue showed, and here and there a rim of gold hinted at struggling sunshine.

Restlessness in the queue alerted Greer to the approaching double-decker bus. Its number and final-destination marker matched the one she'd been given for

Ferndale, and she shuffled slowly forward until she could climb aboard and up the wooden-slatted stairs. She'd never ridden on the second floor of a bus before and as it swayed away from the curb her stomach rose, making her wonder if she should have chosen the lower deck. She gripped the chrome bar atop the seat in front and watched the scene they passed from a new and quickly engrossing perspective.

After two more stops and only a few minutes, Dorchester receded, to be replaced by open countryside to the southeast. Greer's mutinous insides adjusted to the swinging motion of the bus and she settled back, scrubbing at the grimy window with a tissue to get a clearer view. Again she had the feeling of being separated from what she was about to do, and intuitively she identified the reaction as self-protective. Fine. Whatever it took to allow her the strength to get this all over with was just fine. This was a good day. It was. Without it she would still be where she'd unconsciously chosen to stay for so long — in emotional hiding. Later she must call Andrew.

Rolling hills stretched away as far as she could see. Meadows, separated by woolly hedgerows, undulated like vast patchwork

139

quilts in shades of green and straw blond. The next time the bus stopped, Greer pressed closer to the window. *Bockhampton.* The tops of several heads moved out below. This was where Thomas Hardy had grown up. Mrs. Findlay had missed few details in her chronicles of local attractions.

Jarring vibration rattled Greer's teeth as the big vehicle accelerated. On some of the closer hills Greer spotted clusters of sheep with black faces, their thick winter coats turning them into softly bloated barrels on spindly legs. She sighed. Her roots were here, and her mother's. The thought was bittersweet, unsettling. How was it possible to want to know more about oneself and not want to — at the same time?

A draft corkscrewed up the spiral stairs. She shivered and made a mental note to dress more warmly from now on. Pants and the fur-lined suede jacket she'd brought with her would be just the thing.

She was deep in thought when she felt the bus turn in a more easterly direction. It crested a shallow rise and headed down toward a village bunched around a square-towered church. Ferndale — and St. Peter's. Greer became light-headed before she realized she'd stopped breathing. Her chest ached. Once more she leaned forward to tighten her fingers around the metal bar.

The first few cottages were widely spaced, their thatched roofs covered in protective wire mesh atop white stone walls. Sweet peas and snapdragons hung on in bravely colorful clumps along short garden paths, while fuchsia bushes still showed speckles of red blossoms.

Closer to the village center, shops lined the narrow streets. Turning a corner, the bus leaned, seeming almost to touch the buildings. Outside a greengrocer's, customers picked fruits and vegetables from bright mounds, placing them in the brass scoop of an antique scale to be weighed. Greer captured each vivid cameo and held it, blocking out the other thoughts that tried to steal in.

"All change!"

The bus stopped a second after the conductor's voice boomed the order. She saw him lope to the sidewalk and disappear in the direction of a nearby shop. Greer waited until the rest of the passengers on the upper deck moved and fell in behind them.

St. Peter's church stood at the far side of

a small common square — the village green, Greer supposed. She walked steadily along a sidewalk that skirted velvety grass, edged with knobby old oaks bearing only the occasional flapping leaf. Swooping blackbirds landed in front of her to squabble over a discarded peanut shell, then scattered when she neared them.

A green metal fence surrounded the churchyard. Without pausing, Greer pushed open the gate and went inside. Graves stretched across the grounds on either side of the path. She halted. Where should she start? In her wallet was a card noting the location she wanted, but the numbers meant nothing. The rectory adjoined the church. The vicar could tell her where to find them, but Greer didn't feel like talking to anyone.

Bands of crushed rock wound between headstones and inset markers. Greer began her search, methodically plodding away from the main path, then back, glancing quickly from side to side, stopping only when a name was too faint to read easily. Colin's grave would have a flat marker. He'd preferred the simple and she had ordered a plain stone that should show only his name and Colleen's, together with their birth and death dates.

She almost missed it. Tucked between two large monuments, a small white angel at the base of the grave made her look away, then back again as the end of the name caught her eye.

Carefully, her feet sinking into spongy turf, she made her way to the marble angel, then knelt on the stone rim surrounding the plot. She should have brought flowers. The stone had been engraved exactly as she requested, her own name linked with each of theirs. She hadn't ordered the angel. Perhaps it was a local custom to place one on a child's grave. When she touched it, expecting cold, Greer felt only the softness of the finish. Why or how it came to be there didn't matter, she liked it.

Greer sat on her heels and held the lining inside each coat pocket. She hadn't ordered gravel chips, either, or the two azaleas planted in tubs on top. Someone tended the grave carefully. Perhaps they knew these people of hers were alone here and gave them special attention.

The tears started, as she'd known they would, clogging her throat and blurring her vision. She covered her eyes and bent until her forehead rested on her knees. *I miss you. I miss you. I miss you.*

When she lifted her drenched face she flinched against the sun that had just broken free of cloud. Colin had been an intense man, kind but practical. What had he said after Dianne and Tom Wyatt died within a few months of each other, leaving Greer totally crushed? Grieve, that's what he'd told her, and that she had a right to. If she didn't, getting over the loss would take much longer. But what stuck in her mind were his later words, when he'd said it was time to live again, "Don't forget them, but let go. It's okay to let go now."

If he could speak to her at this moment, he'd say the same thing. And he'd be right. She would never forget him or their baby, but it was time to get on. They would always be where they belonged, in her heart. Her life could never again hold the joy she'd once known, but it could be full and peaceful. Sometimes the pain would flare. But each time it would be less.

For minutes she listened to the birds, watched the shifting sky. This was her turning point. The past must be relegated to its place and she must search out her present. Any living members of her biological family were part of that present, and it was time to look for them.

Greer headed purposefully for the

church. Stained-glass windows reflected the sun, their facets turned to glittering gems. Set in a pointed Norman frame, the great oak doors were studded with tarnished brass. The ring handle turned easily and she entered the building, her nose wrinkling at the strong odor of old books and used incense.

Old books were exactly what she hoped to find. Baptismal records. Her own certificate had been issued by a vicar of this church. Ferndale had been her mother's home once. There could be an entry for her, too.

Her heels echoed on irregular flagstones. Three blocks of wooden benches, separated by wide aisles, stretched to a distant brass altar rail. Greer wandered forward beneath lofty stone arches, their pillars crowned with carved shields and cherubic bodies. Dust motes tumbled in shafts of colored light that pierced the windows to slash her path.

"Afternoon, miss. Can I help you?"

Greer jumped. "What?" She swung around in the direction of the voice to see an elderly man kneeling in one of the pews.

"Sorry if I frightened you," he said. He stood, no taller than she, and smoothed wrinkles from his long black cassock.

"No — er — vicar." With any luck that was the right salutation. "I didn't expect to see anyone, that's all."

"I'm Mr. Russel," he said. "The verger, not the rector. Did you want to see him? I think he's in."

A verger was a sort of caretaker, she knew that much. And this man looked old enough to have been here for a long time. "I don't think so, Mr. Russel. I was hoping to look through the church's baptismal records. Could you show me where to find them?"

Piercing gray eyes studied her face carefully. "That depends. Recent entries are open in the vestibule." He nodded a bald head toward the entry. "Past ten years in the sacristy."

"And before that?" Greer prayed silently that the rest weren't sent far away, or even disposed of.

Mr. Russel scratched his chin. "Locked in cupboards — up in the gallery. Just how far back did you want to go?"

Greer craned her neck, locating the gallery behind its low banner-hung walls. "About fifty or so years. Maybe a bit less." By her calculations, that should be her mother's approximate age now.

For a second Greer thought he would refuse. She saw him deciding what to say next.

"They'll take some finding," he announced at last. "Would you mind telling me why you want them?"

The man was kind. Greer knew so instinctively and decided to be honest and trust he would respond. "I'm trying to trace my family. My mother. I know I was baptized in this church and that she lived in Ferndale. I was hoping to find an address — anything that might give me a lead."

"Ah," he said, then added, "I see," although his puzzled expression suggested otherwise.

"Did you know a Ruby Timmons?" Greer pulled out her wallet and began searching for the sheet of paper where she'd noted what few facts she had on Ruby.

He shook his head slowly, looking at the sheet she offered but making no attempt to take it. "Can't say I remember the name, miss. But I've only been here since I retired. That was twelve years ago. Wouldn't some other member of the family know — I mean — ? You're not English, are you?"

She'd thoroughly confused the poor

man. "I was adopted when I was a baby — by an American couple who took me to the States. They only knew my mother came from this village. Look, if it's too much trouble, I understand. I probably wouldn't find anything, anyway."

A stubby hand on her arm stopped her from backing away. "Nonsense. No such thing, young lady." His ruddy features turned a shade darker. "You follow me and we'll open up those cupboards. I'll have to leave you to it, but you can ferret around as long as you like, and good luck to you. Good luck to you."

The change in Mr. Russel's manner was startling. He hustled Greer ahead of him and up worn steps to the gallery. In an alcove cluttered with piles of threadbare tapestry kneelers, tattered hymnals, even a battered piano, stood two tall cupboards. Only two. While the verger unlocked their doors, Greer cast relieved eyes at the ceiling. *Thank goodness.* She'd half expected dozens of them.

"There you are, Miss — ?"

Greer smiled gratefully. "Greer Beckett. And thank you very much."

"Just leave the key in one of the locks, then." His gentle old face was benevolent. "I'll pick it up after evensong."

★ ★ ★

Greer's fingernails were grimy, her coat smeared with dust. She sat on a miniature chair in the children's corner of the church. The note pad she held listed several names, dates and an address.

Ruby Timmons was born to Mollie and William Timmons of Marsh Cottage, Kelloway Lane, and would now be forty-eight. It was too late to start this afternoon, but Greer would try to locate the cottage tomorrow. Finding Ruby's record had taken more than an hour. The books were dated on each spine, but the older volumes weren't in order and their identifying gold numbers had faded.

Beneath her mother's name on the pad, Greer had written another, with the same address. Kurt William Timmons. *Kurt*. She tried to create an image to fit the name.

Curiosity had prompted Greer to search for the entry of her own baptism. Ferndale was a small village, its population probably not more than a few hundred. The register showing her own oddly impersonal statistics, one page before the last, also contained those for children born in a number of previous years. Flipping backward, another entry for Timmons had leaped at her. Six years before Ruby had Greer, she'd given birth to a boy — Kurt.

Greer stuffed the small book into her pocket and hugged her knees. She wanted to cry again. Just as she'd warned Casey, once they started, tears were hard to stop. The attempt didn't work. After a hiccup, her eyes misted. In one day she'd covered a gamut of emotion enough to exhaust an entire army of people. But these tears weren't from sadness, or confusion — they were happy, happy tears.

Her mother hadn't been married. The absence of a father's name for Kurt or herself made Greer certain of that and it didn't seem important. But she had a brother, or at the very least a half-brother.

Muscles in her arms and legs trembled. Somewhere, if nothing had happened to them, she had not only a mother, but a thirty-two-year-old brother.

Chapter 8

Andrew parked near the bus stop in Ferndale and got out without taking time to lock the car. He hurried around to the sidewalk and scanned the waiting passengers. No sign of Greer.

Getting free at the hospital had taken twice as long as he hoped and he'd already gone through this process of scrutinizing bus patrons, in Dorchester. A quick call to her boardinghouse confirmed she hadn't returned there. She couldn't reach Weymouth by any other route, so he'd waited for the next inbound load from the village before setting out to head Greer off at this end. There was only her chance comment of the night before to go on, but it seemed likely she'd come to Ferndale as intended.

Surely, she couldn't still be at the graveside. He chewed his bottom lip and hooked back his jacket to thrust both hands in his pants pockets. Glancing up and down the deserted street, he crossed rapidly and stood for a moment before entering the churchyard. There was no need to leave the main path to see she wasn't there. He'd only been back once since Colleen's funeral, to bring the azaleas and make sure the angel and chips he'd ordered were in place, but he knew the exact location of the grave by heart.

Where the hell was she? If he never actually saw her again, there was no way he'd ever forget the poignant suffering on her face outside the nursery. Damn. How had she found her way there, and why hadn't someone stopped her? No good looking for a way to shift the blame — he should have made sure she was properly settled before he left her alone in that miserable office. If he hadn't been so preoccupied with Coover and his own problems . . .

He started back toward the street. Better check the shops and cafés. Then, if he had no luck, he'd drive to Weymouth and wait outside her rooms until she turned up.

His hand was on the gate when another possibility struck him. Was she the type of woman who might go into the church to pray? He didn't know for sure, but if Greer *had* been here, she must be emotionally battered and longing for a calm space by now.

Long strides took him quickly to the church doors. One stood slightly ajar and he pushed it inward tentatively, feeling himself slip backward in time. Familiar dank cold crept out at him, and the musty odor that had always sickened him as a boy. "Please, let me get out of here before I keel over," was the only prayer he could remember clearly from those days. He used to repeat it over and over to ward off the dreaded faintness. Morning prayer with his father was a Sunday ritual until Andrew left to become a boarder at Harrow. The church they'd attended, very like this one, had been near Dorchester.

He smoothed the worn door edge, feeling wistful. Ten years since John Monthaven died. The old man had been something, an unchanging rock amid a constantly shifting tide of progress: "Holding the line, Andrew — that's what a fellow has to be sure of. And doing what's right. No hope of holding on to anything without doing what's right."

Andrew smiled and went inside. The place was Norman, graceful in a cavernous sort of way. Candles burned a red-and-white glow on the distant altar. There was little other light now that the afternoon had begun to wane, and only every other wall sconce had been turned on. Peaceful. Unexpectedly reassuring — but empty.

Somewhere, the sound of wood scraping on stone set his teeth on edge. Sounded like a chair leg dragging. He searched around, peering into shadows that spilled from corners and recesses, until a muffled sniff sent him in the direction of a small area separated from the rest of the church by waist-high bookcases.

Andrew approached slowly until he could see over the cases. He ground his teeth. Greer sat with her back to him on a child's chair. Her forehead rested against her knees and her diminutive size struck him afresh. Not much bigger than some children. She must have heard the clipping of his heels, yet she made no attempt to move. Her shoulders rose and fell slightly, regularly, almost as if she dozed. Mentally exhausted, and who wouldn't be?

He rested one elbow on the other forearm, pulling at the front of his hair. All she needed now was for him to startle her out of her wits. Best to wait in the yard until she came out. Then he could insist on taking her home. He hadn't completely turned around when the sound of movement made him look back. Their eyes met. She showed no surprise. Good

Lord. Was she in shock?

"Hello," he said lamely, half-raising a hand, then letting it fall to his side. "Don't let me disturb you."

Her laugh was explosive in the echoing loftiness of the building.

There was something wrong with her. Hysteria about to let loose? Extreme tension brought its own entourage of unpleasant mental and physical ills. "Greer," he said ever so gently. He'd try to ease her out of it. "You probably don't feel like talking after what you've been through today. Just relax and let me take you home. A good night's sleep is what you need."

"You sound like a doctor." She laughed again and covered her mouth. "Silly thing to say. You are one."

Could she be feverish? Her face was flushed, the great eyes unnaturally bright. He smiled with an effort and held out a hand. "Funny lady. Come on, I'll get you to Weymouth."

Her palm slid into his and she stood, close enough now for him to see she'd been crying. He checked the urge to hug her. "Come on," he repeated.

"Uh-uh. I don't want to go home, Andrew. There's no one there."

Tender surges overtook him. "What a

lousy day this has been for you," he said. Half expecting a protest, he caught her neck in the crook of an elbow, pressing her face to his chest.

A fragile moment. This fleeting capsule of closeness was all he must expect, Andrew knew. Greer leaned against him, her hands at his waist, while he made little circles over her back. The downward tilt of his head would bring his lips against her hair, instead he stared ahead. One small suggestion of what he really felt could send her skittering for cover and he'd be back to square one.

"You're so kind." When she spoke, her breath warmed his skin through the fine cotton shirt. "I've never done anything for you. But you don't know how to stop feeling responsible for people, do you?"

Oh, he was a pillar of chivalry. If only she knew. "I like you, Greer. I'd feel good if I thought you liked me, too."

"I do, Andrew. Very much." She straightened and pushed back her hair. "Did you ever get lunch?"

The hair spilled through her fingers — alive. "What — oh, lunch? No. How about you?"

"I wasn't hungry. But let me take you somewhere. The least I can do is feed you.

I've complicated your whole day and caused you to starve, and it'll be dinnertime in a couple of hours. I think I saw a café up the street."

This wasn't what he'd expected. She hadn't mentioned Colin or the baby and although she'd obviously been crying, he'd swear she was elated rather than crushed. This could always be an initial, unconscious avoidance to delayed reaction.

"Are you still with me?" she said, with eyebrows raised.

"Mmm." He needed to stall, to think. "I'd prefer to wait for dinner now. But how would you like to go for a drive along the coast? The sea's stunning right before it gets dark. Particularly on changeable days like this," he said inanely. She was bound to refuse him.

"Sounds great. But are you sure you don't want to eat first? You aren't expected somewhere else — ?"

"No! No. Not at all. Let's go," he said before she could change her mind.

They walked side by side to the car. He only touched her briefly when she got in. Lifting her raincoat clear of the door, he waited until she gathered it around her and their hands brushed. Cool skin. None of this was rational. Single thirty-five-year-old men with enough lovers to their histories to have forgotten one or two were supposed to be blasé about women. Andrew rounded to the driver's side. This must be second adolescence. A glance, an unconscious touch that meant nothing to her, and his body turned to fire. He was in love with a woman he'd never even kissed, and she thought of him only as "responsible." Responsible was about as far from the way he felt as he was ever going to get.

Greer watched the sun's last valiant rays spear an early dusk. Hills to the south of Ferndale were gentler than the ones she'd passed through earlier. She could see the road winding away like a tossed roll of celluloid film. What would Andrew say if she told him what she'd discovered in St. Peter's records? Would he understand her excitement, and the tinge of apprehension mixed with it? He might. He was sensitive and she wanted to share her news with him so badly. Andrew was the only one she wanted to share it with.

She crossed her arms. Of course he was the only one — she didn't know another soul in England. He also knew she was alone here. That's what had brought him after her this afternoon, but she mustn't take advantage of him, or read anything deeper than inbred caring for others into his actions.

"You're edgy, Greer. Want to talk about it?" Andrew said carefully.

Yes. "I'm fine. This is lovely. If I relax much more I'll melt."

"Really?" He looked at her quickly. "If you say so, I suppose. But you might want to uncross your arms before you completely cut off circulation to those white knuckles."

He was right. She laughed and dropped her hands to her lap. "You don't miss much, doctor. I guess that comes from working with a lot of patients too young to answer all the questions you'd like to ask."

"Probably," he said vaguely.

It didn't hurt. For the first time since Colleen died, it didn't hurt to think about children or to talk about them. Greer breathed deeply and the air tasted sweet. Andrew had fallen silent. She'd surprised him as much as herself. From the way she reacted at the medical center he wouldn't expect her to want to discuss his work. But he didn't know what happened since then. She wasn't all the way home, but she'd started back, and she no longer doubted she'd get there in time.

"Hold your hat," Andrew said as he

turned off the paved road, onto a rutted lane between tall hedges and bare trees bent inland by winds off the sea.

Greer laughed, grabbing the dash with one hand, Andrew with the other. Limestone rocks bumped beneath the car's wheels, jiggling her from side to side. After an abrupt right turn they ground to a halt on a wide verge atop beetling cliffs.

"Wow," Greer exclaimed, tightening her grip on him. "It's fantastic. If someone painted this it wouldn't look real."

The light had reached a point between dusk and night, where the land and the ocean beyond took on an opalescent glow. No trace of sun remained, but lemon and rose cloud banks cast moving shadows in every direction.

"I think you're impressed."

Andrew's teasing tone caught Greer's attention instantly and she blushed. Goggling and oohing like a schoolgirl. Good grief!

He sat with one wrist hanging languidly over the steering wheel, the other elbow hooked over the back of his seat. He faced her, grinning, and might have bent the closest leg for comfort — if she weren't grasping it.

"Oh dear," she said, when she, too, noticed and sheepishly withdrew the hand.

Andrew tipped back his head, showing flawless white teeth in a delighted laugh. "Oh dear? I'm proud of your cool. Not even coy. If I didn't suspect otherwise, I'd think you were a dyed-in-the-wool 'leg woman' doing what comes naturally."

She couldn't think of a snappy comeback. She couldn't think of anything, but his eyes — serious now — and the memory of her hand on his leg. Widows and divorcées were supposed to crave a man more than a woman who had never married. Could that be what was happening to her? Greer turned to throw open the car door and climb out. This really had been some day. Overwhelming enough without her inventing more complications. Another man was the one thing she had never longed for after losing Colin.

Bending her head, she picked her way to the cliff's edge. Scalloped coves curled on either side, spume-capped waves gushing over rock outcrops to reach sheltered beaches.

Andrew came behind her. "I embarrassed you. Forgive me?" he said.

"Forget it." Changing the subject quickly, she said, "Just look at all this."

"I know every inch of this coast without

looking, but it never bores me. Here — put this on or you'll freeze."

Before she could protest he was pushing her arms into the sleeves of a tan sheepskin coat, obviously his own. It easily accommodated her thin raincoat, covered her hands and almost reached her ankles.

"What about you?" she shouted, the wind tearing at her words. "You've only got a jacket on."

Methodically, he buttoned the sheepskin, then held her shoulders. "I'm a warm-blooded animal." He turned her firmly toward the open sea. "Take a good look and then let's go back to my place for something hot. It's only a couple of miles from here."

Too easy, she thought. Too enticing. A fire, a warm room and this incredibly appealing man. Heavy layers of clothing separated his hands from her skin, yet it felt naked and electric beneath his touch. She needed a friend now, someone to confide in, and she wished it could be him. Common sense told her the stirrings she felt were the beginning of something that would make simple friendship impossible.

She moved away. "Would you mind if I went down to the beach to get a closer look? You could wait in the car and I wouldn't be long. I can see the path from here."

"It's rough ground. And slippery," he warned her.

"So what? I can walk perfectly well," she snapped.

"Of course you can. I didn't mean — I'd like to go, too."

He didn't mean anything at all. It was just her built-in touchiness. Greer pressed her lips together, smiling directly at him with her eyes. Andrew seemed about to say something. Instead, he went ahead, taking strides that never faltered. The first time Greer slid on the shingle track, he only glanced back, hesitated, then went on. With the next downward cascade of pebbles from beneath her feet, he reached to catch her hand and steady her until she was beside him.

On the beach, Andrew gripped her shoulders while they scrambled closer to the water. The tide was gaining momentum. All about them lay trails of glistening seaweed and with each pounding wave spray leaped high, misting their faces and hair. Greer tasted salt on her mouth and laughed up at him. His ruffled hair was flattened to one side of his head, a jacket lapel caught carelessly inside out.

163

"Pretty wild, huh?" he shouted, rubbing her arm. "This coast doesn't have its reputation for nothing."

"What do you mean?"

He bent, bringing his ear closer to her mouth.

"What do you mean?" Greer repeated loudly. "Reputation?"

"Shipwrecks. Hundreds of men have lost their lives along the Dorset coastline. Every headland and ledge you see has claimed its victims — with the help of some of the worst races and tides you'll find anywhere. Then there used to be wreckers to contend with as well as the storms."

Greer shook her head uncomprehendingly. "I don't think I ever heard of wreckers."

"Locals — villagers usually. They set out beacons to make sailors think they were headed for safe harbor. When the poor devils broke up on the rocks, there was always a reception committee waiting to collect their spoils from the ships' holds." At the horrified expression on Greer's face, Andrew hurried on to explain. "It wouldn't be fair not to mention how many people actually risked their lives to save others from drowning. And still do. But

164

there was a lot of the other."

Watching slate-green walls of water rise, shiver glassily, then crash, Greer had no difficulty imagining the doomed seamen's fate. She drew closer to Andrew, unconsciously slipping an arm behind his back. He must be cold.

"Sounds terrifying," she said. "You're getting chilled, Andrew. I shouldn't have made you come down here like this."

"You didn't make me. I volunteered."

Andrew watched Greer covertly. She was wonderful with her hair tossed wildly about her face, her eyes alternately shadowed and bright as she reacted to the surroundings and his stories. And she was more relaxed. It didn't make any sense, but he could feel it.

Keeping himself in check was becoming more impossible by the second. Far from being chilled, he was almost unbearably hot. Blood pumped through his veins in time with the surf and the rapidly wheeling gulls overhead. His awareness of her was freshly sharpened by every scent and sound. Unless he forced a diversion he would kiss her. He might even get away with that much, but he was only human. She excited him from fifty yards, beneath his lips and hands she was likely to blow away any thought of control . . .

At the light feel of her hand on his sleeve, his stomach muscles contracted as if he'd been kicked.

"Do you feel all right, Andrew?" she said above the noise.

"Of course." He glanced at her quickly. "Why do you ask?"

"I don't know," she hedged. "I guess I thought you seemed tense. You must have gotten my imagination into high gear with your sea tales."

"I'm told I have a wicked way with words." Every time he looked at her she was harder to resist.

His fingers wound between hers and she returned their pressure. She must be totally absorbed. Cold little hands. If he weren't so damn selfish he'd take her home immediately.

Andrew tipped up his jacket collar and watched her. His sheepskin flapped around her ankles, obscured her perfect figure as effectively as a stuffed gunnysack, yet she remained the most desirable thing he'd ever seen. She was driving him mad and didn't even know it — did she?

He wrapped both arms around her. "For warmth," he mouthed into her immediately upturned face. The waves beat relentlessly, their roiling crowns rising in phosphorescent billows. Carefully he leaned to rub his cheek against her hair.

She didn't move.

Her chin was cool satin when he took it between finger and thumb. "Greer, look at me," he urged.

"I feel mixed up," she replied. Her lips remained slightly parted, the expression in her blue eyes veiled. "Don't you ever get mixed up?"

Every nerve in his body was a rubber band stretched to breaking point. "Mixed up?" he nearly shouted. "Just looking at you destroys me. But I know what I intend to do right now. I'm going to kiss you unless you try to stop me."

Greer couldn't stop him — didn't want to. When he framed her face, threading his fingers through her hair, something inside her turned white-hot. He was lowering his head, closer, slowly closer, until she felt his breath, warm and sweet on her lips.

"Kiss me, Andrew."

His mouth was firm, exquisitely gentle at first, a butterfly's caress. She felt herself sinking into him, melting. His tongue at the corner of her mouth startled her — but only for an instant. Her eyes had flown open to find that his were tightly shut, each handsome feature drawn rigid.

He was cold. Through the haze of desire, she felt his cool fingers at the back of her neck, massaging the little dips beneath her ears. Forcing a hand between them, she struggled with his jacket buttons. Andrew appeared too absorbed in an intense study of her lips to notice. With his tongue he followed their outline, then slid between them to her smooth teeth.

Breath came to her in aching gasps. To touch him, hold him — be held. The jacket was undone at last, and her own, until she could wrap him inside, warming him with her body, and the power of what he had ignited.

Standing on tiptoe, she locked her wrists behind his neck, drowning in the feel of him, his fresh scent so like the wind that tangled her hair with his.

"Greer, Greer," he whispered. A hundred nipping kisses covered her face and throat, missing no millimeter of skin until he reached the exposed V at her neck. Immediately he returned to her mouth, opening it wide with his own, delving far inside. Her hands smoothed the hard muscle through his shirt, caressed the hint of roughness along his jaw. And as she pressed more urgently against him, filling her fingers with his hair, Andrew surrounded her waist, sending burning impulses into every part of her.

His thumbs moved in circles over the soft sides of her breasts and Greer shied. Somewhere in her mind a small warning flare burst, but it was very small, then gone.

Their kisses were feverish now, sweet, desperate punishment that forced their tongues together as if there was no getting enough of each other. A storm of desire swept into the depths of her soul. So long since . . .

Andrew raised his face to stare at her. "You are beautiful," he said. "Do you know how beautiful you are and what you do to me?"

The pressure of his thigh between her legs obscured her mind for endless seconds. Beside her ear he whispered, but she didn't hear what he said.

She was wrapped in his arms, molded to him, when the flare burst again — brighter this time and strangely intrusive. And the magnificent male body that embraced her sent its own inevitable message. Greer stiffened, trying not to pull away. *Fool. What did you expect?* Another thrust of his pelvis proved what she already knew. He was fully aroused.

"Andrew." She held his face until he opened his eyes. "Listen to me, please."

The amber eyes were glazed, and he shook his head like a man drunk on heady wine.

"No more talk, lovely lady. I'm taking you home. To my home."

"We have to slow down, Andrew," she reasoned. "Be sure what we both want."

One more hard kiss, full on her mouth, and he started for the cliff, pulling her with him.

"I know what you want, Greer. I can feel it. And you know what I want. To make love to you — over and over again."

Chapter 9

"Andrew. Wait," she said stumbling behind him. "I know how I seem — seemed. This is my fault."

"Right, on point one." Undeterred he forged on, not looking at her. "Wrong on point two," he shouted. "We both know how you seem — present tense — and you aren't pretending, even if it does shock you to admit you're responding to me. But when it comes to fault, no one's to blame. I'm not ashamed of being attracted to you or wanting you. Are you embarrassed because you feel the same way?"

He looked back and Greer met his eyes, then lowered her gaze to his mouth — so sensitive, perfectly formed; so firm and erotic wherever it had touched her. No, she wasn't ashamed of the way she felt. Surprised, but not ashamed. They were both adult and free, weren't they?

He pulled her to his side and held the

sheepskin close to her neck. "You didn't answer me, Greer. Is it upsetting you to be attracted to me?"

"No, of course not," she said quickly. She ached to feel his lips again. "But, Andrew, this is pure emotional release. I'm not sure of all the elements that led up to it for you, but I don't think they're so different from mine." At least she sounded logical.

"Fascinating. Are you going to let me in on this analysis of yours?" he gibed.

The sudden, fleeting brush of his lips at one corner of hers made her sway against him. "You're laughing at me, but I'm right," she insisted. "We've both had a day charged with tension — problems and confrontations. It's none of my business and I'm not prying, but you have things on your mind, too." Greer brushed her hair out of her mouth before going on. "Then there was Ferndale. You couldn't know all I faced there, but you absorbed my feelings just as if they were your own. I know you did because it was written on your face. You don't have the first idea of how to ignore someone in need. I'm amazed you've lived this long and stayed sane with the load of other people's trouble you must have carted over the years," she said, realizing she was unfortunately finished. As long as she kept talking, she'd be safe.

"You're wonderful," he said congenially. "Finished summing me up?" He kissed a spot in front of her ear this time before lifting his head again.

Greer shuddered. It was too easy to respond to this man. "Don't try to distract me. I haven't finished," she warned him. "We came here to the coast. It's wild, intoxicating. Every bit of me gets whipped up by the wind and the ocean. The kisses were natural, I guess. An outlet. Let's leave it at that."

"I went too fast," Andrew asked, bending to study her face. "Is that what you're trying to say?"

"No. Oh, Andrew, I don't know what I'm trying to say." She grasped his lapels and buried her face against his chest. Feeling his heartbeat, steady beneath her cheek, made her more acutely aware of his strength and humanness. "I'm not cut out for casual encounters, Andrew," she mumbled. "I wouldn't even know where to begin or how to react and it would only be hard on both of us."

As soon as he stiffened she knew she'd said the wrong thing. In that instant, Greer realized what should have been obvious.

Andrew Monthaven wasn't a casual man — about anything. This wasn't a spur of the moment attraction for him; mild interest fanned to a need for sexual release that could be satisfied by any woman. It was only she he wanted — had wanted, for how long? The question paralyzed her reason and she clung more closely.

Gradually Andrew's muscles relaxed and he stroked her back and shoulders. "I don't have the stamina for a parade of one-night stands," he said. "And I don't think you really believe that's what I want from you." Tilting her head, he looked deep in her eyes. "Listen, Greer, we were together in some tough times. They're over, but there's no way for either of us to forget them completely. I don't want something frivolous with you. I want a relationship, Greer. You may not be ready, but I can wait — about two minutes." His laugh was strained.

You want to make love to me. You said so. I want it too, but . . . "I don't know what to say," Greer whispered. "It's all in my head somewhere, but nothing makes sense when I try to tell you."

Andrew held her away. "Take your time. We've got all night. Although I am slowly freezing and you may have to borrow a blowtorch to thaw me out soon."

Even in the almost darkness she saw desire flicker in his eyes. This could be the one man capable of reaching the part of her she'd thought — had chosen to believe — was dead.

Once more she slipped into his arms, grateful he seemed to know her greatest need for the moment was to be held. "Maybe it would be better for me to go home now, Andrew," she said softly, playing her fingers along his jaw and down to lay against the pulse in his neck. "Give us both some breathing space."

"I don't want breathing space," he said simply.

"We can't stay here any longer."

"It's better than letting you go."

Was it even possible for her to satisfy another man? She clenched her teeth, rolling her forehead to the hollow of his shoulder and feeling his arms tighten around her. *Another man.* Colin had been the only one in her life. Perhaps, along with her ability to have children, she'd also lost that wonderful spark that made a woman half-magic with a man who aroused her. If that was true, and she couldn't satisfy Andrew, would it be fair to pile yet another of her problems on him? He might think it his fault. Virile, mature, everything any woman dreamed of — he was all of these. She'd have to tell him about the hysterectomy. It seemed unlikely that his maturity and professional experience would allow him to be anything but understanding. But the risk was too great, and she didn't have to take it.

"What are you thinking?" he asked finally.

"That I've made a mess of this evening and I'm not sure how to get out of it." Honesty was supposed to be the best policy.

Andrew found her hand and headed for the path. "If this is what a messy evening is like with you, I can hardly wait for one of your better efforts."

Don't you make this any easier, will you? "Maybe I should say I'm *not* attracted to you," she suggested lamely.

They reached the cliff top. "You aren't the type to lie."

"How about the fact that we only just met?"

"Nothing doing. We're old friends, remember? You said so yourself this morning — to two of my colleagues."

"I guess I did," she admitted. "But it seemed the right thing to say just then." A gust, carrying sand, whipped around them. Greer rubbed her eyes.

Andrew pulled her close, tipping her head forward to shield her from the wind. "It was the right thing to say. Also pretty close to the truth. More than two years is a long time. Any other excuses for escape?" he joked.

The moon had risen, throwing a silver-white crust around crevices, over piles of stones and tussocks of blowing crabgrass. Greer shook her head and made gratefully for the car, hoping not to have to answer any more of Andrew's probing questions.

He had other ideas. When they were both settled, he leaned back to watch her with no evident intention of starting the engine. "You still haven't convinced me that you would rather go to that grisly boardinghouse than come with me to Ringstead Hall. Just come and have a drink, and talk to me," he said casually. "I get lonely in that rattling old house. Then I'll let you go — Scout's honor." His raised right hand obscured half his face, but that didn't lessen the impact of his persuasive smile.

Her long sigh filled the little vehicle. "You make me feel guilty," she said wearily.

"That's the whole idea."

"Dirty pool, Andrew. I'm responsible for a business five thousand miles away, and there's a sister there who relies on me." Greer realized she was beginning to sound desperate.

"So?"

"Let's not start something we can't enjoy for even a little while," she explained. "You said you weren't interested in a one-night stand — neither am I. But that's about all we could have at that distance. You can't argue with the obvious, no matter how badly you'd like to." How much she wished she could let go and take whatever she could from the next few hours.

Her mouth was quickly covered, then he kissed a line along her jaw and down her neck until his lips burrowed beneath her collar for an instant. "For tonight, I told you all I expect — not want, but expect — is the company of a woman who makes me feel good. After that, we'll see. But your sister isn't a kid, is she?" He waited for the reluctant shake of her head. "No. And the airplane's been invented, right." Again he waited for her to nod. "Also, I hope to do research work in the States on a fairly regular basis at some time. When will be up to me." Grinning happily, he

178

chucked her under the chin. "How am I doing so far?"

Greer ran a fingernail over the edge of his tie. "I don't think you're playing fair. But I'm running out of excuses for not being your friend."

"Terrific." In several quick movements he started the car. "I'm dying for that drink."

"You're making this very difficult," she warned him. She felt his excitement. Whatever he said, once they were in the private comfort of his home, a drink and conversation wouldn't be enough — for either of them.

"What's wrong now?"

"All this sparring. It doesn't change what's real."

"I didn't intend it to," he said.

Greer was quickly running out of patience. The best thing to do was lay it on the line. "There isn't room in my life for you now, Andrew," she said firmly. "And it wouldn't be fair to pretend things could change. Why don't you take me back to Weymouth and forget you ever saw me. I shouldn't have come bursting into your tidy existence again."

His laugh was softly derisive. "There's very little about my existence that's tidy.

And your bursting into it again was the best thing that could have happened. I'll take you to Weymouth under protest, but that doesn't mean I'm giving up on you."

"It could take a long time for anything to be different with me," she said halfheartedly. How desperately she wanted him to persist. Why couldn't she just say, *take me with you,* and stop second guessing the future?

He turned the key in the ignition. "We have as long as it takes, my darling."

Darling suddenly sounded like the most beautiful word she'd ever heard. She was almost certainly courting disaster, but she couldn't make herself tell him to leave her alone.

At a truck stop on the outskirts of a tiny place called Winterborne Monkton, Andrew stopped the car and got out without comment. He went inside, his tall body backlit in the yellow light. She watched his movements, the incline of his head, the slight jerk as he laughed at something the proprietor must have said. Then he ran his hand over the glinting dark curls, mussed by the wind. Here was a man with the confident elegance few men ever achieved. She must be mad to hesitate even for a second. Her eyelids closed like leaden weights. Not mad, only scared. It could work out, if . . .

The slamming of Andrew's door startled her. She stretched.

"Taking a little snooze?" He bent to peer at her closely. "Yup, thought so. Exhaustion and starvation — bad combination. Here, time for your introduction to the English version of American fast food. Floppy tomato sandwiches, stale currant buns and good old tea. We built an empire on fare like this. Should pick you up instantly."

Greer blinked and took the plastic-wrapped food and the cup he offered. His irresistible smile marched straight to her defenseless heart. "With a recommendation like that, it's bound to," Greer assured him. No point telling him what she already thought of the tea. "We'd better keep going, though. I can hold yours while you drive."

His wry grimace left no doubt he knew she was determined not to be swayed in her decision to go to the boardinghouse. Handing him his sandwich and watching the steady munch of his jaw reminded her of other trips, one in particular. Nausea twisted tight from her stomach to her throat. She and Colin had usually traded sips of coffee from the same cup and shared whatever they ate while he drove. "Might as well save a hand. I'll risk the bugs if you will," he'd quipped more times than she would ever remember. They'd done the same thing the night he was killed. And it couldn't have been more than a few miles from here. Tears prickled at Greer's eyes. She didn't know the exact spot where the accident happened and never intended to find out.

Her heart was pounding by the time they swept along the winding stretch of Ridgeway, a hairpin bend above Weymouth. A glance into the murky depths of her waxed cup surprised her. It was empty, although she hadn't even tasted the tea.

With an absentminded twist she opened the window and lifted her head to catch the first whiff of salt from the bay. Exhaustion didn't come close to what she felt and even the bracing air current did nothing to clear her fuddled brain.

Andrew's cup was also empty, and he'd eaten every scrap of the food he'd so denigrated. With a sidelong glance, she stuffed the bun into her raincoat pocket and mashed her barely touched sandwich between their two cups. When she got out, the evidence of her ingratitude would go with her.

The dash clock read eight-thirty when Andrew pulled up in St. John's Terrace. A distant, interior light shone through the pebble-glass inserts in the front door of Bay Vista. "Home, sweet home," he said lightly, and slid an arm around Greer's shoulders before she could make a move.

"Thanks for everything, Andrew," she said quickly. "We'll talk again."

"Oh, we certainly will, sweet lady."

"Good night, then."

His fingers braced her head in a gentle vise while he studied her eyes, her mouth. If he'd suddenly drawn away, she might have stopped him, but he didn't draw away.

The first kiss grazed her forehead, the second her temple. Then she lost count, dropping the cups on the floor to circle his neck and find his mouth. He parted her lips wide, pulling her tongue hard against his before smoothing the moist lining inside her cheeks. Blood hammered in her eardrums. Every thought, every physical response, made a lie of her earlier protests. He knew it, and they both knew he did, but she didn't care.

"Greer," he said against her throat. "I'm going to take you in now."

Almost, she felt a space where his body

had been. He got out and came around to open her door.

The sidewalk absorbed the sound of her footsteps until she stood before him on the step. She held herself rigid to hide the tremors that had started.

Andrew touched her cheek lightly. "Tomorrow night?" he said.

She frowned, puzzled.

"We're going to the Wilsons' for dinner, remember?"

"Of course," she said. Relief filled the emptiness inside. "The Wilsons'."

With an effort she turned away, feeling him do the same. At least they would be together again tomorrow night — even if there would be other people there.

"Wait!"

She spun around at the sound of Andrew's voice. He sprinted to the car, opened his door and rummaged inside until he extricated himself with an indistinct bundle.

"Almost forgot this. Seems like a year ago when you bought it."

He returned to hand her the parcel containing her green, market sweater. She'd completely forgotten the thing.

She stared at it briefly before lifting her face and finding Andrew's mouth a scant millimeter from hers.

Cradling the package, she could do nothing while he wrapped her gently in his arms and delivered a totally soul-stripping kiss.

Greer felt him tremble. The firm grip on her shoulders before he stepped away was to steady them both. " 'Night," she whispered.

" 'Night." He stuck his hands in his pockets, backing away. "Dinner's at seven. Pick you up at six, okay?"

"Yes — perfect," she answered, watching until he left. Then she went slowly indoors.

The sheepskin. Greer shook her head slowly and tiptoed upstairs. No good trying to catch Andrew with the coat now. The sound of his engine had already faded.

In her room, high at the back of the house, Greer shrugged off the cumbersome garment, but couldn't resist burying her nose in the collar before draping it over a chair. A trace of her own perfume clung there, but it was Andrew she smelled — clean sea air, pine.

It was early, but this had been a draining day and bed sounded great. She peeled off her clothes until she stood shivering in bra and panties. Hardy breed these Britishers.

185

They even seemed to take pride in throwing open windows to the night air — healthy they insisted. Crazy, Greer thought, splashing cold water into a sink atop exposed galvanized plumbing. There was a faucet marked *H*, presumably for *hot*, but it didn't work. Neither did the radiator, although it occasionally thumped loudly and gave an ominous hiss. She checked the bed quickly for the lump that would indicate her hot water bottle and groaned when she didn't feel it beneath the quilt.

With brisk determination, she scoured a frosty washcloth over her protesting skin. "No showers at night," Mrs. Findlay had decreed. "Don't hold with them then, and they wake my lodgers." Greer had met only one other boarder, a pale young man who was "doing some sort of paper on Roman stuff," according to their landlady. He'd passed Greer in the hall twice, dropping his head in a shy nod each time, and she'd never seen him at breakfast. According to the books she'd read on Dorset, the area was rich in Roman history and artifacts, and from the preoccupied expression on the man's face, the sound of a shower should be the last thing to distract him.

Greer chuckled, grabbing a flannel

nightgown from the rickety middle drawer of a marble-topped dresser. She was falling in love with this quaint country and its determinedly cheerful people. England was in her blood and she felt a growing closeness to everything around her.

Two dormer windows poked out from one wall of the room. Greer knew the scene below without looking. A narrow, concrete courtyard surrounded by woven wood fences, and double gates leading to an alley behind. Swathed in her fleecy aqua bathrobe, knee-high socks pulled up securely and feet jammed into fur slippers, she opened one drape. Night was kind to the plain scene, disguising rows of garbage cans and an array of potted plants, already yellowed by the first frost. Slate roofs reflected moonlight. The few stars that showed were steady, distant pinpricks of polished steel.

Somewhere to the east, Andrew might also be getting ready for bed. She'd never seen his bedroom — had no idea which way it faced. But if he looked up, perhaps he'd notice the same stars, the inky black camouflage of darkness. Would he also think of her, or was she reading too much into the past few hours?

Sleep beckoned and Greer padded to the

bed, winced when she took off the bathrobe and slippers and scuttled beneath the covers. She kept on her cable-knit socks. In the morning her legs would bear their imprint, but she'd wear pants.

Before turning out the lamp, she snuggled deeper and took a last covetous look around the room. Already it felt like home, her retreat. Roses had obviously been the only prerequisite for inclusion in the decorating scheme. Drapes sported a larger and slightly more faded design than the bedspread, and the wallpaper, old as it was, had obviously been chosen for its floppy dog roses. Greer made a mental note to check the rug in the morning. She flipped off the light. In the faint glow from the windows she could see the brilliant white shape of a kitten, pictured on an enameled board used to block off the old fireplace.

What was Andrew's bedroom like? She turned on her stomach, shoved her hands beneath the pillow and pressed it to her face. She tried to control her dangerous thoughts. *Think about tomorrow. Back to Ferndale and Kelloway Lane.* To no avail. His room would be masculine, lots of books, a bit disorganized . . .

The pillow smelled of mothballs. Greer flipped to her back again and stared straight up. Little colored flecks shifted in front of her eyes. Did he sleep nude? *Good Lord, Greer.*

Her nose was cold. She pulled the sheet over her eyes and promptly sneezed. She turned on her side, curling into a tight ball. Immediately, her fingers went to the long scar from hip to thigh, hardly definable through the thick nightgown. Reluctantly she covered her flat abdomen. The cesarean section was a thin, almost invisible line now, but a parallel incision had left a ridge that would take a year or more to flatten and pale. Tightness squeezed her chest. No one could have foreseen the pelvic inflammatory disease that left no choice but hysterectomy. The surgeon who operated on her had waited until any further delay would threaten her life.

Only this recent scar would be new to Andrew — if he even noticed it — he already knew about the others. And all he'd offered was a liaison, not his heart and soul on a platter. She'd told herself she wanted to lead a normal life again. Sex was a healthy, natural part of any human existence. If there was one man likely to help her forget her reservations, it was Andrew Monthaven.

Believing the latest surgery or some

mental injury left over from losing Colin had made her incapable of responding to a man was probably a cop-out. Probably . . .

Dammit! She would never hurt Andrew. But she *would* take whatever happiness she could find with him for as long as they were able to be together.

Chapter 10

Greer waited. Finding Reverend Alec Colyer in the pretty village of Chaldon Herring had taken all morning and part of the afternoon. She was increasingly conscious of time passing and the need to be back in Weymouth and dressed for dinner by six.

The reverend sat in a matching chintz chair opposite her own, staring thoughtfully through rain-streaked windows. The temptation to prompt him made her grip the cup and saucer in her hands tightly. He was walking the old paths of his life slowly, feeling the way. Trying to rush him would do no good.

"Ruby you said? Mmm." His light blue eyes returned to her face. "She was an only child, I remember."

"Yes," Greer said, although she hadn't known. She mustn't break his concentration.

He sipped his tea loudly, wrinkling his

191

snub nose. Always tea. Greer suppressed a little smile and drank some of her own. In time she could start to like the stuff. Carefully she set the cup in its saucer, trying not to rattle the china.

"I was vicar of St. Peter's for thirty-five years, young lady. Knew everyone who came and went in the village."

Greer mumbled that she was impressed, which seemed to satisfy him. He shifted his short bulk to a more comfortable position and put his cup on the delicate Chippendale table beside his chair.

"I'd be there yet if the rheumatism hadn't slowed me down."

"Miserable," she commiserated. *Please, get on with it.*

"Didn't mind moving out of the rectory so much, but I wish I could have found a suitable place to live in Ferndale. Knew everyone," he said with regret.

"You have a very nice place here, reverend."

Greer already knew some of the ex-vicar of St. Peter's pet concerns. She also knew almost every street, lane and alley in Ferndale, and most of the shops. Esther Lyle ran the combination post office and variety store. Alf Gleed was the only police constable, and monitored law and order from the kitchen of his four-room cottage. The closest medical or dental care was in Dorchester.

The villagers had been anxious to talk — about weather and crops, and what it was like in Seattle. Did it rain as much there as it did here? Greer's emphatic yes brought laughs all around. They'd been eager to predict bad winter in Dorset — crows nesting low gave a sure sign. But each time she brought up Ruby Timmons, or Kurt, her questions were met with blank expressions, slowly shaken heads and yet another suggestion for some local monument she ought not to miss.

In Kelloway Lane — her first stop — she had walked back and forth in front of Marsh Cottage until she felt too conspicuous to pass it again. Then she'd stood across the lane to watch, and just as she gathered enough courage to start for the front door, it opened. A flustered young woman shouldering a baby emerged and plopped down two empty milk bottles.

Hopeless. No point even asking someone who clearly could have no connection to Ruby. Greer had headed for the village center once more, dismissing the notion that she was almost grateful not to have to go inside the cottage. Later, when she had been ready to give up altogether, the police constable's suggestion that she talk to the rector had paid off.

The present vicar of St. Peter's dealt with her inquiries briskly. A busy middle-aged man, he showed little enthusiasm for his ten-year appointment in Ferndale. No, he had no present parishioners named Timmons. Probably meant the family had left the area. But his retired predecessor, Alec Colyer, who now lived in Chaldon Herring, might be able to help her. Then she'd been favored with a smile she sensed was rare and a warning, "If you can keep him off his favorite subjects. Missing Ferndale, taxation and his rheumatism."

So far she wasn't doing a very good job. Taxes would probably be next.

"Bill Timmons was a good man. Fine stonemason. He did some repairs around the church. Lived in London as a young man, so he said — had a hand in building St. Paul's Cathedral. Quiet though. He and Mollie came south for the peace, I think, and to get their little girl out of the city."

Greer's cup almost slid from the saucer. She steadied it quickly. Who did he mean? Her grandfather? "What was their little girl's name?"

The old man looked at her sharply.

"Ruby. Ruby, of course. I thought that's who we were talking about."

"We were, are. Did you know her, too — and Kurt?" Her lips began to quiver. She mustn't cry. He wouldn't understand.

Reverend Colyer blinked several times while he rubbed his swollen knuckles. "Did a bit of carpentry myself before this. Decorative stuff," he added, pausing thoughtfully. "Ruby used to come with her mother. Mollie helped clean the church. The girl was a quiet thing with a lot of red hair."

Greer tipped her head and closed her stinging eyes. *Red hair.* She's already said Ruby was her mother, but he seemed to have forgotten.

"She left Ferndale the year she finished school. Must have been coming up to sixteen then, I suppose. Wasn't a year later she was back and the little boy was born."

"Kurt?"

"That's what he was christened. They called him Rusty. Killed Bill, though," he said, clucking his tongue noisily.

She could stop it now. Colin had told her to stop if she changed her mind. Greer placed the cup on the windowsill and half rose. There had once been heartache in that nondescript cottage she'd walked away from this morning. People had suffered — her people. Did she want to know how much?

"More tea, Miss . . . ?"

"No, thank you," she said wearily. She'd come this far. She couldn't run away now. Gathering all her self-control, Greer sat back down. "Please go on, Reverend Colyer."

"Not much more to tell," he said, staring into his teacup. "Ruby's dad died a couple of years after she went away again. She'd left the baby with her folks." Now his balding head wobbled sadly. "Mollie took Rusty around like he was her son instead of her grandson. Then Ruby came with the new baby and Mollie would have done the same for that one, too, if she hadn't been ill by then."

Greer felt her blood run cold. Now he was talking about her. "Do you know where Ruby went afterward?" she whispered.

With a wheezy sigh, he stood and moved to peer at the sky. "More rain coming. Beats the plants down." He pulled at the stretched hem of his blue cardigan. "I don't remember all the details, but after Mollie Timmons died, I think Rusty was put into a school for homeless boys. I never knew what happened to Ruby and the baby."

"But you do know something about Rusty?"

"And you're the baby. Funny world," he said, taking Greer by surprise. Until that moment she had not been sure he was making all the obvious connections. When he turned, his eyes were startlingly clear. "Rusty was a good boy, levelheaded and resourceful. I heard he went into the merchant navy. He probably decided it was best to get away and let go of the past. Maybe he was right."

Maybe he was, but Greer had made a distant sighting of her goal. What could it hurt to at least try contacting the brother she'd never met, never even guessed existed before yesterday? And Rusty could very well know where their mother was. The problem that seemed insurmountable was deciding what to do next.

"You've been very helpful, reverend. Thank you," Greer said as she stood. "I don't suppose you know how a person joins the merchant navy?"

He rocked onto his toes, smiling faintly. "Not really. But if I were a young woman determined to find someone who had, I'd probably contact the Seamen's Union in

Southampton. Rusty would have to belong if he went to sea, and they keep each man's work record — the ships he'd signed on with in the past, and his present vessel, if there is one," he said, scratching his head absently.

Another step forward. If Rusty had gone to sea, she could very well close the gap between them a little more. "Thanks again, very much," she said, impulsively grabbing the reverend's hand. "I'll think about everything you've told me." Her heart flipped about giddily. Silly. She might find out nothing.

At the door the old man waved. Greer raised a hand, then almost ran down the paved path to the gate. Closer and closer. And in a couple of hours she'd see Andrew again. He would understand how she felt. She knew he would. As soon as they had some time alone she'd explain everything to him. Without someone to share her hopes — and reservations — she'd burst.

Greer stopped and lifted her face to the rain. Even if there were a dozen people she could turn to, here and now, people she liked and trusted, she'd still choose Andrew.

One day she'd have her colors done. Greer surveyed the pile of clothing on the bed critically. She liked simple styles, natural fabrics and usually felt confident of her choices. So why was she having so much trouble choosing something to wear to an informal dinner?

Ridiculous. She was behaving like a teenager going on her first date. Too bad the outfits she'd packed were all so practical though. . . .

Greer checked her watch. Five-thirty, and she was standing in a camisole and panties. *Good Lord.* She eyed the blue-and-black-striped blouse — silk always felt good — black angora vest and black worsted pants. Fine. She dressed quickly, hung the rest of her things again and searched for the black pumps she'd bought but had never yet worn.

The shoes were too high. Knowing how poor her balance could be, why had she selected something she'd probably break her neck in?

Her hair had gotten wet on the way to the bus in Chaldon Herring and then there'd been no time for shampooing. She brushed it hard and succeeded only in creating a springy mass of unruly curls. At least it shone.

This condition was known as panic. Greer sat on the edge of an upright chair and took a deep breath. *Twenty-six-year-old widows don't panic over dinner dates.* What little makeup she wore looked just right, the outfit flattered her and the shoes made the most of small feet and narrow ankles. *Andrew Monthaven, you're a lucky devil.* She grinned. When all else failed, she still had her sense of humor, and life was full of promise now. Later she'd share her new discoveries with Andrew.

The distant jangle of the doorbell sobered her instantly. Murmuring voices followed, then the slow clump, clump, of Mrs. Findlay's sturdy leather brogues on the stairs.

At the expected knock, Greer's heart almost stopped.

"Gentleman for you, Mrs. Beckett. He'll be in the lounge," Mrs. Findlay called through the door.

Greer's weak thank-you was lost beneath even, retreating thuds.

She grabbed her beige fur-lined jacket. Didn't match, but it was that or the raincoat, which wasn't warm enough. The only purse she had was the one she used for travel. Brown with a heavy strap. Out of the question. A lipstick, comb and some money fitted easily into the jacket pockets.

Taking Andrew's sheepskin coat, Greer

picked her way carefully downstairs. The thought of making a dashing entry appealed, falling flat on her face didn't.

"Something wrong, Greer?" the deep voice said from the bottom of the stairs.

She jumped. "Andrew! No. Nothing's wrong." *Except you caught me creeping along, staring at my feet like a senior citizen.* "Mrs. Findlay said you were in the lounge," she said as pleasantly as possible.

He smiled and her insides melted. "How much time . . . ?" He leaned to peer down the hall then whispered, "How much time have you spent in the lounge?"

"You mean you don't like the decor?" Greer took the hand he offered and made herself walk confidently at his side. "If I could smuggle out that collection of antimacassars and plaster shepherdesses, I'd be able to auction them to the highest bidder," she said in a conspiratorial voice.

"You're kidding."

"Yep. I sure am."

They both smothered laughs.

"But," Greer said archly. "I like this place, it's comfortable. And I like Mrs. Findlay." Having made her point, Greer quickly changed the subject. "Here's your coat," she said. "Thanks."

Andrew took the sheepskin and opened

the front door. "Beautiful, and loyal, too. A paragon." He ignored her narrowed eyes. "The Wilsons' place is even more remote than mine. We'd better get going."

Everyone here drove faster than at home. Greer fidgeted, trying not to look each time a car passed on the narrow two-lane highway. "It's a prettier night than I expected," she said conversationally. She would watch Andrew instead of the traffic.

"I was inside most of the day."

"You didn't miss a thing," she replied.

Andrew was concentrating on the road, his brows drawn together while he checked the rearview mirror before passing a cumbersome builder's truck. He maneuvered back into place and his expression cleared. An intriguing face — not good at hiding the slightest emotion. He glanced at her and smiled. His pearl-gray turtleneck, beneath a charcoal suede jacket, contrasted sharply with the dark hair. Casual but elegant, and she had the feeling he didn't have to try hard to achieve the effect. Fortunately her own outfit seemed appropriate.

He braked to round a bend and even in the failing light Greer's attention was drawn to the movement of his thigh. She turned to the window. Maybe she was becoming what he'd laughingly accused her of being — a leg woman. Her stomach tingled. This was no joke. She was falling for the man and there was no point pretending she didn't want him as more than a friend. His kisses last night, her own in return — the response of her flesh to his touch. The memories were vivid. She wanted to make love with Andrew. The admission thrilled and frightened her.

Minutes slipped by with rows of houses, red telephone booths, tiny shops and the inevitable corner pubs. Greer settled deeper in the seat when the town was behind them and only hills shrouded by approaching night lay ahead. Her hills, her mother and brother's — where were they now?

Andrew drove past the gates of Ringstead Hall and turned south on a paved lane. "Be prepared for chaos," he warned. "Wonderful hospitality, but bedlam. Lauren believes in houses being homes. Nothing in its place and no place for it, anyway."

"Sounds like fun," she answered. A dip jerked her against the seat belt and she hooked a finger through an overhead strap. "I've always envied people who could relax . . . ouch."

The glove compartment flapped open, sending a shower of books into Greer's lap.

"Damn," Andrew said, slowing the car. "That thing's always doing that. Did you get hurt?"

"No, I'm fine," she assured him. "Just surprised. Keep going. I'll put these back."

She bundled the books into a pile, reaching for several that had slipped to the floor. Children's titles. Inside the cover of the top one she found a library sticker.

"Manage?" Andrew asked. "Slam the compartment hard or it'll happen again."

"These are for children," she said. "Are they Simonne's?"

Andrew shook his head. "No. I like to keep a fresh supply of something interesting in the waiting room at the hospital. The stuff they provide looks as if it arrived with William the Conqueror."

"You go to the library to get them?"

"Mmm. That way I can change them every couple of weeks."

Greer's eyes grew moist. Stupid reaction. She already knew he was crazy about children. Why else would he be a pediatrician? "I doubt if many of your colleagues are so conscientious," she said seriously.

"I enjoy the books as much as the kids do. This is it. What do you think?"

A modernistic house faced them across a bridged ravine. "Wow. It's the last thing I expected," she admitted. "You had me visualizing a Victorian manor, with multiple bad additions."

Andrew hugged his elbows and laughed. "Wait until you see inside."

The front door flew open before Greer and Andrew could get to the steps. Simonne launched herself into his arms. Her cheeks were flushed and long, sparkling earrings waggled from her ears. "I've got a new fish pond, Uncle Andy. Daddy built it up by the rockery. Come and see."

"Simonne. Enough. You can show off the pond later." Bob Wilson disentangled his daughter and set her firmly inside the door. "Come in. Come in," he said to both of them. "She's been watching out the window ever since she got home from school."

Attractive man, Greer thought. Rugged. The child looked too fragile to be his, yet the clear blue eyes, high foreheads and unruly blond hair were the same.

Bob moved to Greer's shoulder. "Let me take your coat, Greer. Lauren and I are delighted you could make it."

She shrugged out of the jacket. He was charming, relaxed. Very different from the anxious impression he'd given on the hospital steps. "Thank you," she said.

"Where is Lauren?" Andrew put one hand at Greer's waist, the other on Simonne's neck.

"In the kitchen. She'll be out in a minute." Bob raised his eyebrows at Andrew and grinned. "You know how she is? Company means we try a new dish, and I'm not sure how this one's going."

He loves her. They're happy. Greer quelled a tinge of envy and felt ashamed.

She was guided from a cathedral-ceilinged hall, topped with skylights, into an extraordinary living room. Black and white, and stainless steel. It was spectacular in its stark design, or it would have been without the clutter Andrew had mentioned. Fabric had been hastily bunched on top of an open sewing cabinet. Spools of thread were scattered all over the plush white carpet. Evidence of Simonne's attempts to entertain herself dotted the ultra-modern furniture.

Simonne bounded into the room demanding the spotlight. "The pond's down there," she said eagerly, pressing her face to the glass overlooking the grounds behind the house. "You *have* to come and see," she insisted.

"There you are Andrew — and Greer." Lauren hustled into the room, swathed in a navy-and-white-striped cook's apron. "Simonne, calm down," she said firmly. "And take off those dreadful earrings. Andrew, look at her. Do you think we've created a monster?"

He appeared to consider, rubbing his chin while Simonne came to stare innocently up into his face. "I'm not sure. There may still be time to save her," he said dramatically. "But I don't think we'll get much peace until I look at these fish. Who's coming with us? Greer?"

Greer shook her head. "I'll help the cook," she answered evenly, hoping Andrew wouldn't notice the slight tremor in her voice. She wasn't as ready to get close to the world of children as she'd hoped earlier.

"Wait until you see this, Andy." Bob was already heading for the hall with Simonne. "They've got this ready-mix concrete stuff now. It's a snap. I even managed a bit of a waterfall."

Andrew hesitated, looking down at Greer. "Sure you don't mind?"

"Of course not," she said.

His expression brightened. "Won't be long." He brushed an errant curl away from her temple, then followed Bob and Simonne.

Greer's fingers went to her face. The sensation of his touch remained. A long sigh startled her and she coughed self-consciously. Lauren Wilson was smiling like an approving mother of the bride. *Bride.* Imagination could be a dangerous, painful thing.

"Is there something I can do?" she asked pleasantly.

Lauren's kitchen was like its owner, bright, busy and cheerfully disorganized. But delicious smells told Greer her hostess was a good cook, even if she was an inveterate culinary gambler.

"Do you like to cook?" Lauren asked, skillfully deveining shrimp.

Greer started drying a pile of draining pots. "I used to."

Lauren's knife slipped briefly.

"Of course," she said. "Silly of me. Bob mentioned you'd been widowed. It can't be the same on your own, I suppose. I'm sorry."

"Don't be. I still miss Colin, but it doesn't hurt like it used to." She chewed her bottom lip thoughtfully as she set down a skillet. It *didn't* hurt the same anymore.

Lauren came to stand beside her at the sink. "I'm glad," she said softly. "Andrew's obviously smitten — something we've waited a long time for. How did you two meet?"

Greer began to panic. She couldn't, wouldn't resurrect all the memories again. "Just by chance when I was visiting England once before." At least she wasn't lying.

"And you kept in touch?"

"In a way . . . something's burning."

Lauren rushed to the stove to retrieve a singed pot-holder and plunge it into the sink. "I think my timing's a bit off." She smiled rather tremulously. "Just like when I was pregnant with Simonne. We're finally going to have another baby."

Tears in the woman's eyes were from pure joy and Greer smiled. "Congratulations. I envy you . . ." She hadn't meant to say that.

"You don't have any children?"

"No."

"I hope you will. You obviously get along with them. Simonne was very taken with you yesterday," Lauren confessed.

Greer knew she had to change the subject. "Did you make it back to your car before the meter ran out?" she said.

"Barely. Look at them." Lauren nodded to the window above the sink. "I never met a man with such an affinity for kids as Andrew. It's time he had some of his own. We just have to get him married off first," she said brightly. Greer felt herself being watched but continued to stare into the yard.

In the spectral glow from outdoor spotlights, she saw Andrew and Bob climbing the rise to the house. Simonne sat on Andrew's shoulders, holding his ears and making whooping noises Greer could hear inside the kitchen. Every few steps, Andrew romped in a circle. Yes, he should have his own family — his own babies to watch grow up. If he didn't, it would be a waste.

"Has he told you much about his family?"

Greer felt remote, almost disoriented. Her thoughts, and the conversation, were becoming confused. "Not really," she said as she folded the dish towel, too carefully.

Lauren didn't seem to notice her discomfort and Greer didn't want to make a scene.

"He's the last Monthaven," Lauren announced. "They were landowners — farmers. A very old family that gradually dwindled until now there's only Andrew left. So it's up to him to make sure there are plenty of heirs to carry on the name, you see?" she said, pausing for effect. "That old house of his is an antiquated barn, but lovely in a curious sort of way. It would be sad if it ended up as a total museum. As long as there's a Monthaven or two around they'll have a right to live in it. Otherwise, it passes to the National Trust completely."

And you hope I'll be the one to provide a bevy of little Monthavens. "I'm sure that won't happen. That the house will . . . I mean . . ." Greer stumbled, wanting desperately to get away. Every word she spoke became unwittingly misleading.

"Are you and Andrew planning — something?" The pleasant glow on Lauren Wilson's face made her thoughts transparent. "Oh, Bob and I would be so happy. We've worried about Andrew being too solitary," she confided. "You'll be perfect together. Wait until Bob hears, if Andrew hasn't already told him. Those two have always been very close."

"Lauren. Please, wait," Greer said instinctively, grabbing Lauren's arm. Greer's fingers turned to ice. "There's nothing like that between Andrew and me," she said as firmly as possible. "We're friends, that's all. I didn't mean to give you any other impression."

In a short silence, the sputter of boiling water seemed deafening. "I'm sure you didn't try to give me any impression." Lauren's gaze was surprisingly penetrating. Greer dropped her hand as Lauren began bustling once again. "We'd better get these on the table if my mousse isn't going to fall," she said briskly. "Could you grab the rolls? I'll have to send Bob for the wine." Lauren picked up a tray of shrimp cocktails in smoky stemmed bowls and waited for Greer to open the door.

They met Bob and Andrew in the hall, where Simonne was bargaining for an extension on her bedtime. Greer gathered the child had already eaten.

"Go on up, kiddo," Andrew was saying. "And when we've finished dinner, I'll come and say good-night." He met Greer's eyes and his smile widened. "I'm sure Greer will, too."

These people had what he wanted. And there was no way she could give it to him. Each glance, whatever he did and didn't say, suggested he was beginning to cast her in the role Lauren had just been talking about. Greer lifted her chin. She couldn't let him hope for the impossible.

"All right," Simonne agreed, walking slowly upstairs, looking back at every step. "As soon as you finish, though."

Andrew and Bob laughed. Greer caught Lauren's appraisal and forced herself to chuckle.

Forget it. Get out of his life before it hurts too much — for both of us.

Chapter 11

"Won't she be asleep by now?" Greer said as she followed Andrew reluctantly from the Wilsons' dining room.

He stood back for her to pass him at the foot of the stairs. "Not this kid. She'll have propped her eyelids open with matchsticks if necessary."

The staircase rose to a second story at right angles to the living and dining rooms. Greer hadn't seen the rest of the ground floor but guessed there would be a study and, perhaps, a game or family room. Lauren had promised to give her a complete tour later.

"Which way?"

Andrew came behind her on the upper landing. "Left. All the way to the end. What do you think of the place so far?" he inquired.

"Interesting, if you go for ultracontemporary stuff. I prefer a softer feel to my surroundings," she said.

"I'm glad to hear you say so. I do, too."

Greer caught his smile and couldn't help giving one of her own. He was mentally pairing them, measuring their compatibility and finding the positive answers he wanted. She sensed it, but didn't know how to reverse the process or disillusion him. Later. Later there would be an obvious way.

Hall floors in the bedroom wing were glimmering oak. Probably Swedish-finished, Greer decided. Their heels clipped sharply to an open doorway where pinkish light cut a red swath over the dark wood.

Simonne, surrounded by a circle of stuffed animals, lay against plump pillows in a high brass bed. Bronzed lashes shaded her cheeks and her unbraided hair spread wide in shiny ridges. A hollow sensation twisted Greer's stomach.

Andrew put an arm around her shoulders. "I guess you were right. She's fast asleep."

He moved to sit with one thigh along the edge of the bed, a foot tucked behind the other knee. Without the jacket, Greer could see that his sweater fitted over his muscular torso like a second skin. Greer's spine tingled. She reached for a windup teddy bear and studied it closely.

"She's a neat kid," Andrew said. He leaned to kiss Simonne's forehead, then studied her with a slight smile.

Unconsciously Greer turned the metal key in the teddy bear's side.

"Brahms' Lullaby."

The child stirred and opened her eyes. "Hello, Uncle Andy. You came."

Andrew was staring at Greer and the smile had vanished from his eyes. "Right, Simonne. We came." He watched Greer and she vaguely noticed that his face seemed paler. "Time for sleep, young lady. I was going to see if you wanted to go out on Saturday. Maybe to Lyme. Does that sound good?"

"Mmm. If Greer comes."

He avoided Greer's eyes. "We'll have to ask her." He kissed the little girl again.

"I'm glad you're coming, Greer. Uncle Andy thinks you're great, doesn't he? So do I. Will you give me a kiss good-night, too?"

Greer hesitated, then bent to brush the soft fragrant cheek. "Good night, Simonne. Sleep tight," she whispered.

"That's enough, young lady." Andrew pulled the sheet and blankets up.

Another turn of the key in the bear's side increased the music's volume.

"I like that music, too," Simonne said sleepily. "Uncle Andy has a music box in his bedroom that plays the same thing."

"Does he?" Greer asked, but the child was asleep. Greer looked at Andrew through shimmering tears. When she tried to speak again, she couldn't.

"Greer. Oh, Greer," Andrew whispered as he rose from the bed. "It still hurts you, dammit. And this probably doesn't help much," he said, nodding at the sleeping child. "I'm an insensitive idiot."

She set the stuffed animal on a chair. The lullaby's last notes faded into the night. *Help me say the right thing.*

He reached out to her tenderly. "I could never bring myself to get rid of the Hummel box," he said. "Would you like to have it now?"

Greer turned toward the door. "No, thank you. I don't think so."

His hands on her shoulders were so comforting she closed her eyes. Would he feel the same about her if she told him about the hysterectomy, or would he be disappointed? She wasn't ready to find out.

Gently he pulled her against his body.

217

"The last thing I wanted was to upset you. For some reason Simonne reminds you of Colleen, doesn't she?" he asked very gently.

The name, on his lips, made the past rush around her like a suffocating blanket. "A little bit, but it's all right. Please stop worrying about me." At least he hadn't mentioned her having other children as he had done after Colleen died. She couldn't take that again.

He cupped her face and made small circles on her chin with his thumbs. "I can't help worrying. You matter to me."

The expression in his eyes warned Greer that he intended to kiss her. "Bob and Lauren will be wondering where we are," she said quickly. She took a step backward, breaking contact. "I'm supposed to have a house tour, and we shouldn't stay too late." She tried not to notice the hurt in Andrew's eyes.

They returned to the stairs in silence, just as Lauren started up from the bottom. "There you are," she said. "Andy, Bob's in the study. If Greer's game, I'm going to show her the illuminated parts of the grounds. It's a marvelous night."

"Sounds great," Greer said, with more enthusiasm than she felt.

Andrew helped Lauren into her coat, then held out Greer's jacket. He slid it up her arms and squeezed her shoulders briefly. "Watch your step out there. The paths are uneven in places."

"I'm not —" She rounded on him and stopped. "A cripple" would have ended her retort. But his concerned face told her she would be selfish to overreact to the simple kindness that came so naturally to him. "Thanks, Andrew. I'll be careful," she said instead.

Once outside, Greer raised her face to the stars and willed the velvet night to absorb her. Soft lights concealed in planting areas gave rocks and leafless shrubs an eerie glow.

"Isn't it super?" Lauren said as she overtook her. "I often come out here when it's dark. Bob's always talking about getting a telescope. We're so far from town we'd have a fairly good view of the sky. Very little artificial light to interfere."

Lauren Wilson wasn't the mental lightweight she seemed determined to project. "You're right," Greer said, following thoughtfully in the other woman's wake. Throughout dinner it had been obvious that her host and hostess cared deeply for each other, although Lauren consistently

219

deferred to Bob, agreed wordlessly in a way that suggested she always left original idea and comment to him. Curious. But it seemed to satisfy them both.

"Come up here," Lauren said, scrambling over limestone outcrops to a ridge.

Greer cursed the high heels and used both hands to steady her on the way up. By the time she reached the top she was breathless.

"I'm sorry, Greer." Concern edged Lauren's voice. "Your shoes aren't meant for climbing. And I'd forgotten —"

"Don't worry. I'm fine." Greer didn't want to talk about her injury. Lauren was sure to have noticed the limp, but that didn't mean she knew of the accident. Andrew might have explained it to the Wilsons, but Greer doubted if he had, and there was no need for them to be told. "It looks like the dark side of the moon up here," Greer said, effectively bridging the awkward moment.

"Exactly what Bob and I call it." Lauren's voice rose. "See how the hills become rounded cones and the valleys are craters — with a bit of imagination?"

Greer laughed. "I think you must be a thwarted astrologist."

"Astronomer. But I do believe in following one's own star sometimes, don't you?"

Stupid mistake. The perfect excuse for another probe of your defenses, dummy. "I haven't given it much thought," she said vaguely.

"How long are you staying in England?"

Here it comes. "I'm not sure. Depends on how my business goes. My sister and I run a shop in Seattle. We deal in British goods and I'm here to look for new ideas." And a few other things she would never readily confess to Lauren Wilson.

"How interesting. I must hear all about it. Could we have lunch one day?"

"I'd love that." Greer responded automatically, then cringed inwardly. Lunch with Lauren probably would be fun. Another grilling session wouldn't.

"Where's Andrew taken you so far?"

Greer smiled despite herself. This woman wasn't at all dumb. "Nowhere, really. He just took me to the market to help me get my bearings. Wherever you decide we should go will be fine."

"Andrew's very dedicated, you know," Lauren said, skillfully directing the conversation.

"Yes." She already knew.

"Sometimes too much so. He forgets

that a man needs to play as well as work."

Determined not to be led into dangerous waters again, Greer decided to take control.

"Maybe work is what makes him happiest," she said, turning carefully to study the house's dark outline. "We should start back."

"I've never seen him look at a woman the way he looks at you."

Please, don't. "Lauren, I understand how you and Bob feel about Andrew, and I agree he's a very special person. But as far as I know, Andrew's perfectly content. And so am I. We like each other — but that's all. We really should get back."

"Sometimes — Would you look at that child?"

"Where?" Greer stared at Lauren's upturned face, then at the house where the silhouette of a head showed above an upstairs windowsill. "Oh, dear," Greer said. "Simonne. She was asleep when we left her. Maybe she heard a noise."

"I'll have to get her back to bed. It must be almost ten and tomorrow's a school day."

"You go on, Lauren. I'll find Bob and Andrew."

Lauren moved ahead with surprising rapidity. Left alone, Greer went slowly. On the path, she took off her shoes to make walking easier and winced as the cold seeped up through her feet and legs. She was glad to get inside the warm hall.

She wiggled her toes for several seconds before stepping back into the pumps and going to hang her jacket in the closet once more. The rumble of men's voices filtered from the wing beneath the bedrooms.

Bob's baritone came to her clearly when she started along a corridor beside the stairs. "I'm asking you to reconsider, Andy. For your own sake."

In the short silence that followed, Greer reached a door that wasn't quite closed. She touched the handle, then froze.

"There's no question of turning back," Andrew said shortly. "And we're going to drop this, now. If I were likely to change my mind I'd have done it during one of the dozens of discussions we've already had on the subject. I'm totally sick of hashing and rehashing the thing with you. It's my problem, and my decision."

"Damn it all, Andrew. You're too hard-headed to know when you're flirting with disaster. Let it go, will you. The boy's dead. Trying to prove it was Coover's fault will only bring your life down around your ears. Believe me. Winston's got all the cards."

A sharp sound startled her.

"The hell he does," Andrew exploded. "Bob, you know I'm right. Why don't you get behind me. We all know that mistakes are made in medicine, just like they are in any other field. Mistakes are one thing — willful neglect of duty is another. Winston Coover was too busy entertaining cronies to go into the hospital and examine Michael. People don't die of a ruptured appendix these days. It just doesn't happen. Or it shouldn't."

"It does happen," Bob insisted. "And the only reason you're so all-fired worked up about this one is because you were in London at the time. This is your way of punishing yourself for daring to take a couple of days off. You're driven, Andy. Obsessed with duty. And you expect everyone else to be the same."

"Are you saying Coover didn't cause that boy's death?"

Greer wanted to retreat but she couldn't seem to move.

"I'm saying that it doesn't matter anymore. And it might have happened even with you on call."

Andrew made some derisive comment

and this time Greer was sure she heard a glass being set down hard. He was drinking — they probably both were — and getting more and more enraged.

"Let's back up and take this slowly." Bob's attempt at reason sounded strained. "If you don't give up the hearing, Coover will use it as a weapon against you. The next step won't be what you want — his license revoked. Instead it'll be a disciplinary action brought against you and if *you* come out of it with *your* license, I'll be amazed. Please — don't — *do it,*" Bob said emphatically.

"I don't believe this, friend." Andrew's tone dropped to an intense whisper. "You and I were going to set the world straight. Remember? No backing off. No compromises."

"That was a long time ago," Bob snapped. "We were kids then. This is life, Andy — the big time."

"And that means we bend our beliefs to keep the going smooth — the old bank account intact?"

"You sound like what you are. A man who never knew what it was to go without. I'm more realistic. I wasn't born with a silver spoon in my mouth, so I've had to keep both feet on the ground."

"You've changed. Standing up for what's right doesn't mean losing what matters to you, or it shouldn't."

What were they saying? Why was Bob trying to persuade Andrew to back down from something he believed in? Greer rolled against the wall, pressing both wet palms into its coolness.

"When I called you the other night, about Neil, did you understand what I was saying?" Bob's voice was low and she had to strain to hear him.

"I understood," Andrew shouted. "But I think you're cracked. What harm could Neil Jones possibly do me? I pity the poor bastard, that's all."

"Sometimes I think you missed a phase when you were growing up. You never learned that half the world doesn't give a damn about truth and honesty. The *poor bastard,* as you call him, can always use money. He moves on the fast track. He'll say anything if they make it worth his while."

Several seconds passed. Greer's stomach lodged beneath her lungs. She yearned to be at Andrew's side. He was being threatened by something she didn't understand and her instinct was to protect him.

"What can he say, Bob? That we had lunch."

Bob's expletive retort made Greer cringe, then she was coldly aware of every word. "Andrew, if your name is linked with that of a confirmed homosexual like Neil, your integrity will never recover. What parent would want you as a pediatrician? What examining board would run the risk of openly backing you, anyway?"

"It's not going to happen. Proving myself won't be difficult. Bob — drop it," Andrew said firmly.

But Bob had no intentions of dropping it.

"Proving yourself?" he shouted. "Is that what this sudden infatuation with your glamorous American is all about?" His voice was full of contempt. "Forget it," he said bluntly. "The convenient new girl-friend is just that — too convenient. She won't help and she could even work against you." There was a long pause during which Greer could hear their heavy breathing.

"Andrew," Bob said softly. "If you don't call off the hearing, Winston intends to prove you're an active homosexual."

Chapter 12

Greer felt faint.

"Leave Greer out of this," Andrew said at the top of his voice. "How will Coover possibly prove I'm gay on the strength of my knowing Neil?"

"As long as you insist on remaining Neil's staunch buddy, that's all it'll take. Am I getting through to you?"

"I'm not the man's staunch buddy. Just an acquaintance who feels secure enough to be civil to him. This is mad. Michael Drake's death is the issue, nothing else." Andrew's voice was growing hoarse.

Hurrying footsteps jarred Greer's brain. "What on earth's going on in there?" Lauren said as she ran along the corridor, breathing heavily. "I could hear the yelling all the way upstairs."

"Just got here," Greer lied. "They're probably arguing about sports."

"Sports?" Lauren's expression was incredulous. "What do you mean?"

"I don't know." The problem was she knew too much.

Lauren swept open the door and marched into an austere room, paneled in ash. A billiard table dominated the center and floor-to-ceiling windows butted at a corner. The men faced each other, their erect postures exuding hostility.

"You two can probably be heard in London," Lauren said, barely managing to suppress her anger. "Simonne couldn't sleep and Greer's standing in the hall like a piece of fossilized wood. Care to tell us what's going on?"

Andrew's back was to Greer. He swiveled rapidly and frowned. "Just a difference of opinion," he said absently. "Nothing to worry about." His eyes met Greer's and held them.

"Good," Lauren sighed. "How about a liqueur and some music before you go home?"

"I don't think so," Andrew said as he looked at Bob who stared into an empty fireplace. "Greer and I ought to start for Weymouth."

"But . . ."

"It's late." Bob interrupted his wife brusquely. "We mustn't keep you."

"Thanks for everything, Lauren," Greer said awkwardly. "Dinner was lovely, and so were the grounds."

"Yes, Lauren. Thanks." Andrew echoed.

His blank expression confused Greer. She was whisked into her jacket and to the car with a sensation of being born along on a flash flood. Her last impressions of the Wilsons' house were of the open front door and Lauren's troubled face. Bob didn't join in the hasty goodbyes.

As the car door slammed, Lauren's faint, "I'll call you about lunch," faded away. Greer lifted a hand in acknowledgment but couldn't tell if it had been seen.

"Bloody rain again," was all Andrew said when he started the Mini and spun the steering wheel with a flattened palm. He didn't speak again while they jolted over the bridge and into the lane.

At first only a few large drops splattered the windshield, but soon the rain became torrential. Clouds obscured the moon. Thick darkness closed them inside the car with a sound like a million spoons hitting tin. Constant rocking of the tires into water-filled ruts sprayed high wings of mud.

She wasn't afraid — or upset. Greer assessed her feelings calmly and decided she was angry. Damn angry. A few more minutes and it would choke her. What happened back there? How could anyone dare to suggest Andrew was gay? And Andrew. Why did he sweep her from the Wilsons' house without clearing the air — or attempting to? And all he could say to her when they were alone was something inane about the weather. Okay, if he dropped her off in Weymouth without another word it would be just as well. A lot of explanations would be saved all around.

"You heard most of what was said, didn't you?"

Greer jumped and looked at Andrew. "Yes," she said feeling the blood drain from her face.

"Shocking I expect."

"Yes. I —"

"You don't have to say anything else." He cut her off. The faint glow from the dash etched deeper lines beside his eyes and mouth.

What on earth did he mean? "I want to say something else," Greer insisted. "I want to say a lot of things."

"I bet," Andrew said sarcastically. "How did it feel to hear yourself described as a convenient cover for a homosexual? If you can stand being with me, I'll get you home

231

as quickly as this rotten squall will allow."

Anger turned to rage. Cheeks that had felt clammy, blazed. "Are you saying you think I believed Bob's crap?"

"It wasn't his," Andrew said harshly. "The esteemed Winston Coover is responsible for my new classification. If it is new. There's always a possibility my true colors are simply being exposed. Is that what you think, Greer?"

Greer could not believe her ears.

"How dare you?" she said in a low dangerous voice. "What kind of fool do you think I am? I know what you are, Andrew. You're gentle and sympathetic, because you can afford to be. You don't have to prove anything — to anyone." Her throat closed painfully and she smothered a cough. "I resent your implications. No one would believe such garbage, and even if you thought someone might, I should be about the last candidate."

Greer's voice echoed in the long silence that followed. Just as she wondered what in the world Andrew must be thinking, he spoke.

"Thanks for the vote of confidence. It's nice of you."

Nice! Greer crossed her arms and went limp against the seat. She rolled her head toward the door, feeling the surge of adrenaline that had fueled her outburst ebb away. He didn't trust her. Instead of gratitude for the perfect excuse to exit from Andrew's life, she ached for his confidence.

Brambles scraped the windows. The lane was a black canyon augered by the car's yellow headlights.

"Greer," Andrew said quietly when they turned west.

She didn't look at him. "Yes."

"Would you come back to Ringstead with me? I think I need coffee — or a stiff drink. It would be good to have you with me. I'll understand if you don't want to."

She should end it now if she were smart.

"I'd love to," she answered. *Oh, Beckett.*

They didn't speak while Andrew negotiated the remaining rough terrain to Ringstead Hall's open gates and the tunnel of yews. Greer could feel their separate minds racing. She should have asked him to take her home, but his loneliness and hurt were so compelling they became her own. He needed her.

"We'll use the sitting room," he said, trying to restore normal conversation. "It's warmer. I don't have a kitchen upstairs so we'll have to brave the old one in the basement. You may even find it interesting."

He spoke in a rush, as if greatly relieved. Andrew hadn't wanted to be alone tonight, and she'd saved him from that for a while. "I saw the kitchen when I first visited the house," Greer said, following his lead. "It's super. What a kick to be there without fifty 'oohing and aahing' tourists. Do we have to light the wood range to boil water?"

Andrew laughed. "The microwave is carefully hidden on tour days. And I do have a percolator." He drove to the side entrance. "Wait for me to help you. It'll be muddy."

Without giving her time to protest, Andrew came around and scooped her into his arms. She vaguely heard his feet squelching in the mud. The feel of him, the scent, obliterated all other impressions until he set her down on the stone tiles inside the door.

"There. I wouldn't want you to ruin those tantalizing shoes," he teased.

He smiled into her upturned face and she saw him swallow, hard. There was nothing abnormal about Andrew Monthaven's instincts — or her own apparently. And this was all becoming more dangerous than she could handle.

"Lead me to the kitchen," she said with false lightness.

Surrounded by almost poignant evidence of what the great house had once been, Greer temporarily forgot Andrew and herself. He rummaged for the percolator, started coffee and began to assemble mugs on a tray.

Greer scraped a chair away from a scrubbed wooden table in the middle of the room and sat down. Banks of iron pots hung above the range and in an alcove used to store wood. Double sinks stood on exposed legs against one whitewashed wall, and she could see another sink in a small sunken room to the right. The scullery, she supposed.

Glass-fronted cabinets filled with china and utensils covered the walls. Counter tops were also of scrubbed wood, worn thin at the edges by years of use. Greer had a mental image of rotund women in floppy white caps and long cotton dresses laboring at their tasks. A meal appropriate for the formal dining room she'd seen on the tour must have taken many hands in the making.

"Hungry?"

Startled from her reverie, Greer looked at Andrew. "Oh, no," she said. "Not at all. But don't let me stop you from having something."

"I don't feel like anything, either. Coffee's ready if you are." Leaning against the counter and looking at her speculatively, he added, "You were miles away just now, weren't you."

She laughed self-consciously. "Years away would be more accurate. I was imagining this kitchen as it must have been during a big party when the whole house was in use."

"Most of that was over by my time," Andrew said without evident rancor. "Good thing, too. A lot of conspicuous consumption and empty posturing in many cases. I'm sure it would be fascinating to observe, but there's no excuse for that kind of waste anymore — never was really." Indicating for her to follow, he led the way out of the kitchen.

In Andrew's wing, they passed his study and entered a small room where pale umber walls were embossed with molded loops of laurel leaves beneath a carved plaster ceiling. He placed the tray on a mahogany writing table and went to set a match to the logs in an elaborate black fireplace.

Folding shutters stood open at a recessed casement where plump pillows surrounded an enticing window seat. The drapes were floral in shades of gold, dark blue and garnet, and when the fire caught, rosy shadows leaped around the walls and over the well-worn furnishings.

"There." Andrew announced. "Choose your spot and I'll pour the coffee. I'm going to put a shot of whiskey in mine. How about you?"

"Fine." She turned toward an over-stuffed couch and caught sight of another room through double doors. A wide bed with a simple cream bedspread. A chest of drawers. Oil paintings on the walls. And books — everywhere. Andrew's bedroom. She swallowed hard and headed for the window seat.

He came to sit beside her. "This is my favorite place," he confided. "My window on the world. When I was a kid I came here at any excuse. To think. To hide when I didn't want to be found. To feel sorry for myself."

When he passed her a mug, their fingers brushed and she noticed how cold his hands were despite the warm room. He was upset, even if it didn't show. Greer craned her neck to peer out the leaded glass windows. Treetops and outbuildings were hazy shapes below. In daylight there must be a clear view of the ocean.

"I like it here, too. If I ever need to hide, I'll know where to come," she said lightly.

"And I'll know just where to find you." His absent laugh told Greer he was preoccupied.

Would he share his problems with her? Greer clenched her fists. She yearned to touch him, to smooth the furrows between his brows. He rested one ankle on his knee and leaned forward. Space and silence gaped between them although only inches separated their bodies.

"It might make it easier if you talked about what's happening to you, Andrew," she said very softly. She held her breath, watching his shoulders hunch.

Andrew took a slow swallow of coffee, then held the mug up to watch steam rise. "If I could talk to anyone it would be you. But this stinks, Greer. You don't want any part of it," he answered gruffly.

Impulsively she rubbed his back with long rhythmic strokes. "I do. I might even be able to help. Sometimes another point of view changes the perspective. When I go inside myself with a problem, it seems to swell until I can't think straight."

His eyes closed and she massaged the back of his neck. The vibrant dark hair was soft between her fingers. "You could try sharing whatever's going on," she repeated. The heavy heat was spreading through her limbs again. A slight move and she could lie against him, rest her cheek on his shoulder. She clamped her teeth together.

"I don't know where to start."

"You're asking for an investigation into that Dr. Coover's treatment of a patient, right?"

"Michael Drake was the patient. My patient. He was fifteen and he died because Coover couldn't be bothered to make a ten-minute drive and examine him."

Lithe muscle became rock hard under her hand. "Would the boy have lived for sure if he'd been seen earlier?" she wondered.

"You sure know the right questions to ask," Andrew said as he straightened. "Yes. As far as I'm concerned there was no excuse for what happened. And I intend to prove it."

"That's why people are trying to throw you off by threatening you with lies?"

"Winston Coover is the only one at the bottom of this attack on my reputation. He's the one who stands to lose if he can't find a way to stop me. So far he's got all the proper people in his pocket, but he's running scared. He knows I'm right and that I can probably prove it. His only hope is to head me off before there can ever be a hearing."

"He wanted to talk to you yesterday," Greer reminded him. "He said so. Have you confronted him with what Bob told you?"

He reached for her wrist and held it while he leaned against the cushions. "I don't have to confront him yet. That'll come later."

"If he's doing or saying what you think, it's blackmail. Winston Coover didn't seem the type to go in for blackmail and I don't see why you accept someone else's word for it that he is. All this might be . . ."

"By someone else, do you mean Bob Wilson?" Andrew's grip on her wrist tightened.

He was going to defend Bob, despite what she'd overheard. Suddenly, she was totally irritated. "Yes, I mean Bob Wilson," she said sharply. "If he were any kind of a friend he wouldn't allow things like that to be said about you. He was a human bulldozer tonight."

"I wouldn't say anymore, Greer," Andrew warned her. "Bob's been my friend as long as I can remember. He's worried about what may happen to me, that's all."

"You're blind, Andrew Monthaven," Greer insisted. "He may be your friend. But what he said to you this evening was indefensible. I could tell he knew your arguments were valid, but he wouldn't agree to support you." She slammed her mug on a small table and stood. Andrew's hold on her wrist was a vise now.

"Stop it," he demanded, pulling her close to his thigh. "You don't know what you're talking about."

Greer's breath came in little gasps. "I know what I heard. When he made that crack about me, he meant it. He was telling you that my sudden appearance on the scene wouldn't change anyone's opinion of your character — including his. He sounded as if he believed the stories about you, no matter who started them." Dammit, she was going to cry. "It makes me so angry."

With a jerk, Andrew brought her beside him. For a moment, the air sizzled around them. Without warning, his anger evaporated like scattering thunderclouds, to be replaced by compassion. Greer knew he had seen the tears in her eyes. "Shh. Shh. You're getting too upset," he said gently. "You'll make yourself ill."

"Don't patronize me," she answered.

241

"I'm not an invalid."

"I didn't say you were." He trailed the back of one finger down her cheek.

"But you won't let me do anything for you and I want to. You helped me once — remember? I was alone and you tried to make it easier. Then I threw it back in your face and it must have hurt you. I'm sorry I did that. I've never stopped being sorry."

Andrew stroked her hair, the side of her face. "It's okay. Really. I just don't want you to misunderstand Bob. He almost lived here when he was a boy. He's like the brother I never had. And you're wrong when you say he believes the rumors that are circulating. His attack was intended to shock me out of doing something he thinks could spell my professional ruin. Bob cares about me. Accept that."

"He'd better care about you," Greer said threateningly. "A lot. Or I'll find a way to make him wish he did."

Andrew moved swiftly, cupping her face to bring it within an inch of his own. "Oh, my darling, darling lady." His eyes deeply probed her own before their lips met.

The kiss was different from those on the beach. He covered her mouth with barely restrained wildness that sent an electric thrill to her core. Nuzzling her head, he lifted her chin and pressed his lips into the hollow of her throat, from where he laid a swift map of kisses over her jaw, the soft skin in front of her ear, her temple and closed eyes. The edges of her mind became fuzzy, the center a spinning whirl of color. She slid her arms around him, felt the staccato rhythm of his heart answer her own. Would it be so wrong to just be with him; to take what he offered and give all she could in return? She knew the answer had already been decided. What she didn't know was if this was the right time and place.

Slowly, slowly, Andrew thought — don't rush her. He kissed her lashes, then smoothed his thumbs over her cheekbones. She cared about him. Her earlier defensive barrage and the way she responded to him physically proved that. But there was something else, natural shyness, perhaps. In time he'd figure it out.

"Let's sit on the couch," he said as he took her hand, pretending not to notice how she'd stiffened. "We can see the fire better from there."

When they were seated, he continued to hold her hand, but she put several inches between them and stared fixedly ahead. What was she afraid of? "Would you like more coffee?" The first mug was barely touched but he couldn't think of anything else to say.

"No, thank you," she answered politely. "I should probably be thinking about leaving."

"Not yet, Greer." He couldn't let her go yet. "We have a lot of things to talk about. There may never be a better time or place."

"You said you didn't want any more discussions," she hedged.

"About my current problems. It's all been said. But we've carefully avoided what happened to you, and to me, two years ago. I can feel it growing with every minute we avoid the subject."

"Me, too," she said, glancing at him. "When I decided to come back to England, one of the promises I made myself was to thank you — and to apologize for the way I treated you."

What would she do if she knew how badly he wanted her? "You already did, although there was no need. I understood perfectly at the time. But — Greer, I —" He must say it, for both of them. "I've never felt so helpless as I did that night. Guilty, too. I should have been able to save Colleen. You can't know how that haunts me. I don't blame you for hating me then — but I couldn't take it if you still did."

"I don't," she whispered. "Even when it happened, I wasn't really blaming you. Everything was too much. Losing Colin was like losing my heart. As long as Colleen was alive I hung on to her and tried to concentrate on our future. Then she was taken away, too, and you were the most convenient focus for all the anger and helplessness I felt. But it's gone now, Andrew. You must feel that."

She didn't draw away when he kissed the corner of her mouth. Sweet. The taste and scent of her tightened every muscle in his body. "I do," he assured her. "But I needed to hear you say it."

Greer turned to him and cautiously slid her arms around his neck.

"Have you ever considered that you may care too much about everyone else's troubles?" she said softly.

The sensation of her fingers in his hair made his insides shudder. "It has occurred to me," he admitted, smiling against her cheek. "Unfortunately I'm getting a bit old to change." Greer nipped his ear playfully and he knew he had to have more of her.

When he undid her vest buttons she

sighed and arched her back slightly. Through the smooth silk shirt, he cupped her breast and felt the nipple crest. She found his mouth and strained against him, pitting her slight weight against his own bulk. His gut was afire. He tried to relax, allowed her to push him against the couch and open his mouth with her lips and tongue. Every instinct pressured him to respond as he wanted, to make love to her in all the ways he'd imagined for so long. A struggling speck of logic warned him that she might not be as ready as her beautiful body suggested.

Carefully he circled her sleek ribs beneath her shirt. "I love the way you feel," he murmured. "So soft." He wanted them both naked and fused together. The thought sent heat darting across his skin.

She pulled away and shed her vest and blouse. Andrew swallowed around a lump in his throat. *Oh, God.* Without looking at his face she tugged his sweater up and bent to kiss the sensitive flesh above his belt. Was the timing right? Every move she made said yes. But the expression on her face, the way she avoided meeting his eyes — She could be forcing herself, trying to prove something to them both.

Another second and he'd lose control.

With her head bent, her lips pressed repeatedly to a hundred fiery spots on his chest and belly, her small body was a living aphrodisiac. Instead of a bra, she wore only a camisole of some gauzy pale blue stuff. It fell from the tops of her breasts, revealing thrusting nipples.

"Sweetheart, sweetheart," he whispered, pushing her gently away to pull the sweater over his head. "Now you." First he soothed her by stroking her soft flesh, molding her with his hands until she looked directly into his eyes. Then he lifted the camisole and she raised her arms for him to take it all the way off.

Gazing at the beauty before him, he felt whatever he said would be inadequate. But he had to try. "You're perfect. Absolutely perfect," he managed.

Her slacks fastened in front. Andrew eased the button free and slid the zipper down. Tiny waist but flaring hips.

She wrapped her arms around him so suddenly, so fiercely, he grabbed the couch to steady them. "Greer," he murmured into her hair. "Are you okay, my love?" He could hear the thud of his heart, feel hers. She didn't answer, only held on more tightly.

"What is it? Has something frightened

you?" *Good God, she was petrified of actually making love.* "Please say something to me. Whatever's wrong, we can work it out."

"No." The word was muffled against his shoulder and the moisture on his skin told him she was crying. "I'm not the same as I was," she said brokenly.

"None of us is." Did she mean because she'd already been married? It couldn't be that.

"You don't understand," she insisted.

He didn't. But he would, if it took forever. "I will," he promised. "We'll understand each other perfectly if we just let it happen."

"There are things you don't know about me."

"We both have a lot to learn about each other."

Trembling overtook her and he crossed his arms over her back. There hadn't been another man since Colin Beckett. Andrew lifted his face, feeling first bemused at how long it had taken him to realize the truth, then incredibly, foolishly happy. Greer hadn't made love since her husband died and she was probably fighting two demons: loyalty she still held for him and insecurity about her ability to fully respond to another man.

"Hey," he said softly. He found her chin and raised her head. "You aren't ready for this, are you?"

Tears streaked her cheeks. She shook her head and he placed a soft kiss on her trembling lips.

"I'm not, either." If he wasn't careful, the happiness would show in his eyes. "And it's too cold for nudist activities," he said with an exaggerated shudder. "But don't get dressed. I'll find us a couple of robes and build up the fire."

A puzzled frown creased her brow. "Andrew. Aren't you angry with me? And shouldn't you drive me home?"

He tried not to look at her breasts, but failed. "I couldn't be angry with you, darling. I'll be right back."

The camisole was in place when he returned, but the blouse and vest had been neatly folded on top of his sweater. "Here. It'll wrap around three times but at least you'll be cozy." He helped her into a gray robe, turned her to face him and secured the belt. "Walk slowly, kid, or you'll fall over the hem."

"I must look like Sweetpea in 'Popeye.'" She laughed and Andrew felt as if the air became softer.

"Much more appealing. The coffee

should still be lukewarm at least. Or would you like some brandy." He shrugged into his own robe and threw another log on the fire.

"Nothing — or yes. A little brandy does sound good." Her eyelashes were spiky from crying.

Somehow he was going to bring it off. His world had been steadily turned upside down in the past few weeks. But he wasn't going to lose this woman again. Just having her with him as often as possible would be enough until she could accept his love-making and return it fully.

He poured brandy into two goblets and came to kneel at Greer's feet where she sat on the couch. She took a glass and smiled at him over the rim. "To you, Andrew. You're unique."

"Thank you. And to you." Clinking their glasses, they both sipped the golden liquor.

"It must be very late," Greer said at last. "I'm not wearing a watch."

"Very, very late," he agreed.

He waited, then heard her clear her throat quietly. "I don't like asking you to go out again, but . . ."

"Then don't."

Her eyes darkened and he moved to sit beside her. "Stay with me tonight. Lie in my arms, nothing more. I just want you with me. Will you stay?" He was pleading but it didn't matter.

She tipped her head. "I never meant to tease you, Andrew. Frustrating a man is a new experience for me, and I don't want you to go through it again. You're wonderful." Her mouth came together tremulously for an instant. "But you're also human and I can't do this to you. You matter too much to me."

It was happening. He almost whooped. "Come with me, lady," he said firmly. "You and I are going to help each other make it through this night. Sex isn't the only thing a man needs from the woman he cares for."

Greer let Andrew lead her. Instinct told her she was totally safe with him. She used the toothbrush he found for her and stripped off her slacks and hose in the bathroom before swathing herself in the robe once more.

When they lay side by side beneath the quilt he reached for her hand and laced their fingers together. "Want to talk or just sleep?"

"Talk," she said, turning her face to his. "Do you know I'm English, too?"

He lifted his head. "You must have had

too much brandy. What do you mean?"

She told him about her adoption out of a foster home in Weymouth, and about Ruby Timmons and Kurt. After minutes of totally one-sided talk she stopped awkwardly and tried to read his expression in the darkness. "So you see, I'm English, as well, in a way. And maybe I'm going to find my biological family. What do you think?" *Did he know how much his answer mattered to her?*

"That it's wonderful." He leaned to plant a kiss on her mouth. "Will you let me help track down your people?"

Greer's stomach felt odd and quivery. She didn't remember so much happiness since before Colin died. And she realized it without wanting to cry.

"I'd like that," she responded eagerly. "Ever since this afternoon I've been waiting to tell you. Yesterday, at the church, I was still too muddled to talk about it."

Andrew pulled her head into the hollow of his shoulder. "When I saw you sitting in the children's corner, I thought of Colleen. It brought back the day I went to her funeral."

A lengthy pause followed as the implications sank in.

"You — Thank you," Greer whispered as she rolled against his side and buried her face. "I wish I'd known. It always bothered me that no one was there."

"I couldn't bring myself to come and tell you afterward," he said, stroking her hair.

"No. And I don't blame you after the way I behaved. I don't suppose you know anything about the little white angel on the grave or the plants?"

"Don't suppose so."

"You had them put there. I know you did."

He rubbed his chin against her forehead. "It must be at least four. Can you sleep? I think I can as long as you're with me."

"Mmm." She snuggled closer, wrapping an arm around his waist. Tears burned her eyes and throat but she didn't want him to know.

Andrew fell silent and soon she heard his regular breathing and felt the steady rise and fall of his chest beneath her ear. Cautiously she pushed up on an elbow until she could see his face. Faint light from the sitting-room fire penetrated the open doors and threw shadows across his features. She could see his dark, arched brows, the straight nose and high cheekbones — and the clear outline of his mouth. The urge to kiss him while he slept almost overpowered her. Moving smoothly, she curled against him once more.

She had come close to telling him about her sterility. Fate had caused him to interrupt and misunderstand, she was certain of it. Earlier, Andrew admitted he felt guilty over Colleen's death. Not his fault, anymore than Michael Drake's death was, but still the man berated himself. Feeling responsible was part of his makeup. A dear but potentially destructive part. If she told him of the hysterectomy he was likely to feel more guilt. Colleen had been the only child she would ever have. After what happened at the Wilsons', Greer was almost glad she hadn't managed to get her message across. Andrew had suffered enough for one night.

They had something incredible together. Perhaps he could help her through her reservations. As she'd told him, he was special. Lots of people found happiness when everything wasn't as perfect as they might have wished. But before her relationship with Andrew went any further, he must know about the surgery. He would have to come to terms with what she told him and decide if he still felt the same about her.

Greer's eyelids drooped. Slender gray lines painted the wall on each side of the drapes. Dawn. Night's end and another day's beginning.

Chapter 13

C

Her nose tickled. Greer rubbed it with the back of a hand and turned over. She burrowed into the pillows, and smelled — Andrew's after-shave. *Andrew.* She sat up, pulling the quilt close to her neck and looked around. An old-fashioned travel alarm on a bedside table ticked loudly. Ten-ten. He must have left for the hospital. No, he wouldn't. She'd have no way of getting anywhere without him unless she walked.

"Morning, sleepyhead," Andrew greeted her as he scuffed barefoot into the room. He was wearing one towel draped around his waist while he dried her hair with another. "Sun's shining. It's going to be a beautiful day. But we already knew that, didn't we?" he added, giving her one of his devastating smiles.

"I guess so." Greer leaned back, wondering what to do next. She felt like taking a shower, too, even in Andrew's intimidating bathroom, but the idea of getting out of bed in front of him made her uncomfortable.

He obviously didn't share her reservations. He continued to vigorously towel his muscular shoulders and chest, moving to where the dark hair she remembered so well arrowed to a diminishing line at his navel.

"I'll go down and start breakfast while you get dressed," he offered. "Have you adjusted to English fare in the morning, or do you prefer something different? I don't think I can manage those pancakes you eat at home."

"I've converted," she said, laughing. "My ancestry is showing. I've got a thing for bacon and eggs — unless it's too much trouble," she finished hurriedly.

"Nothing's too much trouble." His hand went to his waist.

She managed to avert her eyes a second before the tug which would leave him naked. Greer studied a large landscape above the fireplace similar to the one in Andrew's sitting room. The painted shapes kept blurring together. Listening to the snap of fabric, a zipper, the swish of a belt passing through loops, was slow torture.

"You can look now," he said, unable to

conceal his amusement.

"I wasn't . . ." She turned and caught the devilish glint in his eyes. "You enjoy making fun of me, don't you?"

"Ah, my dear," he said, approaching the bed with mock stealth. "You're so much fun to make fun of." His kiss was quick, but thorough before he left without a backward glance.

Greer pressed her fingers to her mouth. She still felt the burning imprint of his lips.

Half an hour later, her skin tingling from a lukewarm shower, she trotted downstairs in bare feet. Her damp hair curled mutinously and wet the shoulders of her vest and shirt. Applying lipstick to an otherwise clean-scrubbed face had seemed a waste of time. Andrew was about to see her as she really was. She hesitated, watching the sun send spiraling prisms through gem-colored stained glass above the front doors. When he'd first seen her she probably looked awful, frightening, yet it hadn't discouraged him. Her heart flipped. Andrew must have felt something for her even then or he wouldn't have spent so many off-duty hours on the surgical unit.

The last flight of steps to the basement was stone. Cold made her lift each foot quickly and she almost fell through the

257

kitchen door at the bottom. Andrew, red-faced from standing over the crackling stove, turned with an iron skillet in one hand. He watched her hop to a chair and plop down.

"That'll teach you," he said, chuckling. "You could at least have borrowed a pair of my socks. Ouch!" The pan clattered on top of the range while he examined his palm.

Greer tried not to laugh. "Are you burned?" she inquired sweetly. "You could at least have used a pot holder."

Andrew glared at her, then went to run cold water on his skin. "I suppose you think that's funny, you sadist."

"Let me see what you've done," she said, trying to make amends. She walked to his side and looked at the reddened area. "Should I get something to put on it? Butter, maybe?"

"Oh my God," he said theatrically. "Preserve me from old wives' tales." He circled her shoulders with one arm and brought his face close to hers. "I shall have to give you a crash course in basic first aid. Cold, my dear. Cold for burns. Ice if possible, otherwise water. Never, never any form of grease. It has a similar result to frying meat — sizzle, sizzle." His raised eyebrows made her mouth twitch.

"I'll remember that, doctor. And speaking of sizzle, sizzle, breakfast smells well-done."

"Hell . . ." Andrew swore, leaping for the stove.

They both swung around at the same moment as an elderly man in shirtsleeves, tie and pin-striped vest and slacks, came into the kitchen. "It's all right, sir." He crossed quickly to remove the smoking pan. "I've got it."

"Thanks, Gibbs." Andrew said calmly, repositioning his arm across Greer's back. "I want you to meet Greer Beckett. Greer, this is John Gibbs, my forever friend, adviser and housekeeper. He could say — quite correctly — that he changed my diapers. Only he's too polite."

Greer contained her surprise. She never remembered meeting a male house-keeper — or a housekeeper at all come to that. The man was taller than Andrew and cadaverously thin. His beaked nose and bushy white brows gave him a scholarly appearance. "How do you do, miss," he said with a movement around his wide mouth that was probably a smile, she decided. "Dr. Monthaven, sir — if you'd told me you were expecting a breakfast guest I'd have seen to this for you."

While he spoke to Andrew, he looked at Greer with soft dark brown eyes.

She nodded and pressed her palms together.

"Nonsense, Gibbs. You've got more than enough to do and I like messing around in the kitchen, as you know."

Gibbs opened his mouth, then shut it again firmly. Greer had a hunch he had been about to express surprise at Andrew's announcement. Again the deep-set eyes fastened on her face. John Gibbs was assessing her, but he seemed puzzled about something. *You're too sensitive, Greer,* she thought. Any strange woman in his boss's house — one who had obviously spent the night — was bound to raise interest.

She returned to her chair at the table. "You've known Andrew for a long time, Mr. Gibbs?" It seemed essential to say something, anything.

"Since he was born, miss." This accent was different from Andrew's. Less clipped, the *a*'s drawn out. Pleasant. She'd heard it wherever she went in Dorset.

While Gibbs deposited the blackened pan in the sink, Andrew took another and began cracking eggs against its side.

"Well, sir," Gibbs said. "If you're sure you can manage here, I'd better get to the packing. How many nights did you say you'd be gone?"

"Ah," Andrew glanced up, running a wrist over his brow. "Four. I'll be back on Wednesday afternoon."

The housekeeper gave Greer a last, penetrating stare and left. He didn't dislike her, she was almost sure — It wasn't important. But the prospect of Andrew being away for several days was. "You didn't mention that you were leaving," she said a little sharply. Immediately, she wished she hadn't spoken. What he did was none of her business.

"I would have," he replied easily, seeming not to have noticed her tone of voice. "We were caught up with so many other things, I forgot until Gibbs mentioned it. I'm giving a lecture series up north. Four days, four cities. It'll be grueling, but it's always worth the effort." He set two plates on the table and covered her folded hands. "I don't want to go, Greer. Not now."

So, stay, stay. "You'll soon be back." Did she sound convincingly cheerful? "And I have some work to get done, too. Maybe I'll have more news when I see you again."

"If I get back to my hotel in time each evening, I'll call."

261

Eleven white lace antimacassars. Greer counted the handmade cloths protecting Mrs. Findlay's lounge furniture for the third time. Wednesday morning. Andrew was due back in Dorset this afternoon and she hadn't heard a word from him.

Trusting innocent. Colin had called her that many times, and just as often his eyes and lips told her he loved her lack of sophistication. Apparently Andrew Monthaven hadn't felt the same way. He wanted, and needed, a normal woman with normal reactions. Not a shrinking violet who couldn't face consummating a relationship with the most desirable man ever likely to come her way. Damn. And she'd actually expected him to waste his time and money on long-distance telephone calls. But he'd said he would.

She tucked her feet beneath her on the couch and stared through the window at the spire of St. John's. The church partially obscured Greer's view of the Georgian buildings that fronted the ocean. When she craned her neck, Weymouth Bay was just visible to the west.

Her days since Friday had been busy. Even Sunday, when she visited the artist whose paintings dotted the walls at Bumble's tea shop. The man had agreed to sell her a small selection of his work immediately and supply more if it sold well in Seattle.

After battling with insecurity Greer had taken a train to Southampton the previous day and visited the Seamen's Union. And now she was really no further ahead than when she left the Reverend Colyer in Chaldon Herring. Kurt Timmons spent ten years at sea, from the age of sixteen, until he was twenty-six. His last voyage had been to South Africa, via the Canary Islands. The trail ended when he signed off in Southampton after the return journey. There was no mention in the Union records of his present whereabouts.

At the sound of the door opening Greer turned to see the man who, according to Mrs. Findlay, was "doing a paper on Roman stuff." The woman always referred to him in this way, as if she didn't know his name. He bobbed his head to push his glasses up and immediately dropped all but one of a pile of books he carried. "Sorry," he mumbled as his pale face flushed. "Didn't know anyone was here."

Greer went to help him retrieve the heavy volumes. "I was just leaving. Where shall I put these?"

"On the floor by the couch — if you don't mind."

She did as he asked and escaped the dusty room. Shy man. He plainly preferred Roman artifacts and books about them to people. Which might not be such an unsound idea.

In the hall she eyed the black pay phone. The contraption was positioned so that any conversation was bound to echo through the house like part of a theatrical production. Greer checked her watch. Casey should be at home now. It would be late, but she never went to bed early. Suddenly Greer needed desperately to speak to her sister. Finding enough coins was out of the question. The cost would have to be reversed.

Without giving herself time to reconsider, she placed the call, listening to the almost instant sound of lines popping open halfway around the world. Casey's voice was clear and calm when she answered, then excited when the operator asked if she'd accept the charges.

"Greer! Is that you?" she shouted.

Greer smiled, feeling happy and intensely lonely at the same time. "The same, sis. Thought I'd make sure you were behaving. How are things going?"

"Terrific," Casey enthused. "How are things going with you? Made any headway? Met a stupendously wealthy baron to marry, maybe?"

Same old Casey. "Loads of new ideas for the shop," Greer began. "They don't have too many barons in England. And I appear to have arrived at a dead end with the Timmons family. Things started to move, but my lead petered out yesterday, so I feel a bit glum."

There was a short silence.

"You still there, Case?"

"Listen to me, Greer," Casey responded. "Remember what dad used to say about setbacks being temporary pauses meant for catching your breath?"

"I remember."

"Right. This is one of those. Take a few deep ones and get back out there. If you made a start, then the answer's around somewhere. Start at the beginning and work through again," she said logically.

Irrepressible. Greer grinned wryly, wishing she had half her sister's optimism. "Yes, ma'am. But I can't stay away indefinitely. Don't you miss me?"

Another silence.

"Casey Wyatt. What's with you?" Greer demanded to know. "You're supposed to say you're pining away without your big sister."

"Of course I miss you," Casey said sincerely, but there was obviously something else on her mind. "Greer, something's happened — something wonderful. I don't know what you're going to think, but I've fallen madly in love and —"

"You've what?" Greer shouted. "Good grief. Who is he? Should I come right home?" Greer's mind turned upside down. *"Who is he?"*

"Do everything you set out to do in England, then I'll tell you," Casey insisted.

"Tell me *now*. I can't stand the suspense . . ." Suddenly, Greer was struck with a horrible thought. "Case, you wouldn't get married without me there, would you?" she asked nervously.

Casey's laughter shot across the wires. "No way. We're not tying the knot until June. I want the whole works. White dress, church, reception and . . . well, anyway, he says that's the way it's going to be. And I need you to help with everything — and give me away."

"Ooh, Case," Greer fumed. "You always were a tedious little pest. You're not going to tell me, are you?"

"No."

"Then I'm coming home."

"Greer." Casey's tone became serious. "Please don't until you've reconciled everything. When you do get back, we'll have a wonderful time. Okay?"

"I don't know —" She threaded the cord through her fingers. "Well, okay. But let me know if you decide to do anything rash."

"I will. Too bad you haven't found a baron though — would have done you good."

Greer stared at the phone for a long time after she hung up. She made a mental catalog of the men Casey knew and couldn't think of a likely marriage candidate.

It was more important than ever to finish what she'd set out to do and get home quickly. *Start from the beginning,* Casey had suggested. That's what Greer would do. This afternoon she'd return to Ferndale and ask more questions.

Greer practically jumped out of her skin when the phone rang. She glanced around, but Mrs. Findlay's door remained shut. Another ring came and she hesitantly lifted the receiver. "Hello," she said quietly.

"Greer?" Andrew's deep voice was unmistakable. "Thank goodness you answered. I was afraid I'd get Mrs. whatever

267

her name is or one of the other boarders. How are you?"

Her brain blanked for an instant.

"Is something wrong?" he asked urgently.

"No." The word came out too loudly. "No, everything's just fine. How are you? How was the trip?" *And why didn't you call me?*

"Exhausting. I got back so late each night I didn't dare phone you. I had visions of waking the whole boardinghouse. Have dinner with me tonight — please. There're one or two things I've got to take care of this afternoon, then I could pick you up. Will you come?"

Will I come? "Yes. I'm going to take another run into Ferndale. I could be ready by seven," she offered.

The pause was slight, but it was there. "Greer, I've loathed the past four days. Sweetheart . . ."

She waited.

"I hate to wait until seven," he said, "but I'll see you then."

After Greer replaced the receiver, she covered her face with both hands.

Sweetheart.

"Why are you looking at me like that?" Greer asked.

Andrew rested his chin on his fist. "I was trying to decide how I feel about the new hairdo."

Greer sipped her white wine. "Makes me look more sophisticated when I put it up," she said airily.

"Who says?"

"Me."

He grinned and wound a red curl around his index finger. "Then it must be true. And that dress is stunning," he added.

"Thank you." She toyed with the stem of her glass.

Thank goodness he'd never know the classic Charmeuse outfit had been hastily bought during a change of buses in Dochester only a few hours earlier. Or that she'd felt slightly dizzy when she converted the price-tag figure from pounds to dollars. "A little black nothing."

They both laughed. Andrew had brought her to an old pub a few miles outside Weymouth. The Elm Tree was hidden away among a warren of lanes and scattered cottages.

Their circular table and spindle-backed chairs were near a fire that glowed beneath a copper-trimmed hood. Pewter mugs and glittering horse brasses crowded a heavy oak mantelpiece, and Greer could have stood upright in the stone fireplace alcove. She breathed in the ambience. Occasional bursts of laughter punctuated a subdued hum of conversation. The place was perfect, she decided, unforgettable.

"Good," Andrew said, as the waitress approached the table. "Food. I didn't have time for lunch. How about you?"

Greer studied the huge slab of game pie the woman set in front of her. A slice of egg had been baked in the center and the flakey crust was golden brown. "I wish I hadn't eaten lunch," she said regretfully. "This looks marvelous."

"It is. Save room for a rum baba."

She raised her brows.

"Dessert. You'll see. Now, what else has happened since Friday?"

In the car she'd explained her disappointment in Southampton. But she'd insisted on waiting to share her latest news.

A bubble of nervous excitement rose in her throat. "You're not going to believe this," she said.

"Try me." Andrew watched her unblinkingly over the rim of his whiskey glass.

Greer colored. He made it difficult to concentrate. "I went to Ferndale this afternoon. I told you I was going to. My grandparents lived in a place called Marsh Cottage in Kelloway Lane. Something Casey — I spoke to her on the phone this morning — something she said made me decide to try retracing all my steps. Anyway, I went back there."

"Kelloway Lane?" He frowned. "That's where . . ."

"I know," Greer interrupted. She held his wrist. "John Gibbs lives there. Oh, Andrew. He looked at me so strangely in your house, I wondered if he liked me. I couldn't believe it when I walked all the way to the end of the row of cottages and saw him working in his garden."

"I'll be damned," Andrew said, squeezing her hand. "Of course. Why didn't I think of Gibbs? But he's only lived in Ferndale eight or nine years. He used to have quarters at Ringstead until a couple of years after my father died."

"I know, I know." Her hand was surrounded by both of Andrew's now. "But as soon as he saw me outside his fence he looked as if he'd had a visitation. It was funny. He's the nicest man," she confirmed.

"The best." He played his lips along her fingertips, always gazing into her eyes.

Greer tried to ignore a heated sensation

271

in her thighs. "He said 'ahh' about three times and kept nodding. Then he asked me in and I sat on a step while he finished pruning back his roses. Andrew, Kurt was there a couple of years ago. *Kurt.*"

"Good Lord," he whispered. "Your brother."

"Yes. Mr. Gibbs said a man who reminded him of me came by asking questions about a family who used to live in Ferndale. As soon as I mentioned Timmons, he remembered that had been the man's last name and the name of the people he was looking for. Kurt didn't ring a bell. But when I suggested Rusty, he was sure he recognized it. And do you know what else?"

Andrew inclined his head and turned her hand to kiss the palm.

She took a shaky swallow of wine. "If this is my Rusty Timmons, and I'm sure it is, he could be a hotel keeper in Bournemouth. Mr. Gibbs said he remembered Rusty telling him that. Andrew, I think I'm going to find him. How far away is Bournemouth?"

"About an hour by train. Go tomorrow," he urged her.

"I won't know where to look."

"What's wrong with the telephone

book?" he said, not giving her a chance to back out. "I'd come with you, but I've got a consultation in Salisbury and I'll be gone until the following day. You could wait for me, if you like."

This was something she intended to do alone. "I'll be fine," she assured him. "Then I can tell you about it afterward. I'm so darn muddled up, though. One minute I'm praying I find him and he tells me where my mother is. The next I'm in a cold sweat in case he does."

"You mean you're normal," Andrew needled her, kissing her jaw. "Eat up. I've got a few things to tell you, too. But they aren't as pleasant and I don't want to ruin either of our appetites."

Greer managed half of her pie and declined the rum-soaked cake Andrew had wanted her to try. On the return drive to Weymouth the pleasant effect of good wine and food were edged with apprehension. She made inconsequential comments about her purchases for the store, and some of the places she'd seen, certain that Andrew would tell her his own news when he was ready. But by the time they parked outside her boardinghouse a leaden weight had formed in her stomach.

"Feel up to a walk?" Andrew asked, as

he opened her door.

Greer tilted her face to his. All trace of humor had disappeared. "Absolutely," she said. "I need to use up some of those calories."

They crossed the wide street in silence. A building on stilts pierced the perfect arc of the bay and Andrew helped her over a wide pebble bank to the hard-packed sand at the water's edge. "Let's head toward the town. Easier going," he said.

He threaded her arm through his. Though he strolled at a leisurely pace, Greer could feel the underlying tension in his posture.

"Look at the moon on the water," she sighed as she tugged them both to a halt. "It ripples up the beach with the tide."

Without warning, Andrew pulled her into his arms with crushing force. "I call it a moontide. It used to be the most beautiful thing the night had to offer, before you came along. Oh, Greer — I needed you with me tonight."

She pushed her hands beneath his jacket and clung to his sides. "I'm here," she said intensely. "Something's gone wrong, hasn't it?"

He disentangled them gently but kept an arm firmly around her waist when they walked on. "I had a run-in with Bob this afternoon."

"Again?"

"Again. Only this one had a different twist. Evidently I'm not flamboyant enough with what little family fortune I have left."

Only the sharp line of his averted jaw was visible when she looked up. "Meaning?"

"Meaning I should buy a Rolls Silver Cloud and go in for mink-lined overcoats."

"I don't understand," she said.

"How could you?" His hard little laugh sent goose bumps across Greer's skin. "Bob says Coover has a new angle. Not instead, but in addition to the existing line of attack. This one suggests that because my home is open to the public, I'm short of money."

"But even if it were true, what could that possibly do to help Coover?"

"Give him a chance to suggest I want him out so I can have his job and the fat salary that goes with it."

"That's disgusting." Greer planted her feet and stuck both hands into her jacket pockets. She almost asked if Bob had tried to defend Andrew, but thought better of it.

"Yup," Andrew agreed as he turned to

stare over the ocean. "But it makes me even more determined not to give up. Only a frightened man sinks so low. Friend Coover's days are numbered."

Tenderness swelled inside Greer. She moved close to Andrew's back, rubbed his shoulders, then wrapped her arms around his waist until her cheek rested on the smooth surface of his jacket. Andrew pulled her in front of him.

His eyes glinted in the moonlight and she saw a flicker of white as his lips parted. "Kiss me, Andrew," she whispered. She stood on tiptoe and brought his face down to hers.

For seconds he seemed to fight his own response, kissing her with a restraint that laid raw every nerve ending in her body. Then, his arms around her, he lifted her against him until her feet cleared the sand. The gentleness fell away and his mouth became forceful, his tongue making desperate forays past her teeth. Greer met his ardor, filling her fingers with his hair, forcing her aching breasts against him, rubbing, touching.

Their breath came in rasping gulps between kisses. Greer lifted her head and shuddered when Andrew repeatedly kissed her neck from the point of her chin to the low, loosely draped neckline of her dress. She took his hands and held them over her breasts. The night was alive with the sound of waves on the shore and another noise Greer realized only she heard — desire's steady thrum.

Abruptly he moved his hands behind her, pressed them into the firm flesh of her bottom until she was molded to him. "I love you," he said passionately, "I want you with me all the time."

Greer's heart bounded. She clutched his sleeves and felt his insistent erection against her belly. *Just admit you love him, too.* She bent her forehead to his chest.

"Greer." His breath moved her hair. "We both need more than this."

She must answer him. "I want to be with you, too," she assured him. "But it isn't clear-cut, Andrew." How was she going to tell him what he deserved to know, must know before he committed his life to her? And even if he accepted her physical limitation, there were other considerations. She couldn't get swept away too quickly.

Soft laughter penetrated her whirling thoughts. "You're embarrassed to say you need more time. Don't be, my love. As long as I know we'll be together in the end, I can wait." He took a step backward and gripped her shoulders. "But not if we don't slow this down. It's cold here, and could become public at any moment, and there's a danger that even my iron will's about to crack. I'm going to take you to your castle and get back to mine while I'm still sane."

His kiss when he left her felt as tremblingly vulnerable as Greer's heart.

Chapter 14

First day of November. Greer sat on a bench and squinted through bare tree limbs at a blue-and-white sky. A lovely early winter day, a day that reminded her of Seattle at the same time of year.

She thought through her brief telephone conversation with Rusty Timmons. The silence after she first told him who she was had lasted so long she almost wondered if they'd been cut off. And he hadn't wanted her to come to his hotel. Tears burned her eyes and she blinked. He'd made a new life, just like the old vicar had said. Probably decided to forget his beginnings. A sister popping up from the past could be an embarrassment he'd rather avoid. Greer didn't want to do anything to hurt him.

A bus had brought her from Bournemouth station to a shopping square in the city's center. She'd called Rusty from a red telephone booth on a steep and busy street lined with shops. Even with the door shut, traffic noise had made it difficult to hear clearly. After several lengthy pauses he'd told her to go to the gardens in the middle of the square and wait by the river in the vicinity of a putting green. He'd be there as soon as he could. Yes, he thought they'd recognize each other.

Ducks bobbled in close groups on the shallow water, occasionally flurrying to shore after crumbs tossed by two toddlers crouching on the bank with their mother. An older boy, in short gray pants and a navy striped school blazer, poked at a toy sailboat with a long stick. His peaked cap was pushed back on his head and his pursed mouth clearly showed his displeasure at the lack of breeze to fill the miniature sails. Greer listened to the group talking. "Here comes another duck, mummy." "Yes, dear. But let him get a bit nearer." All so calm and uncomplicated.

"Hello, Greer."

She looked up sharply into a pair of eyes as blue as her own. "Hi," she said. Her chest ached.

"May I sit down?"

"Please."

They sat half-facing each other, separated by a giant barrier forged from twenty-four years, and two entirely different lives. Greer took a shaky breath before speaking. "I shouldn't have come," she blurted. Her throat was so dry it hurt.

"Don't say that." Rusty spoke with the soft accent she'd heard and liked in Dorset. He held out a hand and she shook it. "I told you we wouldn't have any difficulty finding each other."

The stinging moisture in Greer's eyes welled and spilled over. She wanted to hug this strange man, but knew she mustn't. "You've got the freckles, too." Inane. His face blurred when she tried to smile.

"And the red hair. Although yours is prettier," he added, crossing his arms and looking away. "I couldn't believe it when you said who you were. How did you manage to track me down?"

"By accident in the end," she said simply. "I reminded someone else of you."

Rusty turned back sharply. "Who?"

She *was* some sort of threat to him. "Just an old man who lives in Kelloway Lane, in —"

"Ferndale. I know where Kelloway Lane is."

One of the toddlers howled but Greer hardly heard him. "Did you ever find what you were looking for?"

"You mean, who, don't you?" Rusty corrected quietly.

A wave of nausea engulfed her. "Yes," she murmured. "Did you?"

He pushed off from the bench and stood with his back to her, watching the children. "I'm married now," he said. "We've got two sons and a steady little business. Nothing that's going to set the world on fire, but enough."

"I'm glad, Rusty," she answered sincerely.

"My wife knows that I was bounced around a bit as a kid. She had to know the rest, too, for the forms when we got married, but we don't talk about it. We'd both rather the boys never found out."

Greer shoved her hands deep in her jacket pockets. "And you're afraid I might tell them?" she guessed. "Don't be. I didn't even know you existed until a few days ago. Then I just wanted to see you — once, if that's what you prefer."

"It's too late for anything else between you and me." He squatted on his heels in front of her so that she looked down into his troubled eyes. "I don't know what made you decide to come digging around after so long," he said, shaking his head sadly. "The same thing that bit me a couple of years ago, I suppose. But forget it, Greer. Go home. I never saw you again after you went into the foster home as a baby, but someone told me you'd been adopted and taken to the States. I was glad. You were free — out of it. Stay out of it," he advised her.

"Of course," she said, standing abruptly. "We're strangers, nothing more. I'm sorry I've upset you."

A hand on her shoulder made her jump. Rusty stood beside her, a slender man, taller than she'd expected. "It isn't what you think," he said in a much gentler tone of voice. "I'm not hiding from my past for my own sake. But the kids are secure. As far as they're concerned, my parents are both dead. It seemed easier that way. How will I look to them now if they suddenly discover it's all a lie?"

"There's no reason for them to discover anything. Not from me." Greer studied his face intently, then dropped her eyes. She'd been unconsciously committing him to memory. "I'd like to meet my mother," she said softly, but firmly.

A long breath whistled past Rusty's teeth. "I can't help you."

"You never located her?"

He wouldn't meet her eyes. "I can't help you."

Greer touched the sleeve of his tan rain-coat. "You did find her, didn't you? Why don't you want to tell me where she is?"

"Because some things are better left alone," he said loudly, then dropped his voice. "She's not every child's dream mom. No cottage with roses around the door. No smell of baking pies drifting through homey rooms. She didn't want us then, damn it. And she doesn't want us now."

The words jolted Greer. So did the tear her brother wiped angrily away. "I'm sorry," she said. "I can't seem to think of anything else to say, but I *am* sorry. And the last thing I intended was to bring back bad memories."

"I know that."

"But, Rusty, this is something I have to decide for myself. Will you tell me where she is?" She touched his hand for emphasis.

"You shouldn't go there. She's — she's got another life, too."

"Please let me have her address. I may never use it, but at least it'll make her seem more real."

Rusty reached slowly into the breast pocket of his shirt and brought out a folded paper. "I had a feeling you'd ask for this and that changing your mind would be

284

impossible," he said. "At least I tried, and I can always hope you don't go."

Her fingers closed over the sheet and Rusty surrounded them, holding on. Desperation and sadness mingled in his expression.

"Don't worry," she said, managing a smile. "I'm a survivor, like you. Nothing's going to happen to me."

"Babies weren't my favorite things when you were born. I thought you were ugly and made too much noise. But our mother said you were the loveliest baby she'd ever seen — like an angel. She never meant to hurt us, but she was too young and poor to do much about it. Can't we just leave it at that?"

Tears pricked at her eyes again. "I don't know," she answered. "I just don't know yet."

Rusty checked his watch. "I'm due back. There's one thing I'd like to ask you."

"Anything." They'd never meet again.

"If you do decide to see our mother — her last name's Hawker now, by the way, married a London railroad engineer —" He reached for her hand again. "If you see Ruby, don't tell her where I am. I can't imagine she'd want to know, but I'd rather she didn't."

Greer nodded her head and impulsively

reached to hug him. To her surprise, Rusty met her halfway.

"Goodbye, Rusty. Give your boys an extra hug and think of me."

He turned and ran. Greer watched while he crossed to the far side of the putting green and leaped a flight of steps in several bounds. At the top he looked back and raised a hand. She waved and pressed her fingers to her sore eyelids. When she removed her hands, Rusty was gone.

Greer paced between her bed and the window. Not until tomorrow afternoon, Andrew had said when he called from Salisbury. They would be together then.

When she'd walked in, after taking a bus from the station, Mrs. Findlay had been about to hang up the phone. Andrew had found out the train schedule from Bournemouth and guessed, successfully, what time Greer might arrive home.

His main concern seemed to be their missed outing with Simonne, which he'd arranged to make up at the end of next week. There wasn't time before his afternoon consultation for deep discussion of Greer's day, and as soon as he had hung up, she felt resentful, then lonely. Tomorrow was too far away, she wanted him with her now.

She was being foolish. Mature women dealt with their own problems. What happened with Rusty should have been predictable. He'd been right. The arrival of a sister he had never mentioned to his family was a complication he didn't need.

Ruby Hawker's London address was pinned beneath a ceramic poodle on the windowsill. Greer pulled the slip of paper out and tucked it inside her wallet. Emotional tension had caught up with her. A nap and then a walk into town to eat dinner would clear her head. Eventually she'd know whether or not to complete the quest for her mother.

Greer had wrestled off one boot when she heard Mrs. Findlay's toiling footsteps on the stairs. "A Dr. Wilson to see you, Mrs. Beckett," she wheezed through the closed door. "Shall I send him up?"

"*No.*" Greer's mind ground to a halt for an instant.

"In the lounge, then?"

Why would Bob Wilson come to see her? "Yes. Ask him to wait and I'll be right down," she called through the door.

Clutching a chair back for balance, she tugged the boot on again and straightened the skirt of her camel suit. The train journey had left her feeling grimy. She ran a brush through her hair and quickly washed her hands. What was it about the thought of carrying on a conversation with Bob Wilson — alone — that reduced her insides to a Jell-O?

The lounge door was open. With a confident smile, Greer strode into the room, then stopped abruptly. Bob was seated on the edge of the couch, his head bent while both hands sagged between his knees.

She cleared her throat. "Hello, Bob. This is a surprise."

Original.

When he lifted his face, purplish smudges beneath his eyes and the shadow of far more than a morning's growth of beard shocked her. He wore faded jeans and a dark blue turtleneck that bagged at the elbows.

"Surprise?" He stood as if every move were an effort. "Yes, I apologize for dropping in on you like this," he said. "But I thought it was time we got to know each other better."

Greer frowned. The man made no sense and he looked as if he hadn't slept for a week.

"Because Andy seems so fond of you, I mean," he added, his eyes sliding away. "Is there somewhere more private we can talk?" A jerky motion of his right hand took in the cramped little room.

Not if I can help it. "Oh, no, no. We won't be disturbed in here." She shut the door firmly and went to sit on a chair opposite the couch. Her heart thumped like a wild thing.

Bob's smile didn't reach his eyes. "I expect you're wondering why I came."

That was the understatement of the century. She studied her fingernails, searching for something to say.

The couch creaked as he slumped back into its hard upholstery. "You don't mind if I sit down?"

Greer shook her head. He was nervous — more nervous than she. "What's wrong, Bob? You didn't come here to make small talk," she said, hoping he would get to the point.

"Of course I didn't," he answered, his voice rising with each word. "Excuse me. I didn't mean to shout, but this is important and the past few days haven't been easy. Just hear me out. It won't take long. Then you can make up your own mind what to do."

When she didn't answer, he turned sideways to anchor an elbow over the couch back. "I don't know how much Andy's told you about this thing with Coover. The hearing and so on. But you do matter to him and that may be the only thing that'll stop him from chucking his career away."

Greer shivered, although she wasn't cold. "Go on," she said evenly.

Without warning Bob shoved his big body upright and started to pace. "A boy died — you know that already. Sad. But there isn't a damn thing anyone can do to bring him back. But Andy won't let it be. He's out for blood and revenge — honor and all that crap." He paused, running a hand through his ruffled hair. "I came here to ask you to help me stop Andy from destroying himself."

"Bob." Greer was on her feet and beside him. "Andrew's told me all about the case. He believes he can win it. Why don't you support him?"

"Support him with *what?*" he shouted, towering over her. His pale eyes pierced her heart. "There isn't one substantiated fact on his side and Coover's got *his* deck stacked. If Andy isn't stopped, in less than two weeks he's going to get nailed to the wall. And if he does, it's going to kill a part of me, too. Do you understand what I'm telling you?"

She'd been wrong about Bob Wilson. He did care about Andrew. He cared enough to be distraught. "Yes," Greer answered. She touched his arm, made long comforting strokes between shoulder and elbow. "I do understand. But I don't know what I can do about it. As you've said, Andrew's determined. He believes in what he's doing, and I'm not sure anyone can shake that kind of conviction."

"But will you try?" He grasped her hands and squeezed. "Will you?"

By the time she closed the front door behind Bob, Greer's temples throbbed. Yes, she would talk to Andrew, she'd agreed. No, she didn't know what she would say or how. And, above all, he'd never learn Bob had come to her.

She climbed the stairs slowly, her hip aching for the first time in days. What *was* driving Andrew to pursue the hearing? It had to be his sense of justice and a concern over the possibility of a tragedy similar to Michael Drake's death. Yet Bob knew the facts, and he was a principled man, too. Surely he'd be as worried as Andrew if he thought Coover was a potential threat.

After a restless night, plagued with muddled dreams, Greer could hardly wait to dress and go down to breakfast. Even the thought of seeing Mrs. Findlay's dour face was comforting.

Twenty minutes later, the sound of the phone ringing shattered her nerves and Greer watched the dining-room door with trepidation. She wasn't ready to speak to Andrew. Or was she? She waited, pushing toast crumbs around her plate. When the landlady launched into her latest list of complaints, Greer knew the phone call had not been for her.

The day dragged by and with each minute, her tension mounted. The only one who could sort this out was Andrew. Until she could see him she'd continue to feel like a pawn in a game she never agreed to play.

Chapter 15

Greer hammered on the side door of Ringstead Hall for the fourth time, then stepped back to stare up at Andrew's windows. No lights. But there wouldn't be at three in the afternoon.

The Mini, slewed at a haphazard angle near the garage, suggested its owner had arrived home. Where was he? She should have tried to telephone Andrew before paying a fortune for a taxi to bring and leave her here.

He could be in the shower. Impulsively she tried the door handle. It turned easily and she stepped into the passageway.

"Andrew!" Her voice bounced off the walls. "Andrew! Are you here?" Lonely place, she thought. Cold and silent.

Pressure built in her head and she gnawed at her lips. Too much. This last day had loaded her down with too many decisions and possibilities to consider.

She walked rapidly to the stairs, her pace increasing with every step until she half-ran into the private wing. "Andrew," she shouted along the corridor. His study, bathroom, sitting room and, finally, the bedroom. All doors gaping, all rooms empty.

"Where are you?" she muttered aloud. His medical bag and an overnight case stood at the bottom of the bed. She lifted the case — still full. But his raincoat and suit had been thrown over an easy chair in one corner, and dress shoes lay on their sides beside the open closet.

Greer picked up a striped silk tie that had slid to the floor and went to the window. The air had been oppressively still all day, as if there could be a thunderstorm. But with approaching dusk, a wind had picked up. The storm wouldn't come, she decided. Too bad. Everything around her seemed to be gathering momentum, with no promise of release.

Did Andrew feel tense, too? He must with the hearing looming ahead. And his feelings for her couldn't help. Good grief, he'd made them clear enough and he was plainly very human. Yesterday he'd promised to get in touch when he returned from Salisbury. Evidently something had changed his mind. Unwillingness to face more sexual frustration? She had no right to expect his endless patience. But she wasn't happy about their situation, either. They had to solve the mushrooming chaos surrounding them.

He must be outside. Greer tossed the tie on top of Andrew's suit. As she glanced up, the Hummel box caught her eye. Half hidden by a stack of books atop a small desk, its soft colors were unmistakable. She stopped, determined not to cry. Her chin quivered. He'd kept the wretched, sweet, music box. Despite Simonne's comment, Greer hadn't noticed it the night she stayed with Andrew. *Find him.* The uneven clipping of her heels echoed through the empty rooms as she made her way to the back of the house.

She'd never been through the grounds. Where would Andrew go out here? She surveyed the woods that topped a rise behind the house, and continued along the skyline to the east. Maybe there? Greer hurried up a flight of steps to a grassy plateau where tall, conical topiary edged a pool. The breeze sent ripples across the metallic-green water and shivers up her back. All still. An eerie setting from another age.

Trembling weakened her knees. Gray cloud banks slunk sullenly across the sky. Another hour and it would be dark. Greer turned along the path leading toward the ocean. The descent was steep and gravity pulled her forward at a trot. She should be thinking of a way to get back to Weymouth, not scurrying through empty acres, searching for a man who might have decided he never wanted to see her again.

The cliff, when she reached it, fell away as if a giant cleaver had severed land from sea. Below, a fluted band of pebbles bordered the tawny sand.

Her hair swirled across her eyes, and she wrestled it behind her ears. Then she saw Andrew. His dark hair and tall, lean body were unmistakable as he jogged along the water's edge. Even at a distance Greer could tell he was relaxed, not hurrying.

Damn him. While her insides threatened to explode, he enjoyed an afternoon run that was scarcely more than a saunter. She searched around and located a spot where a mountain goat, or someone very accustomed to the terrain, might get to the beach. Her nostrils flared. Anyone who was angry enough could make it down that steep, rubble pathway.

Small stones began to fly the instant she

took her first tentative, downward step. With the second she slipped, landing with a bruising thump. *Damn, damn, damn.* She *would* get to him — and give him a piece of her mind.

Colored specks darted before her. As a kid, she and Casey had loved to run. Downhill meant fast and don't think. Greer scrambled, gathering speed. Her calves and the backs of her thighs pulled sharply, but she kept going.

Twice she slithered, skinning the heels of both hands. She didn't look toward Andrew.

The bottom. She paused to breathe deeply. Her lungs burned as if she'd been too long under water. The pebbles jabbed at her feet until she reached the sand bar. Andrew was a short distance ahead to her right. She caught up, then passed him, swerving closer to the ocean.

"Greer! Stop!"

A wild impulse engulfed her. Why should she stop? Because he said so? Surf swamped her shoes.

Andrew drew level. "For God's sake," he shouted. "Stop. What's the matter with you?"

"You should know." The words seared her throat. "You don't own this beach and I want to run."

"Your hip isn't strong enough," he insisted. "It should be, but it isn't."

She was openly crying now. So what? "Don't tell me what should and shouldn't be. Or what I can do," she shrieked.

"Stop this," Andrew said firmly. "Unless you want me to make you."

Greer winced at the pain in her hip, but kept on running. Ahead a spit of rocks jutted into the sea. Before she could reach it, Andrew ran to block her path. He faced her and halted, fists on hips.

"Get out of my way," she threatened him. She hobbled sideways to go around him and gasped as he snatched her arm.

"That's it, Greer," he yelled, shaking her angrily. "Enough." He glared and abruptly released her. The force of his thrust caused her heel to turn in the soft shingle and she started to fall.

"You little idiot," Andrew exploded as he attempted to grab her, missed and overbalanced. "Oh, good Lord."

She took the full force of his crushing weight. His left forearm slammed into her diaphragm, winding her and leaving incredible pain in its wake. He shifted swiftly and Greer curled into a ball on her side.

Instantly Andrew knelt over her, brushing back her hair, cradling her head. "Sweetheart," he whispered. "Lie still. Where do you hurt?"

"My stomach," she rasped.

Instantly she felt his probing fingers. "You're okay, thank God," he pronounced. "Just winded. But why the hell did you do this?"

"I'm angry."

"So you decided to come down here and run like a maniac? What are you angry about? And it better be good."

Greer's wind was returning, plus her anger.

"When you called, all you could talk about was Simonne."

He rolled her into his arms and got to his feet carrying her. "You're jealous of a little girl I happen to like? And this is my punishment?"

"Put me down," she insisted. There was no escaping his tightened grip. "I'm not jealous of anyone. But everything's too much for me and I can't go through another day of not knowing what to do about it all."

"Fine." He started to walk. "I know how you feel. We'll get your feet dry and talk about all our troubles. Yours, anyway."

She twisted angrily in his arms. "I'm not

one more silly juvenile, Andrew," she said. "You aren't going to pat me on the head to make it all better. You're in as much emotional hell as I am and we're going to start sorting your problems out by making love."

"Making — ?" He almost dropped her. "I don't believe this," he said as if talking to himself. "Yes, I do on second thought." Hiking her higher against his chest, he pushed her face into his shoulder and marched on.

Greer tried to speak but the fabric of his black sweat shirt and his rapid progress over the pebbles made it impossible. She expected to be set down when he reached the cliff. Andrew only hitched her closer, wrapping one arm around her waist, the other across the backs of her thighs and buttocks, and climbed to the top without a pause.

Not until they reached his study did Andrew finally let loose of Greer. He dumped her in one of the leather wing chairs and yanked off her shoes.

"Andrew . . ." she began.

"Don't say anything."

Misery inched into the spaces where her anger had seeped away. She watched him leave the room and return in moments with a towel. "I'm sorry," she said automatically. He must think her mad. She thought herself mad. Temporarily unhinged at least.

His answer was to apply stinging friction to her feet with the towel.

She sighed audibly and slumped backward.

Andrew plopped down, cross-legged, still holding her feet. Now he rubbed them gently with his hands. "You scared the hell out of me down there, Greer. Then you made me *madder* than hell." Andrew paused to let that sink in. "But you're right about one thing," he added. "This can't go on. We've got to sort ourselves out — individually and jointly."

"Yes," was all she said.

"Ready to talk about it calmly?"

"Yes."

He lifted one foot. "Little feet." His lips grazed the instep. "You go first."

"Oh, Andrew." Blindly, she sought his warm strength, folding her arms around his neck and sinking to the floor until they knelt together, thighs touching.

"Tell me," he said hoarsely. "What's happened?"

It poured out. The meeting with Rusty. His attempt to stop her from seeing their mother. What it felt like to know her brother lived and breathed but she would probably never see him again. And all the time Andrew stroked her back, rocked her gently, until she punctuated her words with tears and tiny sniffling kisses along his jaw.

"I never even asked their names," she said miserably.

"Whose names?" Andrew prompted softly.

"The boys. Rusty's boys. My nephews. Or his wife. He must have had pictures, too. At least I could have seen what they look like."

"Some things are better left alone."

She pulled away abruptly and sat on the chair once more. "Everyone says that. But who decides, Andrew? Who decides what's best left alone? You?"

He frowned and tried to take her hand.

"No." Greer sat straighter. "Your life is rocking like an overloaded teeter-totter, too."

"That's not something you have to worry about," he told her.

"It isn't? You think I don't care about what happens to you? I'm worried sick that you're going to get flattened at this stupid hearing. You love your work and if they say Winston Coover's right and you're wrong and he drags up a lot of lies that a bunch of his cronies may be only too happy to believe —" she said, dragging in a breath.

"They could stop you from doing what means most to you and I couldn't stand that."

"Are you asking me not to go ahead?" His voice was as level as his golden eyes.

Greer tipped her head wearily to one side. "Of course not," she said slowly. "All I want is to be sure that when you do go into the ring, the fight isn't fixed." She found herself seized by panic. "Andrew," she said, leaning forward. "Is it going to be all right? Do you have enough evidence to prove your case? And *is* there any chance Coover can ruin your reputation?"

For agonizing moments he was silent. Then he pulled himself into the facing chair and rested his chin on his hands. "It's going to be all right," he said wearily. "I'm all the evidence I need to prove both my case and my reputation. And every step of the way I'll be thinking of a red-haired woman who — who's rooting for me." Andrew reached across the space to take her hands. "I can't tell you what to do about your mother any more than you can solve things for me," he continued. "But I think you should give yourself plenty of time to decide, then follow your intuition. Rusty sounds like a nice guy. I'm glad you two met even if you don't see each other again — but he can't make your decisions, either. Does that sound sensible?"

"You always sound sensible," she said, grinning wryly.

"Great. Now try this on for size. Since I left you the other night I've been thinking about you and me." He stood and began to pace. "On my way back from Salisbury I went to the Sealink ferry terminal in Weymouth and bought two round-trip tickets for Guernsey."

Greer rubbed the bridge of her nose. "One of the Channel Islands?" she said.

"Right. About four and a half hours from here."

"What are you really saying?"

"Greer. We're hemmed in on all sides by distractions. But there's one thing that overrides them all and we both know what it is. We want each other, and not just as sympathetic buddies. The way we feel — sexually — is there every second we're together. And when we're not together. You didn't include that in your list of frustrations, but the hysterical offer you made on the beach proves I'm not the only one being driven over the edge."

She shifted to stare at the ashes in the

fireplace. "I wasn't hysterical," she answered.

"That's irrelevant." He stood over her. "The tickets I bought are for the Tuesday-afternoon ferry. Come to Guernsey with me, Greer. It's beautiful there — and isolated. We need to be alone and completely separated from anything that distracts us from —"

"Taking me up on my hysterical offer," she blurted out, flushing. At the same time she felt the familiar throb of desire in her lower limbs. She knew he was right.

His fingers brushed her cheek. "I was thinking more of — loving each other," he said tenderly.

"I do love you, Andrew," she whispered and closed her eyes.

She felt him move. His hand slid behind her neck, but she pulled away.

"Greer. Darling," Andrew said, clearly struggling for patience, "I don't understand you. What's holding you back? It's not still Colin, is it?" he asked, as if he were afraid of her answer.

"No, damn it," was all she said. All she had to do was tell him, now — all of it — and let him decide how he felt. "Andrew."

"Yes." He kissed her temple.

"I'll come with you on Tuesday."

Chapter 16

"If it weren't so cold we could pretend it was a summer's evening," Andrew said, smiling. He hooked both elbows over the back of a slatted bench on the huge ferry's upper deck and half closed his eyes.

Greer squinted at a carmine horizon streaked with drifting lumps of miniature clouds. "Is there a name for formations like that?"

"Mmm," Andrew said as he considered the clouds. "Mackerel locally, I think. After the fish. I don't know why. Not my field. We'd better retrieve our bags."

"We can't be there yet."

He pointed over his shoulder. "That's Guernsey. We'll be docking in St. Peter Port shortly."

She twisted to see land and a harbor fronting clusters of buildings. Her stomach lurched. St. Peter Port, and the hotel where she and Andrew would stay. When he picked her up to come to the boat, it was the first time she'd seen him since the afternoon at Ringstead. They'd agreed to spend the intervening time apart, to gain perspective and get some work done. Greer had wandered through the two days devoid of inspiration for Britmania, thinking of little else but Andrew and, when she couldn't shut her out, Ruby Timmons Hawker.

"I half expected that landlady of yours to say you were out when I got there this afternoon," he said suddenly.

Greer turned to him. "If I'd changed my mind I'd have called," she told him. "Anyway, I made the hotel reservation, remember. I wouldn't have let you leave without a place to stay when you got here."

"You think I would have come without you?" He stood and hauled her to her feet. "Where are we staying? I still don't understand why you insisted finding digs was your territory."

She swallowed uncomfortably. "You already asked me that fifty times at least. And, like I told you before, it's a surprise." *To me, too, probably.* Choosing the most inexpensive listing on the travel agent's books might not have been such a good idea. But no way was Andrew going to pay more than half the bill and it was time to watch what she spent more closely. "I'm good at finding little-known gems in the hotel department," she hedged. "That's why I wanted to do it."

His expression suggested he was skeptical. "Like Belle Vista?" he challenged her.

"I like it there."

"Of course," he said, his eyes laughing at her. "You already told me that — must be getting forgetful. I'll put you in line to get off and collect our things."

Few of the passengers appeared to be tourists. Businessmen who might have been dressed for a day's work anywhere in the States, families whose lack of interest in their surroundings suggested they were returning home; only language and accents gave the small crowd a foreign flavor. Greer identified German, English spoken with a French accent and what sounded like a form of French — probably one of the Channel Island patois the guidebook had mentioned. The islands were now a part of Britain but had once been claimed by the Duchy of Normandy.

"What do you think?" Andrew said as he dropped their bags and leaned against the rail beside Greer. "It always seems more continental than English here to me."

She watched the gulls swoosh overhead. "I've never been to the Continent. But the town looks like all those travel brochures for France or Spain. I like the way it comes right down to the ocean."

"Am I allowed to know where the hotel is? So I know what bus to catch from the terminal?"

"We're staying at Phelps in Smith Street," she said. He was close, his elbow touching her wrist. Fading sunlight cast shadows about the clear lines of his face. The salt scent of the air seemed a part of him. And they were going to be lovers on this green island in a cobalt sea. She stared silently at his profile until he faced her.

He reached to take her hands. "Relax, sweetheart. This is going to be a beautiful time for us. The start of the rest of our beautiful times together."

"I hope so, Andrew," she whispered. Her lips parted to receive his soft kiss just as the ferry bumped against the dock. She clung to him, trembling inside, praying he didn't sense her clamoring turmoil.

Inquiry revealed Smith Street to be within walking distance of the jetty. Greer took in the scenery while Andrew carried both bags. Shops and cafés, each with a different and quaint facade, lined the narrow cobblestone streets. Could be somewhere in Brittany, she decided. All the photographs and paintings she'd seen of the northwest peninsula of France showed similar settings.

"This is super," Greer panted, concentrating on the rough pavement. "Slow down or we'll miss it all."

Andrew immediately dropped both bags. "Sit," he invited and pointed to his leather suitcase. "I happened to notice one or two drops of rain and it's rapidly feeling arctic. It's also dark. But don't let me rush you. I'll just use the time while you're sightseeing to catch my breath."

"Comedian," Greer quipped as she punched his ribs playfully. "I guess we can come back tomorrow — or maybe after we've checked in?"

His penetrating gaze seemed to probe every corner of her mind. "Tomorrow, for sure," he said. "I don't think we'll come out again tonight. It's almost six. Let's buy a bottle of wine and some bread and cheese and eat in the room later."

"Sounds terrific," she said, ignoring her racing heart. She lifted a bag but he took it from her.

At a stall heaped with fruit and vegetables, Andrew bought two apples and some grapes. A bakery yielded crusty French bread. Greer spotted the small grocery store where they picked out a box of Camembert, then passed over several fine white wines in favor of a bottle of very dry champagne. When Andrew added plastic glasses and knives to his purchase, the clerk looked amused. He grinned at Greer who promptly blushed.

"You should have seen yourself in there," Andrew said, laughing when they were back in the street. "You were beet red just because some stranger figured out we're going to have a picnic."

"That isn't what he was thinking."

Andrew bent to whisper in her ear. "He was thinking how lucky I am to have such a gorgeous woman to picnic with. And you're imagining things."

His breath tickled Greer's cheek. She arched a brow at him, quickened her pace and changed the subject immediately. "Pollet Street. Le Pollet. Why do they show each street name twice?" she inquired.

"To keep the French as well as the English tradition. I think this is our turn."

When Greer saw Phelps, she opened her mouth in horror, then snapped it shut again. Another Belle Vista, only less pristine. White paint peeled from brick facing below a sagging slate roof. A jutting sun porch at street level could have been attractive — if every window weren't securely covered by grayish lace curtains. Greer hugged the sacks of food miserably to her chest.

Andrew tipped his head, studying the building to its top story, and smiled at her benignly. "I'd have known this was it even if you hadn't told me," he claimed. "A true Greer *gem*. You certainly do have a flair for picking winners."

"Good grief," she breathed. "We could always look for someplace else. I really had no idea —"

"Wouldn't hear of it." The smirk on his lips curled her toes. "If you chose this, I know it'll be great."

The small foyer showed more promise. A copper vase filled with russet chrysanthemums glowed on a highly polished round table. The air was redolent with lemon oil. One ring on the desk bell produced a stout huffing lady who explained with pride that she was *the* Mrs. Phelps. She would take them upstairs herself.

Every few steps the woman stopped to glance at Andrew and Greer, her small black eyes shrewdly assessing them while she fired obsequious questions. "You're sure you won't be needing hot-water bottles — no? I'd be happy to turn down the bed if you'd let me know when you leave for dinner."

A few minutes after showing them their room, Mrs. Phelps returned with a daily paper, then, again, with a tray of tea and cookies. Each time she lingered to size up her guests and their belongings with avid interest. "You're sure there's nothing else I can do for you Mrs. — ?"

"No. But thanks for the tea," Greer said, putting her hands behind her. Andrew hadn't noticed her wedding band was missing — Mrs. Phelps had. Without it her finger felt huge and naked. But she couldn't use Colin's ring as a mock symbol of respectability.

"Thanks very much, Mrs. Phelps," Andrew said as he backed the woman subtly toward the hall. "We'll certainly let you know if we need something."

Greer leaned against the closed door, listening to the landlady's retreating footsteps. "What do you think her next excuse will be?"

"Who knows? If she comes back again, we won't answer the door." Andrew rubbed his hands together and hunched his shoulders. "It's freezing in here," he complained.

"Maybe that's why she brought the tea. She knew we'd need warming up." Hot blood surged to Greer's cheeks. She studied the worn floral carpet, avoiding Andrew's eyes.

His arms were around her shoulders before she realized he'd moved. "What are you afraid of, Greer?" he asked her gently.

"Me?" The fleeting kiss he brushed across her forehead made her already stretched nerves vibrate.

She wanted to say, "Me, Andrew. It's me I'm afraid of." Instead she touched his sides lightly and ducked beneath his left arm. "Don't be ridiculous," she told him. Her voice wavered, and she felt him watch her progress around the room as she pretended to inspect the furniture.

"So, what is it?"

"Nothing," Greer said, too quickly. "Just that this all feels like such a setup."

"A setup?" His short laugh was mirthless. "Does that mean you regret coming? That you feel I coerced you into this — trip?"

The watery sensation in Greer's legs spread throughout her body. "No, no. I want to be here with you," she assured him. "I even arranged the hotel, remember? If anyone's guilty of carefully planning an interlude, it's just as much me as you."

He went to the window and lifted a lace curtain to peer into the night through rain-splattered glass. "Speaking of which. What did make you choose this wonderful establishment?"

"Please, Andrew. Not now."

"Seriously," he insisted. "Why this one?"

"How can you switch topics like that?" she said, clamping her teeth shut to still the trembling in her jaw.

He wheeled around. "Humor me."

Greer sat on the edge of a chintz armchair beside the unlit gas fire. "It had one star in the book. Said it was clean with an ocean view." She brought her eyes to his, aware that he would see her defiance. "And even if you do need a telescope to see water, it's cheap," she snapped.

"That's good," he said objectively. "Now you're angry."

"You like me to be angry?"

"It's an excellent start. Sometimes we have to work our way through a pile of emotions before we can get where we want to be," he explained.

"I thought you were a pediatrician, not a psychiatrist."

"There's a repressed psychiatrist inside every doctor. The really good ones, anyway."

A sigh slipped past her lips. "One of the traits I admire most in a man is humility. And you are so humble."

His rumbly baritone laugh seemed to warm the room's cold air. "See," he teased her. "Anger to disgust. Moving right along. Work on feeling disgusted while I figure out how to light the fire. I thought this kind went out of use years ago. Do you have any matches?"

"What comes after disgust?" she asked dryly.

"Matches, I hope."

"I don't have any reason to carry matches. Maybe we should call Mrs. Phelps. She'd probably volunteer to come up and help us out."

Andrew crossed the room and knelt at Greer's feet. "Forget it. If necessary I'll break off a couple of chair legs and rub them together. I tried it a few times when I was a kid — with sticks, not chair legs."

"Did you manage to start a fire?"

"No. Not even a spark." He rested a forearm on her knees. "But we could forget the fire and see how much body heat the two of us could generate," he said suggestively. His head was bent, his face averted.

He was trying to take the tension out of the moment, but she couldn't laugh. Blue-black hair curled over the high neck of his cream sweater. The brown corduroy jacket he wore made his shoulders seem even broader. Greer stroked his hair tentatively, rubbing the skin behind his ear with the backs of her fingers. The shudder she felt pass through him was almost imperceptible. "I wanted us to be here, alone, so badly," she whispered.

"And now you're not sure it's what you want?" Andrew dropped his head farther forward.

She replaced her hand with her cheek, wrapping her arms around his shoulders. Slowly she nuzzled her face back and forth. "I've never been more sure of anything," she murmured. "But I don't want to disappoint you. You're so good, Andrew. You wouldn't say or do anything to embarrass me — including refusing to tolerate a skittish woman who puts you through hell every step of the way even though she wants to make love as much as you do," she confessed.

"What?" In a move that shocked her, he twisted around and caught her face between both of his hands. He studied her eyes, then her mouth. "Oh, darling lady," he told her. "You couldn't disappoint me. And if this is being put through hell, I hope it happens daily. You're something," he concluded, sealing his words with a brief but poignant kiss. "Just a minute," he said, leaping up and going to the tea tray the landlady had left. "Brain wave pays off. Matches on the tray. Don't move a muscle while I light this monster. Keep the thought patterns on hold, too — they have definite promise."

With a twist of a chrome key on the right side of the hearth, Andrew turned on the gas. He struck a match and the hissing settled to steady popping sounds as the flame immediately ignited. "There," he said, thoroughly pleased. "This place will warm up in no time." He tossed the matchbook on the mantel and faced her, elbows akimbo, his fine hands spread wide on slender hips beneath his jacket. "Now, where were we?"

"Already out of my depth, I think," she said nervously.

"Give me your coat."

"I'm still cold."

"No more excuses," he insisted. Andrew shrugged out of his jacket and held out a hand. "Up. I'll hang these in the wardrobe if that's what that thing is. Looks a bit like a Grecian casket on end." He tipped his head to one side, apparently concentrating furiously. "Possibly Roman — they were the ones into fruit."

Greer stood, laughing, and let him help her out of her raincoat. The heavy walnut closet was narrow and freestanding. Carved bunches of grapes encrusted the front. "I'm beginning to believe you really are very bright."

"Good," he replied. "I've been telling you as much all along. But what made you decide to agree at this particular moment?" He arranged their coats on hangers and reached to push them on the closet rail. The inch of taut flesh exposed at his waist sent a heavy spiral of heat into Greer's abdomen. She wanted this man. He awakened instincts she'd repressed too long.

She laced her fingers together to stop herself from touching him. "I read a book about types — of people," she explained.

"And?"

"It said that brilliance and a tendency to make irreverent connections often go together. So . . ."

"I know," Andrew said, cutting her off.

He took their suitcases and pushed them beneath a high rickety table by the door. "I make Roman artifacts out of twentieth-century wardrobes, so I must be brilliant." His smile was lopsided and totally charming.

Suddenly Greer felt as if a million fluttering moths had been released inside. She was light, so light she might float away. Nothing was real but Andrew's supple body moving around her, capably performing insignificant tasks to fill gaps in their conversation. She squeezed her eyes shut and folded her arms tightly across her chest.

"Greer. Greer, what is it?" Andrew said in alarm.

When she lifted her lashes he was a few inches away, staring at her, his wonderful, golden eyes darkened with concern. The moths burst free, and with them the emotion she'd tried to suppress. "If you don't hold me, now, I'm going to break into little pieces," she told him urgently. "I need you. There's so much I want to tell you, but every time I try, I talk in circles about things that don't matter. Andrew, is there something wrong with me?"

He swiftly wrapped her in his arms. Her ear pressed hard over his heart and she heard its steady beat, a strong, calming rhythm that seemed to urge her own to slow down. "There's nothing wrong with you, my darling," he soothed her. "Nothing except that you've been alone too long, and now you're a bit frightened to allow yourself to feel again."

His chin rested atop her head while he made broad circles over her back. Their scents mingled, a mysterious and heady combination. Greer was aware of her own perfume, subtle, faintly reminiscent of sandalwood, but it was Andrew's after-shave, a hint of leather — so masculine — that wound threads of heat into her thighs. Heat and need, and longing. Greer stood on tiptoes to lock her wrists behind his neck. His jaw was tantalizingly rough from a day's growth of beard, and she followed its angular lines with a row of tiny nipping kisses.

Andrew lifted his chin to allow her to press her lips to his neck, but when she stretched to take his earlobe in her teeth, he twisted his head until he could capture her mouth. His kiss was gentle, an erotic movement with firm, barely parted lips. Then the tip of his tongue found a corner of her mouth and traced the line of her lower lip before he carefully drove deeper, skimming over smooth teeth to the sensitive inside of her cheeks. Greer sensed his conscious restraint. Andrew would never push her faster or farther than he thought she was ready to go.

"Sweetheart," he breathed against her mouth. "I'll take away the doubts, if you'll let me. It's okay to love again."

The uncertainty had gone. She wanted to tell him that, but buried her hands in his hair instead, pulling his face against her neck. "Andrew," was the only word she could form.

He moved away from her to pull the sweater over his head. Muscle and sinew flexed as he relaxed his arms, then threw the garment aside. When he looked at her, his hair was mussed, his eyes alight with a sensual glow that penetrated her heart, her soul.

As if she had no will to decide what she did, her fingers sought the textures of him. His skin was drawn tight over well-developed shoulders, rough where the dark hair on his chest narrowed downward over his flat belly to the low waist of his jeans. At his sides she found a smoothness that extended to his back. She held him, stroked him slowly and kissed a flat nipple. Nothing but Andrew mattered. With him she felt a new freedom and rightness she'd never dared hope for.

"I want to feel you against me, Greer." Passion thickened his voice.

Greer started to take off her sweater, but Andrew stopped her. He lifted her and carried her to the bed, setting her down like fragile china. Each contact produced an electric charge. When he removed her shoes the arches of her feet tingled, then tickled as he kissed each one. She wriggled and laughed, and their eyes met, gold with vivid blue. The laughter caught in her throat.

The lithe economy of his motions fascinated her. Under his deft fingers, her skirt zipper slid noiselessly down, followed by the skirt itself, her half-slip and panty hose.

At Greer's automatic attempt to hide her scars, Andrew shook his head. He captured her hands and carried them to his mouth. "Don't," he said. "You're beautiful. Absolutely beautiful."

"Thank you," she said brokenly. "So are you." Nerves in her cheeks quivered when she tried to smile.

Andrew kissed the tips of her fingers, then released them. Her green sweater was slipped over her head and discarded. Then he knelt before her and filled his hands with her hair. His kisses became a gentle storm that covered her face, her neck, her shoulders. He drew back to study the tender flesh above her low-cut bra. Almost reverently he stroked a line along the lace trim that barely covered her pulsing nipples.

Their sighs mingled as Andrew continued making his chart of kisses over her body. With both hands clasped around her ribs, the moist trail passed lingeringly from the tiny flower that joined her bra between her breasts down to her navel. Skimpy white bikinis couldn't shield her from the heat of his quest. When he found the soft insides of her thighs, his warm breath sent an erotic dart to her core and she reached to draw him to her.

"Lie with me, Andrew," she whispered. "Let me watch your face. I want to see it when we make love."

He stood, his movements suddenly fevered as he took off the rest of his clothes. But he didn't stop looking into her eyes. When he was naked, she feasted on the sight of him. His body was totally masculine, speaking of his need for her in a way that left her breathless.

"Darling," he said, so low she scarcely

heard. "God, what you do to me."

Then he pulled her to her feet, flung down the bedcovers and lay her against the pillows. At his single urgent tug, her bra was undone and her aching breasts, already swollen with desire, burned under his circling palms. He slid the panties away and kissed her waiting body until every cell begged for release. His lips and teeth seduced her nipples to even tenser crests while the heel of one hand pressed into the softness between her legs. She arched against him, searching blindly to touch and hold.

"You are the loveliest woman I've ever known," he admitted. "What I feel with you almost scares me. I can't lose you again, Greer." He stared into her eyes as he spoke, then lowered his head to her belly and beyond. The molten spear his tongue created shot to her center, turning her mind blank, and although she heard her own strangled cry, she never knew what she said.

A second hung, suspended, throbbing, before Greer urged Andrew over her, parted her thighs and lifted her knees. "I want you Andrew," she breathed. "Now."

His face above hers was dark, the veins in his neck corded. Every feature was radiant and dear, the features, the expression of a lover. He entered her slowly, carefully. A tiny unexpected pain made her gasp and he paused until she moved against him, smiling, giving him her joy.

Their pace speeded, Greer reaching to meet each thrust, matching his passion, certain that his ecstasy equalled her own. And at their climax a sob broke from her throat, joining with Andrew's groan. She looked at his face, as she tried to stem the explosion that threatened to tear her apart. Andrew's eyes were closed, his lips pulled back in a lover's grimace. *I love you,* her heart told him, but she didn't say it. Later she would tell him.

Andrew became still over her, his weight supported beside her head on his outstretched arms. Greer could see the pulse in his neck, the rapid beat of his heart.

"Hold me, please," she asked softly. "Need me. Let's stay like this forever."

Their damp limbs remained entwined when he slid beside her and folded her into his arms. "I'll always need you," Andrew said. "I love you. Oh, how I love you."

With a sigh he hoisted himself to one elbow and looked into her face. He wound a tendril of hair between his fingers. "Wouldn't it be something if you were already pregnant?" he said wistfully.

"What?" Her mind blanked, then came slowly into focus. He couldn't have suggested she might be pregnant.

No!
Andrew smiled and nuzzled her neck. "It's supposed to only happen in the movies. But pregnancies do occur the first time a couple makes love. We can hope, can't we?" he asked tenderly.

Greer gripped him tight. He hadn't taken any precautions or asked if she intended to. It crossed her mind that it was something a doctor ought to think of. *Fate, you fool. Didn't you think it would catch up with you?* He must want children — his own children — at least as much as he wanted her.

"You aren't saying much, sweetheart," he said, caressing her neck. "I thought you'd like the idea as much as I do. It's time, my love. I've seen the way you look at children. You need another baby."

"Oh — Andrew." She cried and couldn't stop, didn't try. He would never guess that instead of joy she felt crushing pain and emptiness. The sudden tight pressure of his arms seemed to hold together the parts of her that threatened to fly apart. "I love you," she said, wanting to tell him there would be no child — ever — but unable to bear what his reaction might be. And she couldn't walk away from him, not now when they'd found such ecstasy in each other's arms.

Andrew's mind fumbled through the day while he smiled and talked — and waited for Greer to admit the truth. In the evening they ate a late dinner at a small Italian restaurant near the harbor and returned to their room at Phelps for the last time. Only the irresistible power of their lovemaking temporarily blotted out his creeping anger and confusion.

Afterward he lay silent while she burrowed into the hollow of his shoulder. When her breathing slowed he knew she'd drifted asleep.

His head pounded. Did she think he'd ever guess about the hysterectomy? Why hadn't she told him? Damn it all, why hadn't he figured it out sooner?

Her reaction to his suggestion of pregnancy had clued him in. Desperation might sometimes be mistaken for happiness, but not this time. All day he'd tried to draw her out, tried to reach beyond the fixed smile and distant gaze that never quite met his eyes. The only definite reaction he'd gotten had come from his reminder of their date with Simonne on Saturday. At that, Greer had forgotten to smile for an instant. Her throat had moved convulsively as she swallowed. But then she'd smiled and chattered about where they would take the child.

He'd noticed the newer scar near the section site immediately. Secondary complications had occurred to him, possibly adhesions, but not hysterectomy. And that's what it was — he was sure of it now. Greer would never have another child and it destroyed her every time he mentioned the subject. He felt tears run hot to his temples and closed his eyes.

No children of their own. It hurt. How it hurt. But it completely tore him up that she hadn't trusted him enough to be honest. This was the only woman he wanted, would ever truly want again, but it wasn't up to him anymore. He couldn't make her confide in him, and unless she did they had no basis for a lifetime commitment.

Simonne's face was wind burned. She backed down the beach, shovel in hand, making a trench. "This'll let water into the moat, Greer," she yelled.

Greer shivered inside her jacket. The wind made her eyes water. Andrew would have to be called away on an emergency when they were due to take Simonne out. She bent to dig up several half-buried shells, then pressed them into the upper bastions of the sand castle she and Simonne had spent the past two hours making.

"Here," the child said, arriving back panting. "Scrape the trench a bit deeper so the tide can swoosh down harder when it comes."

"Yes, ma'am." Greer watched the spindly figure whirl away, arms flapping, as she revolved in circles. "Yes, little one," she whispered.

Her nails were crammed with sand and it stuck to the damp palms of her hands. She started to work at the dip Simonne intended the water to enter. The girl had already been with Andrew this morning when he picked Greer up in Weymouth. He ran them back to Ringstead, explaining he must visit the hospital before they went to Lyme. As soon as he left, Simonne talked her into clambering to the beach to build a castle.

She hunkered down and looked over her shoulder. The tide was coming closer —

threatening to rush at her before she was ready. Like everything else in her life.

Simonne was sweet. It hadn't been so painful to hold her little hand coming down the steep cliff's path, or to rebraid a pigtail. Greer hugged her shins and rested a cheek on her knees. The tight knots she'd tied around the sensitive spots of her heart were gradually loosening. But would there be any way to hold on to what mattered most to her now — Andrew's love?

"That's perfect."

Wiry arms, wrapped around Greer's neck from behind, landed her on her rear with a thud. Simonne's cold face was pressed to her ear.

"It's going to be *stupendous*," the child announced noisily.

Greer held the wrists beneath her chin and laughed. Thin sun blinded her as she sensed another presence and looked up. "Andrew, is that you?" she said. His silhouette was unmistakable and when he didn't answer immediately, she shaded her eyes to make out his face. "We didn't hear you coming. What do you think of this palace?"

"Fantastic. The best." He smiled, but not before she saw his drawn, almost haggard expression. Every muscle in her body clenched. Despite all her efforts, her anxiety of the past forty-eight hours had been transmitted to Andrew. She'd suspected as much on the quiet boat ride back to Weymouth. He was trying to pretend, too, without even knowing why he should.

"We've had so much fun, Uncle Andy," Simonne chirped. "I wouldn't even mind if we didn't go to Lyme. We could watch the moat get filled up, then have tea in your kitchen."

"Sounds good to me," he told her. "How about you, Greer?"

She brushed at her jeans and went to stand in front of him. Simonne concentrated on the frothy water bubbling nearer her castle with each wave.

"Was she too much for you?" Andrew asked softly.

"I loved being with her. She's wonderful." Something caught in her throat and she tried to clear it. "I think I've decided to go to London tomorrow."

Andrew turned her toward him. "To see your mother?"

She nodded. "If I can. She may not be happy when I show up. She might even tell me to get lost, but at least I won't have avoided her," she said, hoping Andrew would say something encouraging.

He stared at the sky for a long time, then

into Greer's eyes. "We can't avoid anything forever. We have to get the tough stuff out of the way if we're ever going to be happy."

Chapter 17

Greer knew Ruby was forty-eight. She looked older.

"Have you lived in Walthamstow long, Mrs. Hawker?"

Andrew's voice was polite, level, designed to help steady the woman's nerves. He shouldn't be here.

Ruby's hand shook as she lifted the cigarette to her mouth. "Eighteen years," she said. "Ever since I came to London." A nerve twitched beside her left eye.

A wooden clock on the sideboard chimed, startling Greer. "I'm in England on a visit," she said. "I thought it would be nice if we met."

"Yes." Ruby glanced over her shoulder at the door for the third time in as many minutes.

The room smelled faintly of cooked cabbage and seemed to get smaller and smaller. Greer's eyes flicked from ocher walls to a square dining table on bulbous-footed legs, to Andrew's gold brocade chair, the double of the one where she sat. Everything threadbare and faded — like this nervous, sullen woman who was her mother.

A train rumbled past behind the house. Greer had seen the elevated embankment from the street. "If this is a bad time I could come back," she suggested. "Perhaps you're expecting someone. I tried to call first, but there wasn't a listing."

The cigarette tip glowed red again and another thin line of smoke streamed upward. "My husband will be back from his club shortly," the woman answered enigmatically.

Damp silk stuck to Greer's back. "When would be a good time for us to talk?"

Ruby bent her head, rubbing a stained finger rapidly across her brow. Gray streaked her short red curls, but the hair was still vibrant.

"What — ?" Greer began, before losing her train of thought. Had she been going to ask when to come or what she should call Ruby. It didn't matter.

Andrew leaned forward, tenting his fingertips. "Mrs. Hawker," he addressed her in a calm, clear voice. "I'm a good friend of Greer's and I know this is very hard on her. That's why I insisted on coming. You must be upset, too. Perhaps if you could both relax a little things would be easier."

Always in control, Greer thought, as dull heat flooded her cheeks. Dr. Monthaven playing the psychiatrist again. An interesting study in plebeian behavior, would probably be his conclusion. She glared at him. They were from different worlds — no common ground except the bedroom. The flush turned cold on her skin.

"Yes," Ruby was saying with a subservient edge to her voice. "But we shouldn't be long, see, because my husband's coming back and — well — there never was any reason for him to know about — her." Greer stared hard at Ruby's eyes. They were lighter than her own and deep set above wrinkled cheeks. This visit was another terrible mistake. All it could possibly achieve was more anguish for both of them. "We'll go," she said abruptly.

"No." Ruby waved Greer back into the chair. "No. You came a long way. It's just that Bill has one too many sometimes and I wouldn't want to upset him," she explained in a hurry. "There isn't a lot to say, but I don't mind talking about it. Did — ? How did you find me?"

"I made some inquiries," Greer said promptly. Ruby had almost mentioned Rusty, she was sure of it. "Andrew and I came to London by train, then caught the underground out here to Walthamstow. I've been to Ferndale and seen Marsh Cottage. I also met the old vicar of St. Peters and he remembers your mother and father — and you as a little girl."

"And you saw Rusty, didn't you?" The pale eyes softened. "That's who gave you my address." The woman shook her head sadly. "I'm sorry, Greer. That's what I told him, too. I never meant to hurt anyone. If I could change it all I would, but they don't give you a second chance."

Greer's eyes stung and she pressed them with her fingers. "I didn't even know I had a brother until I went through the baptismal records at the church," she told her.

"He's your half-brother," Ruby clarified. "I named him after his father — Kurt Stevens. He was a sailor when I worked in Portsmouth. He went to Australia before Rusty was born. Never came back." Greer heard Ruby give an uneven sigh. "Said he would. We were going to get married after his trip." Greer waited as Ruby collected the memories she had tried so hard to forget. "I waited, but he wasn't on the ship when it came in and they all — the other men all said they didn't know where he was. We were kids, sixteen and seventeen. He was tall, like Rusty, with black hair and those dark blue eyes. You've got them, too, but I don't know —"

Who my father is — or was. "Are you happy, Ruby?" She couldn't call her anything else.

"Yes!" she answered without hesitation. "I've done very well, considering. Me and Jim never had any kids — We couldn't seem to, but we've got this house and he makes a steady wage." She sniffed suddenly, then coughed. "Everything's fine with you isn't it, Greer? You're happy? They've been good to you?"

"Of course." Greer heard her own voice crack. "They've been very good to me."

"That's all right, then," Ruby said gratefully. "Rusty was too old — nobody wanted him. That's what I feel worst about. He got pushed around."

"I'm sure he doesn't blame you for that anymore," Greer said instinctively. It was all so hopeless and pointless.

"He does," Ruby insisted. "He didn't say so, but I could feel it. When I saw him on the doorstep with my hair and Kurt's eyes — Kurt said he'd come back. We had plans. We used to dream." Ruby rubbed teary eyes. "Bunch of childish nonsense. I took too long to grow up, that's all. You're not married yet, then?"

Greer touched the back of her naked ring finger, trying to ignore Andrew's intake of breath, his sudden shift in the chair. "I was. My husband was killed," she said simply.

"I'm sorry. It's bad when you lose the one you love."

"You get over it."

Ruby's expression became distant. "Sometimes you do." She winced as the cigarette burned down between her fingers. "Jim's bound to be back any minute."

Andrew stood immediately and offered Greer his hand. She hesitated, then took it.

"There isn't anything else to say," Ruby concluded. "You won't mind seeing yourselves out?" She sat rigidly in her cane-backed chair. "Good luck to you."

"Good luck," Greer echoed faintly.

The front door was open when she pulled away from Andrew and returned to the back room of the house. Ruby was staring straight ahead, her eyes dry. Lipstick had run into the little lines fanning out from her mouth.

Greer's nose felt stuffy and she opened

her mouth while she fumbled for a tissue. "It's all right," she said, dropping to her knees. In an awkward motion, she hugged the woman quickly and kissed her papery cheek. "You did what was best, mom."

Ruby never moved.

On the way back to the underground station Greer rushed ahead of Andrew. The streets were grimy, some shop windows boarded. Newspaper rolled like tumbleweed along the sidewalks, curling into untidy cylinders in gutters and around lampposts. She hated it all. What she'd come from. What she really was. She was the lucky one who'd escaped and now the smart thing was to get out — go back to the States and forget all this. Ruby's dreams died with a young man, a boy, who'd sailed out of a harbor over thirty years ago and never returned. The woman she might have become disappeared with him, leaving her with nothing to give — to anyone.

Casey and Seattle. Greer pictured Britmania and the other store owners she'd come to know in Pioneer Square. There was nothing here for her, no future, certainly not with Andrew who couldn't possibly want her now he'd seen the background she sprang from. And it was all for the best. Time to go home.

On the tube-train, Greer avoided looking at Andrew. Steady and rattling vibration made conversation unnecessary, so she concentrated first on other passengers, then on advertisements pasted near the ceiling.

The cars hurtled repeatedly between tunnels and yellow-lighted stations until Andrew leaned close, pressing his shoulder to hers. "This is it," he said.

She moved mechanically to a platform before noticing the sign read Bond Street. "We're supposed to go to Waterloo," she told him. "We can't catch a train to Dorset from here, can we?"

"No. But we're not going back yet."

Greer watched the last train coach disappear into its inky burrow. An acrid blast of air shot back, driving grit into her eyes. "I want to leave, Andrew. And if we miss the seven-ten there's nothing else until early tomorrow morning," she complained.

He took her arm. "We're going to walk, and eat — and talk."

"I'm going to Weymouth."

"You're trying to hide from what happened out there. It's no good —"

"Save it for your patients," she snapped. Her face felt stiff. "I didn't ask you to

341

come. And I'm not asking you to play shrink for me now."

The pressure behind her elbow was steady, propelling her through an archway to the escalator. "Playing the shrink, as you put it, is the last thing I want to do with you," he answered firmly. She couldn't help but feel badly for everything she'd put him through. "Don't shut me out, Greer," he continued. "You may not have asked me to come, but I'm glad I did. I can tell you feel like running for the closest foxhole right now, and you shouldn't be alone."

A steady drizzle peppered them when they climbed to the street. The sky was a slate backdrop to solid rows of buildings. Small shops at ground level were already closed.

"What time is it?" Greer said, yanking at her jacket sleeve for a look at her watch. "Seven? It can't be."

"We couldn't have made that train," Andrew said. "I know a little club off Berkeley Square. The food's good and later there'll be music. Do you like jazz?"

"Yes," Greer answered absently. "But I'm not dressed for a London club." She glanced down at her navy gabardine pants and flat shoes. "Why are we even discussing this? We've missed the train, Andrew. Is there a bus or something?"

He pushed a hand beneath the hair at her neck. "There's a warm club a few blocks away where you'll knock 'em dead in what you've got on. You would in anything."

Greer sighed audibly. "You aren't about to budge, are you?"

"Nope." He shook his head and wrapped an arm around her shoulders. "You're in my stomping grounds, so you might as well enjoy it. I'll make sure we get home."

The club proved to be an elegant room in the basement of an old hotel. Candlelight flickered over black-and-white ink sketches drawn directly on the wall. Chairs with wide curving backs turned circular tables into secluded islands. A soft buzz of conversation blended into the taped reggae music. A small dance floor, surrounded by mirrors, was empty, except for a cluster of draped instruments.

When they were seated and a waiter had taken their order, Andrew lifted her hand from her lap and pressed the palm against his cheek. "What did you expect to find in Walthamstow?" he asked softly.

She tried to pull away.

"Relax, darling. I only want you to be objective."

"I can't talk about it now," she replied firmly. The music's insistent beat made her temples throb.

"I'm glad you went, Greer," he insisted. "If you hadn't, you'd have spent the rest of your life wishing you had and wondering if you still should. It wasn't so bad, was it? She was honest, and —"

"Stop. Please, Andrew, stop."

He lifted her chin and waited until she finally looked at him. "We will talk about it — when you're ready," he added.

The waiter returned with fluffy crab mousse with asparagus sauce and Marfil Seco, a dry white wine from Spain that Andrew explained was rarely exported. Greer didn't feel like eating, but the wine tasted good. It warmed her veins and slowly melted the tension from her leaden muscles.

"Dance with me," Andrew said suddenly.

Greer started and looked uncomprehendingly at him.

He stroked a knuckle across her cheek. "We've never danced together." His mouth trembled slightly and her heart squeezed.

She fingered a spoon. "I don't —"

"You don't dance," he said cutting her off. "Likely story. Come on."

They were the only couple on the

shadowy dance floor. Andrew folded Greer close, massaging her back, stroking her neck, until she softened and put her arms around his waist. She loved him. She always would. But there could be no mistake about the differences in their backgrounds or what they meant to their future. He behaved as if nothing had changed between them when he must think of her as part of a life-style he knew little about. He'd witnessed the sorry scene with Ruby. Heat flashed over Greer's neck and face. There were no family portraits to document her heritage.

Andrew danced smoothly, using his whole body to guide her around the floor. He held her against his length, turning them both with the rhythmic pressure of his hips and thighs.

"You know I've got a flat in London," Andrew whispered against her hair.

Greer frowned up into his face. "You never told me. How would I know?"

"I didn't think I'd mentioned it," he explained. "But I thought maybe Lauren said something at her house."

What would he say if she told him what Lauren had really said — and about Bob's visit to the boardinghouse? "Nobody told me. Where is it?" she asked reluctantly.

"About four blocks from here."

Greer's insides began a slow burn. He wanted to sleep with her tonight — to make love. Her nostrils flared and she closed her eyes. She imagined him around and inside her, and every female urge sprang to life. He'd planned it this way so why not go along with him? Memories would be her keepsakes and there would be too few of them.

She pushed her hands beneath his jacket and watched his eyes darken. "Kiss me, Andrew," she told him urgently. "Kiss me, then I want to go to your flat and make love." *For this one last time, my darling.*

He trembled, swung her back to the room and encircled her gently, gathered her to him until her toes barely touched the floor. "I love you." The whispered words escaped through his teeth before his lips covered hers. When he lifted his head she was dizzy. Andrew buried his face in her neck, still swaying faintly to the music. Over his shoulder, Greer saw their bodies reflected in the mirrors like a single piece of sculpture. Tears sprang to her eyes. Every line, every texture and scent of him was dear. Would she ever smell a breeze off the ocean, hear a man's deep laugh, or see a pair of golden eyes and not think of Andrew? But Andrew must never suspect — especially not tonight.

"I want to go now," she said evenly. Blinking rapidly, she touched his cheek. "Take me home, please."

It wasn't nine, yet the streets were deserted. This was Mayfair, Andrew told her. The flat he owned had belonged to his father before him. John Monthaven had used it when he came up to town for plays and the horticultural shows he enjoyed. Now Andrew found it useful when he had a consultation or simply wanted to get away for a few days. The quiet elegance of the area spelled wealth and the remnants of a more graceful era to Greer.

"It's a mews flat," Andrew said, steering her into a quiet alley lit by old-fashioned streetlights shaped like carriage lanterns. "Years ago they were servants, quarters. There are garages on the lower floor that might have housed horses once. The rooms are upstairs," he explained.

The flat surprised Greer. Rather than the antique pieces she'd expected, it was furnished in Oriental style. A low, red lacquered table dominated the living room. The couch and chairs were deep blue splashed with giant Chinese peonies. An exquisite Oriental screen inlaid with gold and mother-of-pearl fanned across one corner and the deep-piled rug was the same dark blue as the furnishings.

"This is fabulous," Greer exclaimed. "You did all this?"

"It took a while," Andrew said dryly. "When dad had it, the place looked like something Sherlock Holmes would go for. Can I get you a drink?"

Greer went to the window, slipping off her coat. "No thanks. But don't let me stop you." Her breathing became suddenly shallow. "Looks a bit like Baker Street on a Sherlock Holmes night outside. Misty rain on slick cobblestones."

"And I thought I was the one with an overactive imagination. Do you want to listen to some music?"

"No."

His sigh was audible. "Will you come to bed with me?"

"Yes, Andrew."

She turned and he held out a hand. "I'm never going to get used to having you," he said. "I keep being afraid you'll disappear."

Greer felt as if she'd been kicked. Why would he say such a thing — now? As panic tried to invade her mind, Greer forced herself to think logically. He wasn't thinking past this moment and the desire that brought them here in the first place. She took his hand and they walked into the bedroom.

"I feel filthy, Andrew. Could I take a shower first?"

He spread his fingers over her collarbone on top of the white blouse, then looked at her breasts. "If I can come with you," he answered.

Carefully she stepped away and loosened the buttons at her wrists. Andrew's throat moved convulsively. Inch by inch, the blouse parted and she slipped it off, dropping it to the floor before kicking aside her shoes and unzipping the pants. Sweat had broken out on his brow. Greer kissed his jaw and dodged his reaching hand. Something primitive drove her on, made her want to excite him past the limit of his restraint. The slacks' silk lining swished past her thighs and calves to join her blouse. Panty hose followed and she stood in a white satin teddy fastened from neckline to navel by a row of minuscule buttons.

"Greer." Andrew's voice broke. "You're an enigma. Fire inside a fragile shell of shyness. You are so beautiful, my darling."

She came close. "I don't do very well with tiny buttons."

He looked into her eyes, then at the

teddy. "You're driving me insane." With shaking fingers he pushed each satin bead through its hole until only ribbon straps and Greer's distended nipples kept the garment from dropping away.

"Take it off, Andrew," she whispered.

With finger and thumb he pulled down first one, then the other strap. His palms stroked the smooth fabric from her flesh, followed it over her ribs and waist, her hips, and let it rustle to her feet.

Andrew tore his own clothes off and lifted her into his arms. Cradled against his naked body, she turned to press her breasts to his chest while he carried her to the bathroom.

They washed each other, reverently, paying rapt attention to every millimeter of skin, touching, holding — following fingers with lips.

"I can't take this any longer," Andrew breathed against her belly. "I want you now."

Greer didn't answer. She dropped her head back, allowing water to beat down on her face and neck, and guided his mouth to a nipple. He shuddered, pressing the heel of one hand between her thighs until she cried out, then he lifted her and Greer wrapped her legs around his waist. Andrew entered her with a single thrust, wrenching sobs from her throat. In seconds her fingers were sinking into his shoulders for support. She bent her face to the side of his head and felt him fill her again and again, drawing raw breaths from her lungs. When their climax came they almost fell. Andrew clasped Greer in one arm, supported his weight against the wall with the other and slid her slowly down until they both stood beneath the cooling spray.

"Lady," he gasped at last. "We'd better lie down before we fall down. My God, woman — no wonder all I can think of anymore is you."

Greer hardly felt the towel on her skin or Andrew rubbing her hair. She dried him haphazardly, but wouldn't allow him to do it himself. They fell into bed and as she drifted asleep she wondered what the bedroom looked like, or the bathroom. Had she even seen them?

"Sweetheart."

She began floating up from a great depth.

"Greer, darling. Wake up."

"Yes. I'm awake," Greer answered, sitting abruptly and looking around. Dawn was barely poking its fingers through tiny holes in rush blinds. "What is it?"

"I want to talk to you and I can't wait any longer," he told her.

Andrew's flat in London. She shook her head and shivered, then realized she was naked to the waist. Before she could pull up the sheet, he pressed her against the pillows and kissed her soundly. For an instant he raised his head to rake her body with his eyes, then rolled onto his back with her wrapped in his arms.

"Mmm." His fingers were buried in her hair. "You smell wonderful in my soap. We should always share showers."

Greer turned to nestle against his chest. "I doubt if either of our constitutions could take it for long," she murmured contentedly.

"Shall we give it a try?"

"You want to shower again — now?"

"No. But I thought we might consider taking lots of them together in future. *Will* you marry me, Greer?"

Chapter 18

She held him very tight, pressed her lips into the hair on his chest. If only — Greer rolled away, pulling up the sheet.

"Greer?" he said as he shook her gently. "What's wrong, darling?"

"Nothing." She splayed a hand across her face.

Agonizing moments passed before he leaned over her, sweeping back her tangled curls. "I asked if you'd marry me." He eased her fingers away. "Look at me, Greer — for God's sake."

Totally bereft of words, she lifted her face to his, knowing he'd see the tears.

"You will, won't you?" he said hopefully. Slowly he lowered his mouth to hers. His lips and tongue moved on Greer's, caressing, beginning their magic. She turned into his arms and filled her fingers with his hair.

When he propped himself on one elbow

to look at her, Greer was breathless and throbbing.

"We don't have to wait," he began. "I'm not sure of the formalities with your being American, but I don't think they'll take long to deal with."

Greer took a deep breath. "I'm leaving for the States on Friday," she said bluntly, moving closer to the edge of the bed. "There are too many reasons why we can't go on."

"I don't get this," Andrew answered. "I just asked you to marry me."

She swallowed the lump that rose in her throat. Please, let her make it through this quickly and cleanly. "It's been something special, Andrew. Now it's time to call it quits and get on with our responsibilities. When's the hearing?"

"Tomorrow," he said mechanically.

Greer sat up. "Good timing." Her heart was running away, faster and faster. "I'm planning to spend the next few days finishing the arrangements for my trip home."

She swung her feet to the floor and immediately found herself flat on the bed with Andrew's strong fingers clamped over her shoulders. "Not good enough, Greer," he said, barely containing his fury.

"You said you loved me."

Her insides clenched. His face was suffused with color, his eyes unnaturally bright. "Love?" She laughed, wishing her breasts weren't heaving with each painful breath. "Probably the most overused word in the dictionary. I love ice cream. I love that dress. I love —"

"Enough." Andrew's brows knit together and he dropped his forehead for an instant. "You took off your wedding ring. Why?" he demanded.

"It was time," she said without expression.

"After two years it was suddenly time? And it just happened to coincide with — us?"

She'd never seen him so angry, but she must press on. "It didn't mean anything."

"I see." He released her and turned away. "It was time to take off your wedding ring and it had nothing to do with me. And saying you loved me meant nothing, either. You're purely hedonistic — is that what you want me to accept? A pleasure seeker, and a taker who doesn't like strings?"

Oh, Andrew, Andrew. "Let's not spoil what we've had," she answered with much more emotion than she should have.

"No," he said sourly as he clasped his

shins. Muscles in his back stood out, rock hard. "Sex is an activity for you. Something not to be confused with feelings. That's what you're telling me?"

She was weary. "Passion shouldn't be confused with love. That's all I'm trying to explain. Tomorrow — next year — you'll be grateful we didn't get into something we'd both regret."

"Little liar," he said, as if the only way to get satisfaction was by provoking her. "There's something else. Why don't you give it a shot, Greer. Tell the truth for once," he challenged her.

"Okay," she snapped. "You want it, you can have it." In seconds she'd left the bed and gathered her twisted clothes into a pile. "We have nothing in common other than sex. We turn each other on. And now I want to catch the first available train for Dorset. You should, too. There's a lot to do in the next few days." Greer thought the silence that ensued would drive her mad. When he spoke, his voice sent shivers down her spine.

"Tell me one thing," he said.

"Sure." There could be no tears yet.

"If you're a woman who can have a casual affair and walk away — someone who enjoys sex as a separate entity — why did it take you two years after your husband died to sleep with another man?"

Greer's hands felt like paws. The teddy gaped away from her breasts while she struggled with its buttons. Don't say any more, she ordered herself silently. Don't let your voice give you away.

"Convince me, Greer," he demanded. "Make me believe you mean all this crap. Why was I the first?"

He came to stand over her and she couldn't resist lifting her eyes to his lean face. Yes, she could have taken what he offered now — but how long would it have been before she became an embarrassment, before physical attraction wasn't enough?

"What makes you think you were the first?"

The deep hurt and disappointment in Andrew's eyes made her look away.

"I'm not a fool," he said finally. "Hurry up. I want out of here before I suffocate."

Somehow Greer had dragged herself through the rest of the day and the longest night she remembered. On the train to Weymouth, Andrew's silence had hummed through her blood. He'd parked the Mini at the station while they were in London and, when they arrived, insisted with distant politeness on driving her to Belle Vista. Then she was alone with countless hours yawning ahead in which she could only try to cope with the beginning of her memories.

This morning the airline had confirmed a seat for Friday. She'd go to London on Thursday and stay overnight at the airport Holiday Inn. That left today and tomorrow to firm up any outstanding contacts she'd made for Britmania.

At lunchtime she walked along the beach toward the town center. She wasn't hungry — hadn't been for days — but she stopped at the seafood hut and tried a little bowl of cockles. The orange-tailed shellfish were surprisingly pleasant, chewy and tart, sprinkled with vinegar and pepper.

Greer finished eating and trudged on, the heels of her boots sinking into wet sand. Fog billowed off the ocean, blanketing the traffic sounds on the promenade. She stopped and faced the fuzzy bay. Ever since Colin died and she'd lost Colleen she'd felt half-alive. For a little while, with Andrew, the dead parts of her had been resurrected. But what she had to offer him couldn't be enough for a lifetime. Fear of loving and losing was destructive in itself — she knew that now. But even if she could cope with the possibility of another personal disaster, she couldn't willingly bring one on Andrew. He'd never let her know when he began to feel cheated. In time their different backgrounds and her inability to have children would have become an issue, but Andrew wouldn't tell her outright. She'd simply know it because his feelings were something he couldn't totally hide.

In the town she visited a fishermen's supply store to finalize arrangements for a shipment of oiled wool sweaters. She'd seen them in Guernsey, the exclusive source, and been told they were available in Weymouth. They'd sell well — particularly to the younger set. Pottery from the Isle of Wight came next. Handmade by a couple, the smooth work reflected an African sojourn. Greer took a carefully packed box of samples with her. Later she'd send for more.

Nothing took long enough. By three she was in her room once more, too tired to pack, too afraid of her own imagination to lie down and think. She wandered downstairs to the lounge with a book. The preliminary hearing on the Michael Drake case would have started. How was Andrew doing? She bit her bottom lip, yearning to be with him.

Mrs. Findlay's door slammed and the woman came into the room rubbing her hands on a tea towel. "Made your arrangements, Mrs. Beckett?" she inquired.

Greer nodded. She didn't feel like talking.

"Did you call that Mr. Gibbs back? He sounded upset."

Gibbs? "I didn't know I'd had a call," Greer told her. "When — was there a message?"

"Just wanted you to get in touch with him. Said he'd be at Ringstead Hall and you had the number. I left a note on your bed," the woman explained.

"I didn't notice. Thanks, Mrs. Findlay."

Ten minutes later, Greer sat on the bottom step of the stairs, fighting down waves of panic. Gibbs had arrived for work this morning to find Andrew's bed untouched. The kitchen bore signs of his having eaten dinner, but Gibbs was certain he'd left shortly afterward, in a hurry. The clothes Andrew wore to London were thrown aside. And at the medical board they said he'd called the previous afternoon to postpone the hearing for a day. No one had seen him and Dr. Wilson didn't answer the phone.

Gibbs's agitation had worried Greer. He was an old man — too old for pressure like this. She'd tried to reassure him and told him to go home, promising she would let him know the instant Andrew showed up. And he would, she insisted, as much for her own sake as Gibbs's. This was her fault. Andrew had gone somewhere to lick the wounds she'd inflicted.

She should contact the Wilsons herself. There was no reply at their house and when she called the hospital the switchboard operator informed her Dr. Wilson was out of town for the day. An invisible hand squeezed her throat. Someone must have seen Andrew since he dropped her off at Belle Vista. She telephoned his number and let it ring fifteen times.

Greer took a taxi to Ringstead Hall and told the driver to wait. Gibbs would have locked the door. Without transportation she'd be stranded if Andrew weren't at home. She beat on his private door and waited, sweeping the grounds for a sign of him. At the front door, the bell jangled hollowly in the great hall and Greer didn't bother to try it again. Breathing raggedly, she ran to the cliffs and scoured the misty beach, knowing instinctively he wouldn't be there. He *wasn't* here. Her nose ran and she blew it on a crumpled tissue. *The car. Andrew's Mini.*

Her breath rasped through her clenched teeth while she rushed up the steps and across the lawn. At the back corner of the house she leaned on a drainpipe, peering through watery eyes. His car was gone. At least he wasn't lying somewhere in the house, unconscious, or — The only thing to do was try all the places he might be, then it would have to be the police. She instructed the taxi driver to take her back to Belle Vista. She'd make her calls from there.

At eight o'clock Greer gave up on getting help. There was still no reply at the Wilsons'. Andrew hadn't even called his service or the hospital, and the police clearly thought they were being asked to deal with the aftermath of a lovers' quarrel. A few more hours, the constable had calmly suggested. She should wait a while longer to see if the "gentleman" turned up. If he didn't, then she could ask for assistance. The police weren't authorized to act until the reportedly missing person had been gone twenty-four hours, anyway. And since the lady knew the subject had eaten dinner at his home the night before, wasn't she being a bit premature? Probably gone for a little drive to "calm things down a bit."

She would go back to Ringstead Hall and wait — all night if necessary. Sooner or later he'd have to show and his home was the logical place. The same taxi driver took her. When she got out of the cab she saw his quizzical expression. "There's someone home here now, miss?" he asked when she paid him off and said he could leave. "It's pitch-dark out here and the house looks dark, too."

"There's someone here," she said lightly, certain inside that she was wrong. "I'll be fine. Thank you."

She watched his taillights swing out of sight in the yew tunnel and turned to the house's oppressive hulk. Without a moon, its size was something she felt rather than saw.

Doggedly Greer went through the same motions as before, knocking and ringing and circling the building. She balked at ranging the grounds or approaching the cliffs, afraid of falling and of the gnawing apprehension growing with each second that passed.

The car was still missing. She sat on the step to the side door and bundled her jacket more tightly to her neck. Droplets of moisture in the fog wet her face and clung to her lashes. When the idea came, it was slowly, held back by her own unwillingness to consider it.

Treading carefully to avoid turning an ankle on the gravel path, Greer retraced her steps to the back of the house and opened the door of the outbuilding that doubled as Andrew's garage. She'd only seen him use the makeshift shelter that first day when he drove her home to Weymouth. He always left his car out.

But not this time. The Mini was pulled inside between stacks of garden tools.

Greer floundered in a paralyzing concoction of fear and confusion. Andrew had come home yesterday, eaten dinner sometime later and left. She rounded the vehicle and felt its hood. Cold. The engine was cold and there were no lights on in the house. Wherever he'd gone, she was certain it had been on foot. Her breathing speeded up, coming in shallow gasps from the tops of her lungs. Something had happened to him. She knew it.

She ran. Up to the glistening jet-black pool.

Sweat bathed her body. At the pool's edge she stared down into barely shifting nothingness. She shut out the thought of Andrew lying at the bottom and struck out for the woods at the top of the rise. If only she'd had enough sense to bring a flashlight.

As soon as the trees enveloped her she knew it was hopeless. Brambles scratched her face and hands and clawed at her hair. "Andrew," she called, and listened to her own voice ricochet between dense trunks. Her skin crawled, but she refused to cry.

She followed the tree line to an easterly ridge, stumbling every few paces on uneven ground. He'd come out here to walk and gotten hurt. The conviction grew and grew until it pounded in every brain cell. Would he go to the beach on a foggy afternoon? Her heart plummeted. Unless he'd gotten up early this morning and carefully made his bed, Andrew had been missing since last night. The moon glimmered through a slim break in the clouds and she peered at her watch. It was almost eleven — three hours since she'd left Weymouth for the second time.

Greer didn't have any idea how far the tide came in when it was high. She must find the way to the beach and search for him there. Forgetting caution, she took several running steps and pitched forward.

Pain shot through her middle as the force of hard earth meeting her chest exploded the air from her body. She lay still, panting, until she could roll slowly onto her back. Every muscle and joint ached. Sharp pains seared her hip.

Far above, a blue glow came and went as the cloud layer wafted across the fickle moon. Water gathered in Greer's eyes. She did love him — so very much. And she'd hurt him, driven him out to wander over this deserted place. Lord, she prayed, just let him be safe. Tomorrow was something she could cope with when it came — as long as nothing had happened to Andrew.

Breathing was agony. Gingerly she got to her feet and started for the cliffs. She fell again when she drew near the house, tearing her slacks. Warm dampness seeped through at the knee. Blood.

Helpless sobs erupted from her raw throat. She sat huddled on the path, her cheek cradled in her elbow.

Then she saw a light.

Chapter 19

At ground level a yellow sliver glimmered above a basement window shade. The kitchen? Greer stood, adrenaline pumping along every vein. There was a light on in the kitchen — probably had been all along, but she hadn't noticed it. Half-running, choking back tears, she scrambled to the side door and pummeled it with both fists.

She waited, her whole body shaking impatiently. Nothing. "Answer the door," she yelled, and pounded again. "Be here someone, please."

Abruptly, the door scraped open and Greer's mouth dropped. Andrew, dressed in faded jeans and a partially buttoned shirt, stared out at her. He swayed slightly on bare feet. "Hi," he said, and winced, rubbing his temple. "What do you want?"

Greer found her voice. "What do I want? Andrew." Her voice rose higher. "I've been searching for you for hours. I've been so afraid. Where have you been?"

He smiled sheepishly and rubbed his unshaven cheek. "Want to come in?"

She marched inside and slammed the door.

"Shh," Andrew whispered. "My head's coming apart."

"You've been drinking," Greer accused him. "I don't believe this. Gibbs is worried out of his mind. I'm running all over the countryside thinking you're dead. And you're holed up somewhere tying one on."

"There's coffee in the kitchen," he answered, turning away. Greer followed him numbly downstairs.

Under the kitchen's dim lights they faced each other and gasped simultaneously.

"You're a mess," Greer exclaimed, taking in his disheveled hair and almost two days' growth of beard.

"So are you," he answered. "You're bleeding right through your pant leg. Sit there and let me take a look."

"I'm fine. Your hands, Andrew. How did that happen to them?" His nails were ragged and his knuckles skinned.

He snorted. "I fell, too. Up the steps."

"Where have you been? When did you get back?" she demanded.

"At a club in Dorchester." He tried to straighten the wrongly buttoned denim shirt. "And I've been here for hours — several hours," he added.

"I rang the bell, and knocked — you didn't answer." A soft buzzing started in her ears. Her limbs trembled uncontrollably.

Andrew's eyes slid sheepishly away. "Must have fallen asleep," he mumbled.

"The hearing, Andrew. Gibbs said you postponed it." The buzzing swelled inside her head and she blinked to keep him in focus.

"I needed time, Greer. To get my act together."

Because of her. She felt sick. If the hearing never took place he'd always carry with him the frustration of missed justice. She did believe he should go through with the case. The insight shook her.

"Andrew." Her voice was far away. "I'm going to pass out." Her legs buckled before he could catch her and they both sank to the floor. Greer tried to bend forward, but he tipped her flat and pulled up her knees.

"It's all right, darling," he soothed. "Take deep breaths through your mouth." She felt his fingers on the pulse at her neck. "What's happened to you, Greer?

You're scratched to pieces."

Oxygen flooded back into her brain. She opened her eyes and found Andrew's face scant inches away. "I searched for hours in the dark," she said. "I kept tripping over things. We have to call Mr. Gibbs and tell him you're safe. There wasn't anyone to help. Bob and Lauren aren't home and the police said it was too soon for them to do anything."

"Good grief. You called the police?"

She went limp while he eased her into a chair. "What should I have done? I was frantic. No one had seen you since yesterday." Greer was amazed that Andrew had not considered the consequences of his actions. He was always so considerate. Now she knew how much she had upset him.

He rocked her, nuzzled his rough jaw against her temple. "I needed a few hours to think. I'm sorry I frightened you," he apologized.

Andrew made Greer sit still while he poured her some coffee and refilled his own, then he called John Gibbs.

The phone rang the instant it was hung up and Andrew put a hand over the receiver. "It's Bob," he said. "Says he's been trying to get me for hours."

Greer watched the play of expressions cross his face.

"It never came off — no — no, it's not canceled, just postponed until tomorrow. Where were you today? Ah. Look, I've had a hell of a day. We'll talk in the morning. Greer's with me now —" He smiled at her and raised his brows. "I don't think that's any of your business, Bob. 'Night." He let the receiver clatter into its cradle.

"He asked something about me, didn't he?" Greer probed.

"Only if you planned to spend the night." He interrupted her forming retort. "He and Lauren are dying to get the two of us permanently tucked up, so don't be mad. Let's take the coffee upstairs."

In the sitting room Andrew lit the fire and fetched Greer a robe from his bedroom.

"Here. Take off those slacks so I can get at your knee. I'd suggest a shower, but —"

"Andrew," she said before he could finish. "You may be bionic, I'm not. It's been a long time since I felt this lousy. All I want is to sleep for a few hours — and know you're safe." Her eyes met his and held them.

He touched her cheek, stroked a thumb over her bottom lip, then reached for the robe. When she'd slipped off the torn woolen pants, he wrapped her in warm terry cloth and left the room to return almost immediately with his medical bag.

Greer watched the top of his head while he worked. Deftly he cleaned the wound with medicated pads, then taped a gauze dressing firmly in position. "We'll give it a day or two, then leave it open." He moved his attention to her face and hands, swabbing at scratches while she winced. "These aren't deep. Need to be kept clean, though."

When he'd finished, Greer held his right wrist and flattened the hand across her thigh. She selected a pad like the ones he'd used and tore the wrapper open, sensing the effort it took to let her help him. "It's your turn, Andrew. You can't always be the crusader," she said more brusquely than she intended.

He grimaced. "Ouch!"

"You'll make it, doctor."

She concentrated on finishing her work on his hands. "I'll do this, then I must call a taxi," she told him.

"No you mustn't."

A shuddery breath slipped past her lips. "We can't start that again. Neither of us has the energy."

Andrew flexed his fingers, studying the knuckles. "No we don't," he agreed. "But since I am the doctor, I insist on keeping you under observation for the next few hours." He checked his watch. "Six to be exact. I need to leave at seven."

"It would be a mistake, Andrew. A reaction to stress. Please —"

"We're going to sleep, my love. Nothing more. In the morning I'll go my way and you'll go yours — for a while. No taxi's going to want to come out here at this hour of the morning anyway, so I'd have to drive you. And you wouldn't want to pressure a sick man," he teased her.

Greer was too exhausted to argue anymore. She drank a few more sips of lukewarm coffee and crawled between Andrew's sheets, falling asleep before he'd finished undressing.

The room was cool when she awoke, spread-eagled across the bed on her stomach. With a sleepy sigh she pulled a pillow beneath her chin and squinted. Music, softly played, came from the sitting room. Then Andrew's ancient travel alarm shrilled suddenly on the nightstand and she crammed the pillow over her head.

"Sorry."

Andrew's voice filtered through thick

down and she gave up the pillow after a feeble struggle. "Rotten clock," she muttered. "Why'd you set it to go off after you got up?"

"I didn't," he said. "Unfortunately I can't shut down all mental systems the way you evidently can. I gave up on sleep an hour ago."

She sat on the edge of the bed and groaned at the pain in her knee. "I want to be with you today. If we could stop by Belle Vista —"

"No, Greer," he told her firmly, rubbing her chin. "You'd distract me, my sweet. And there may be some testimony I'd rather you didn't hear."

Greer opened her mouth to argue, but shut it again. What he said was right. He didn't need the added pressure of knowing she was watching and listening. She shunted against the headboard and sat cross-legged while he knotted his navy tie.

A devastatingly handsome man. Athletically lean in a pale blue shirt and a three-piece suit of silver-gray worsted, so fine it glistened faintly. He faced her again, finger-combing his blue-black hair and grinning. Totally masculine. Every clearly defined line of his body complemented by the perfect fit of his clothes.

"Do I pass inspection?"

"Mmm. How do you feel?"

"Better than I deserve." He bent to kiss her lips and she smelled warm sandalwood. Immediately heat suffused her limbs. Could she fight it forever? Did she really have to?

"*Ciao,*" Andrew said cheerfully. "Why don't you rest a while longer. When Gibbs comes in he'll be happy to drive you to Weymouth for a change of clothes. Could you be here when I get back this afternoon?"

She should say no. "I'll be here, Andrew," she said instead. "Good luck."

For an instant he hesitated, his grazed knuckles whitening around the doorknob. "Later, then." His briefcase hit the wall as he left.

Greer tucked up her feet and hugged her knees. Somehow they had to work through the deterrents to their future together. Or at least give themselves a chance to try. She had to give them a chance. Her fears were throwing up the blocks. Fear of rejection. Fear that their diverse backgrounds would eventually destroy whatever they tried to build. Andrew didn't even know what held her back. He did love her. Every look and touch proved it. Didn't she owe him honesty? Was it right for her to second-guess his reaction to her sterility? She could accept it now — he probably would, too. And they both knew she was a passionate woman. Though she had resisted making love, it was clearly evident how much she enjoyed it when they did.

A door slammed downstairs. Gibbs was early. Probably hadn't slept well, either. It was obvious the old man cared deeply for Andrew.

She straightened her sweater, slipped on the ruined slacks and went into the bathroom. In the age-spotted mirror she glowered at her puffy eyes. The brambles had designed a patchwork quilt on her forehead and a long scratch curved from temple to chin. *Mess* didn't come close. Cold water cleared her head and brought a hint of pink to her cheeks. There was a comb in her jacket pocket but she wasn't sure where she'd left it.

Humming in a monotone, she crossed the hall to the sitting room once more. The jacket lay on the couch. Greer reached into a pocket and stopped, an icy sensation climbing her spine one vertebra at a time.

"You might as well put that on, Mrs. Beckett."

Very slowly, she straightened, clutching the coat to her breast. There was no air in the room.

"It's all right. Keep quiet and nothing will happen to you," the strange voice assured her.

Greer turned around, her throat closing, and stared at the man who stood behind the door. He was nondescript, colorless. Average height, average build, thinning sandy hair, eyes not blue or brown. But his expressionless features struck mindless terror into Greer.

"Put on your coat please, Mrs. Beckett. We're going for an outing. You Americans enjoy our English countryside, I understand."

She sank to the edge of the couch. "Who are you? What do you want from me?" she said, stalling for time.

"Don't make this difficult," he answered calmly. "I already told you we're going for a drive. You don't need to know who I am. You'll never see me again after today."

"I'm not going anywhere with you," Greer insisted. "And you'd better get out before Dr. Monthaven gets back."

"He just left and we both know he doesn't intend returning until this afternoon."

Her belly contracted. "Mr. Gibbs is due any minute."

"Not until ten. Let's go."

"Don't touch me," she croaked. "Stay away."

The man let out an exasperated sigh. "Violence isn't what I had in mind — not for you," he said enigmatically. "But if you don't do as I ask, Dr. Monthaven may not be so fortunate."

Greer wanted to scream. She was being used to exert some sort of pressure on Andrew. "Winston Coover put you up to this," she concluded.

"What you choose to believe is your business." He checked his watch. "We have to leave now."

She went. Securely belted and locked into a vintage, convertible Jaguar, Greer watched the hillsides as they passed, and the valleys, the farmhouses and clumps of trees. First north, then east, then north again. After what seemed like hours she lost her sense of direction and put all her energy into musing and trying to control her shaking arms and legs.

Her driver never spoke. He drove fast but skillfully, and Greer had no idea how far they'd gone when he pulled into a lane that was barely more than an animal track and wound for miles between stands of evergreen trees.

After they stopped he got out and went to the car trunk for a knobby bundle. Greer hung back when he opened her door, but one look into his eyes reminded her of what he'd said at Ringstead Hall. If she didn't do as she was told, Andrew might suffer.

Before she had time to consider her next action, he pulled her from the car, twisted her around and tied her hands. "No! Stop!" She kicked at him.

The blindfold came over her head in a flash. "Kick again and I'll tie your ankles," he warned her. He knotted the scarf securely around her eyes. "You shouldn't be too hard to carry. And I will if I have to," he added.

Greer stood still. For an instant she thought of screaming, then changed her mind. He'd probably gag her.

She felt marshy ground beneath her feet as the man appeared to zigzag endlessly, dragging her behind him. "This is it," he said at last.

"This is what?" Sweat soaked Greer's back.

Hands closed over her shoulders and she was forced to sit. "I brought food and water and extra sweaters. There's a blanket, too," he told her, as if she cared. "You'll get free, eventually. Then, if you're lucky, you may manage to find the track we came in on. Nothing comes up here. Making it to the highway would take you hours. By then it'll be dark." He paused to make certain she was listening. "Your best bet is to stay put until early tomorrow morning. You'll be fine here. When you do start out, take it easy and keep calm."

"Keep calm?" she shouted. "Don't leave me here — please."

She heard his retreating footsteps.

Andrew slammed through the corridor and down the basement stairs to the kitchen. "Gibbs," he yelled. "Gibbs. Where the hell are you?"

He smelled meat pie baking in the oven but there was no sign of John Gibbs. At a full run, Andrew dashed to the stairs and took them two at a time. "Greer —" Her name faded on his lips when he entered the empty sitting room.

"Hello, sir." Gibbs came from the bedroom carrying Andrew's dirty shirt and jeans. "You're early. I wasn't expecting you until —"

"Where is she?" Andrew cut him off.

"Mrs. Beckett — Greer. You took her to Weymouth, didn't you? Why did she decide not to come back?"

The old man's forehead wrinkled. "Was I supposed to pick Mrs. Beckett up, sir? You never said."

Andrew ran his tongue over the roof of his dry mouth. "She wasn't here when you arrived?"

"No, sir. I spoke to the lady yesterday. She was most helpful. But she hasn't been here today."

His bones turned to putty. "Thanks, Gibbs. That's all I wanted to know."

As soon as the door closed, he pulled out the note: "If you want to know where Mrs. Beckett is — drop the case." Typed on a sheet of loose-leaf paper and enclosed in a white envelope, it had been put on his chair in the hearing chamber at the administration building during first recess. Andrew had set off for Ringstead immediately, leaving Bob to make some excuse.

He stuffed the envelope into his breast pocket and went to the phone. Mrs. Findlay's sniffs punctuated her replies to his questions. No, like she told the other man, Mrs. Beckett wasn't at Belle Vista. No, she hadn't been there today or called.

What other man called the boarding-house? Andrew ripped off his tie.

Greer was gone. He went to the window seat and stared out at the tree tops. Between the time he had left for Dorchester and Gibbs' arrival someone came here — to his house — and took her away. Good God. She'd been abducted and the reason was so blatant it hurt. The note spelled it out. He was to be stopped from testifying in the Michael Drake case by whatever means necessary. And they'd found his weak point. Greer.

The one element that made no sense was Coover. The man wasn't a fool. And he was the first suspect anyone would zero in on. Coover would never risk a stunt like this.

Another idea took shape and Andrew ground a fist against his mouth. *Oh, no.* His eyelids felt stretched wide open. *It can't be that.*

He left the side door open when he left. The Mini spewed sprays of damp earth behind its rear wheels as he spun it around and peeled out of the gates. Driving west, he tried to put the pieces together calmly, but they kept overlapping, then blurring. His deduction couldn't be true, yet there was no other explanation.

Bob answered the door himself, dark circles around his sunken eyes. He was clean-shaven and still wearing suit pants and a white shirt with a tie pulled away from the collar. He stared into Andrew's face and turned to walk into the house. Andrew followed him silently to the game room.

His heart hammered against his ribs. This had to turn out to be a bad dream. "Where are Lauren and Simonne?"

"Away." Bob's voice was husky. "Visiting Lauren's folks."

"What did you say after I left the hearing?"

"That you had an emergency." Bob went to a bar by the wall. "Want a drink?"

"No, thanks," Andrew answered coldly.

Bob dropped ice cubes, one by one, into the glass, then paused. He looked quickly at Andrew, then stared through the window for an instant before splashing a huge measure of bourbon over the ice and adding a few drips of water from a jug.

Andrew's nerves threatened to snap. "We have to talk, Bob."

The straight back seemed to sag and Bob swung around. "You know, don't you," he said in a quaking voice. "Damn it all, Andy, you know. I can see it in your eyes. I never meant it to go this far. You've got to believe that. The last thing I wanted was to hurt you."

Iron fingers closed around Bob's windpipe. "The last thing you wanted was to hurt *yourself*," Andrew spat.

"No!" Bob insisted, struggling out of Andrew's grasp. He gulped greedily at the liquor. "You mattered most. Then Lauren and Simonne."

"Touching," Andrew said. "I guess the baby who's not even born is in there somewhere, too."

"I didn't want any of this to happen," Bob insisted.

"Why? Because you care so much about me." Andrew's mouth tasted sour. "So much you arranged to take Greer, then left that note in chambers."

The glass dangled from Bob's fingers. "What a bloody mess."

"Where's Greer?" Andrew demanded.

Bob shook his head slowly.

"Where is she, Bob? If you've done something to her I'll — Where is she, damn you?"

"Safe, Andy. You know me better than that."

"I don't know you at all," Andrew snapped. "That note was a death threat. What are you afraid of? Your reputation?

Do you think that if this hearing comes off — which it's going to — you'll be linked to me and ostracized because of it?"

"You don't understand," Bob answered wearily. The glass rattled on the rim of the pool table. "Andy, I wanted to tell you but I knew you'd walk away from me — for good. I couldn't take that."

Andrew watched Bob's face crumple. He cried noiselessly, making no attempt to wipe away the tears. Panic crept over Andrew. "Where's Greer? Tell me."

"I'll tell you, Andy," Bob assured him. "But first you have to know the rest. You love Lauren and Simonne — I know you do. For their sakes you've got to help me through this thing."

"What? What thing? I want Greer," Andrew persisted.

"Look at me, Andy. Listen — hear me out to the end," Bob said, appealing to Andrew's sense of fairness. "I'm bisexual," he announced. "I've been bisexual since Cambridge."

For seconds Andrew stared at his friend's drawn face. "My God," he said, dropping into a chair. "You can't mean that."

"Neil was the first with me," Bob explained. "But there were others. I stopped when I met Lauren. I love her. You may find that hard to swallow, but it's true. And I love Simonne. I'd rather be dead than have this touch them," he said in obvious agony.

Andrew hid his face.

"For years everything went just fine," Bob rushed on. "Then I ran into Neil again about three years ago in London and everything started again. He didn't mean anything to me, just part of something I don't understand. But I couldn't help it," Bob finished, on the edge of fresh tears.

"Bob." Andrew looked up. "You poor stupid bastard. You could have come to me," he told him. "And there's counseling available. What have you done?"

"Only tried to stop the whole world from knowing what I am," Bob said miserably. "How could I have imagined — even in a nightmare — that one of Coover's boys would stumble on Neil and ask questions about you and me at Cambridge." Bob took a shaky breath and ran his fingers through his hair. "Neil blackmailed me. The guy hates me for running on both sides of the track. He played me off against Coover — threatened to tell him everything. I had no choice but to pay him — my reputation was at stake. It was the only way Neil would agree to help me stop the hearing," Bob said bitterly. "You see, even if Neil didn't testify, there was still a danger that Coover might have come up with someone else who would implicate me while he slandered you."

"Someone else?"

"Neil said he had friends who might talk. My only safe bet was to make you call it off."

"I can't cope with this," Andrew said as he stood and paced the room. "I'm going to ask this once more and if you don't answer I'm calling the police. *Where* is Greer?"

"Neil took her away," Bob finally admitted. "She's fine. Andy, are you going to blow the whistle on me?"

The muscles in Andrew's face hurt. He stopped in front of Bob and hooked two fingers over his tie knot. "Bob," he said quietly, and pulled him closer. "If Greer's okay, I'm going to drop this hearing. I can't destroy three more lives because Coover destroyed one." Andrew could not conceal his hostility. "I'll watch the guy every step of the way until he retires, if I have to," he continued. "And you'll take a leave of absence and get some counseling. You'll pull it all together, Bob. Maybe one day I'll even begin to forget what you did to me. But I want you to tell Lauren. It'll be hard on her, but she'll cope."

"Andy. I'm sorry." Bob sobbed brokenly. "I'll make it. I *can* pull my life together. You'd better go after Greer," he told him. "Neil was going straight back to London once he left her."

"Left her where?"

"Someplace north of Trowbridge. I've got a map. Neil used to go there with friends years ago."

Andrew felt his breathing speed up. "A town near Trowbridge? About two hours or so from here — a bit more? Is she at a hotel?"

"Relax, Andy. She's safe."

"*Don't* — say that again," Andrew seethed.

"Okay," Bob said, recognizing Andrew was on the edge. "The map's of a wilderness area. It's very detailed. Neil made sure she had food and water and extra clothing. I'm sure she'll have enough sense not to try to walk out before morning. I —"

"You son of a bitch. Give me the map. *Now!*"

Chapter 20

☾

The flashlight picked up fresh wheel tracks in the turnaround. Andrew spread the survey map on the hood of the Mini and followed Bob's red line with a forefinger.

Bundling the crackly paper together in one hand, he struck out. What kind of man left a woman alone in the dark — in the middle of nowhere? He frowned savagely. He knew the answer to that question.

On the chart the line ran almost straight in from the left side of the lane, but trees and tangled undergrowth made it impossible not to dodge this way and that. At least he'd had the foresight to borrow a compass from Bob. He gritted his teeth and checked it. Still the right heading.

A circle marked the clearing where Neil had supposedly left Greer. It couldn't be far now. Andrew broke into a run, immediately slapping into a bush that poked at his calves through his suit pants.

He moved on more slowly. Bob's confession came and went in snatches. It was unreal. They'd known each other all their lives. How could he have been so blind? Andrew thought of Lauren, then Simonne. That little girl wasn't going to suffer if he could help it. The hearing must be stopped — Greer would wonder about his reasons but at least for now he'd have to put her off. Later, when he was sure there could be no danger of a slip, he'd tell her. She'd understand then.

A clearing opened in front of him. "Greer," he yelled. "Greer." There was no sound and he pressed his lips together. However he approached she was bound to be shocked. How many shocks could one human being take in two days?

Treading lightly, he started forward and circled the spongy area. Nothing. Muscles in his thighs trembled. He shaded the flashlight beam to study the map again. This had to be the right spot. What if she'd tried to walk out and gotten lost? It could take hours to find her. He'd better save the battery.

An instant before he clicked the light off an irregular shape caught his eye. "Greer," he said softly, then he called more loudly, "Greer." When there was no reply he shone a full beam on the silhouette. A bundle of something. With fingers that tangled together, he loosened the string around the package. A jumble of sweaters and carelessly wrapped sandwiches spilled out to the ground. A bottle of water rolled against a rock and broke into a tinkling spray of shards and liquid that hung, glittering, before it fell. How far would she get without food and water?

Andrew picked up an old army blanket. "You did it, Greer," he muttered aloud. "You wandered away in this maze. My poor darling." Which way would he go first?

A tentative touch in the center of his back brought him spinning around.

"I hid," Greer whispered. "I heard someone coming — or something. I was afraid it might be an animal."

"Ahh —" Andrew dropped the blanket and grabbed her. "Oh, Greer. My sweet, my love. I've never been so scared in my life."

She hugged him, laughing and hiccuping. "Me, either," she admitted, tightening her hold beneath his suit jacket. "He tied my hands and blindfolded me," she explained. "When I finally got loose I kept trying to find the way out, but it was dark and I didn't dare get too far from this place. Andrew, I knew you'd come for me."

"It took me forever to find the lane. I overshot it twice and backtracked before I saw any kind of gap big enough for a car." He felt her soft body pressed to his and closed his eyes.

"How *did* you find it?" she asked. "How did you know where he took me?"

Andrew's mind went blank. Of course she'd ask that. "I got a note," he said slowly. "As soon as I arrived at the administration building. It was a warning not to go on with the hearing." He said nothing more.

"Thank goodness they told you where I was. I don't think I'd ever have gotten away from here on my own."

Andrew kissed the top of her head and gazed into the darkness. He hated lying to her, even by omission. But Greer was out of danger now and there were still others to be protected. "All I want is to get you home." It wasn't all he wanted. The thought shamed and amused him.

"Take me there, Andrew."

Her face was turned up to his. With infinite care he lowered his lips over hers, grazing leisurely back and forth until their tongues met. Her belly moved into his hips and the fire in his loins was immediate. "Time out, darling," he said, turning her away firmly, grateful in that instant for the gloom, although she'd probably felt the beginning of his arousal.

Greer leaned against Andrew's side. What she wanted was to stay in his strong arms forever and to be with him when they exposed Winston Coover. They trod cautiously, following the flashlight's beam.

Inside the Mini, Andrew produced a thermos of coffee and two plastic mugs. He added a measure of whiskey from a flask to Greer's. "Drink that," he told her. "Wrap your hands around the mug."

The smell of the liquor wrinkled her nose as she took a sip. "I memorized his license number," she said. "He drove an early model Jaguar — at least I think it was. Dark green with a black convertible roof. Shouldn't be hard to trace."

Andrew snapped on the ignition and shot the car into gear so abruptly her coffee spilled. "Forget it," he said bluntly.

Her head pressed against the seat. "You aren't serious?" she responded. "Some maniac drives me to the middle of nowhere, ties me up and blindfolds me, then leaves. Forget it? No way. This is going to win your case hands down," she insisted. "We get back, give the information to the police, and watch Winston Coover get nailed. He deserves it, Andrew. You said he did and you were right. The man's a criminal."

"It doesn't matter anymore."

Greer looked at Andrew's profile. His nostrils were flared. "Since when?" she breathed. "This morning nothing would ever stop you from seeing the investigation through. Now it doesn't matter? What happened?"

He drove too fast. "It'll be better for everyone if I let it go."

"I don't understand," Greer persisted, unbelievably confused. "I was kidnapped to stop you from persecuting Coover. That means you're right. And I want the whole world to know it."

The car skidded around the intersection of the highway. "It's not necessary," Andrew maintained. "Coover's got less than two years before retirement. I can watch him. Why risk a big flap?"

She took a long thoughtful swallow of coffee. She was beginning to understand. "Why not?" she challenged. "Because of me, right? Andrew . . . they've won. You're backing off because you're afraid they'll try something else with me."

"Not entirely," he said evasively.

"What then?" Greer was not about to drop it.

"There are other elements to consider," he said, beginning to run out of patience. "Can we leave it at that?"

"No," she replied firmly. "We can't leave it at that. These other elements. Is your professional reputation one of them? And what people think of you personally? Has the possibility of scandal finally gotten to you?"

"I didn't say that," Andrew responded calmly.

Blood hammered in her ears. "Andrew, is it all right for you to be with me as long as no one finds out about Ruby? Would it embarrass you if we married and someone discovered I was a bastard?"

"Hell." He braked so violently they both slammed into their shoulders belts. "What made you say a thing like that?"

"Would it?" Greer insisted.

"That doesn't mean a thing anymore," he told her. "And no one's going to find out." Instantly Andrew regretted his words.

Greer breathed deeply. "So it's all right — as long as it never comes out? But it could," she insisted.

The hand brake creaked on and he

flipped off the ignition. "I don't see how," Andrew responded.

"Okay. At least you admit you've considered it and decided the prospect's unlikely. But Ruby could get down on her luck and come looking for me." Greer glanced over her shoulder. "We can't stay at the side of the road like this. It's dangerous."

"She'd never find you." Andrew said, trying to reason with her.

"There's always a chance."

"Stop this, Greer," he shouted, finally exploding. "I don't care who your mother is, or your father." Andrew lowered his voice when he glimpsed the shimmering tears in Greer's eyes. "My mother left us when I was sixteen," he told her. "The man of the moment was twenty years her junior. I never saw her again. She's probably still living it up somewhere in the south of France but I don't even think about it — it doesn't make me feel less than I am."

"That's different." Greer bit her lip to stop it from quivering. "At least you were legitimate. But you might have told me when you knew how low I felt about Ruby, just in case it helped make me feel less of an untouchable."

Andrew put a hand on her shoulder, but

she scooted close to the door. "Tell me what you want me to say?" he said.

"That you've woken up to the fact that you don't want to be a social outcast after all," Greer said flatly. "And that if I show up at the hearing to testify on your behalf, my undesirable past could come out. They'd be bound to ask questions about me."

"This is absolutely insane, Greer," Andrew said, crossing his arms. "How long did it take you to come up with this gibberish?"

Greer rolled down the window and emptied the rest of her coffee. "I need to get to Weymouth," she answered. "My train for London leaves early in the morning and I haven't finished packing."

She jumped when he threw open the car door, then slammed it behind him with enough force to vibrate the steering column. He'd left on the headlights and she watched him stride ahead and stand with his back to her. She wasn't being fair suggesting he was a snob, but it was the only excuse she could think of to separate them. Regardless of what he said, he *was* giving up his convictions out of concern for her. She was trouble to Andrew Monthaven and he deserved better. All she could offer him was sex. Not social support and not the children he desperately wanted. Leaving him would be her gift, and eventually he'd thank her for it. And she had a sister to consider, a business that couldn't be duplicated in England. They had no common ground and she'd already hurt him enough. For his sake, she must make the break quick and clean.

She saw Andrew turn and heard gravel scrunch with each measured footstep. He got in and started the engine. "We're going to Ringstead and then you'll talk to me," he said without preamble. "If it takes the rest of the night and all of tomorrow, we'll end up understanding each other."

"I'm going to Weymouth," she insisted.

"I'm driving, lady. And you'll go where I take you."

In her agitation Greer caught his sleeve and the car swerved. "Sorry," she muttered. "Don't keep this up, Andrew. It won't get us anywhere."

He ignored her and drove on. When she tried to speak again, he turned on the radio and she slumped into the corner. He intended to make his pitch, whatever it cost them, so why fight? Once he gave up she'd leave as planned and work at forgetting. Angry tears smarted behind her eyelids. Again it was forget-and-get-on-with-it time.

Greer was surprised when the car stopped at Ringstead. She must have dozed.

"Wait for me to come around," Andrew said, opening his door. "I'll have to get some sort of light out here. You can't see a thing at night."

She rubbed her forehead wearily. He was going to pretend their last conversation never took place.

"Give me your hand."

Don't touch me — please. When she didn't move, Andrew took her fingers from her face and pulled her gently from the car.

With each step, pressure mounted in her head. Another confrontation — more accusations and denials, and for what? They didn't belong together, no matter how much she wanted to believe otherwise. She had her life thousands of miles away, and his was here. Andrew would be grateful for her decision one day. Why couldn't he see it now and let her go quietly?

He opened the door and led her inside. "Do you want something hot or a drink?" he asked amicably.

"Nothing, thank you." It was easier if she didn't look at him.

"We'll go straight up then." The airiness

in his tone sounded false. "I'm going to have a double of whatever I pick up first." Sighing deeply, he continued. "What a day. What a couple of days — and nights. You must be exhausted. I know I am."

I'm sorry this has to be so hard on you. "Neither of us has slept much for the past two nights, Andrew. I really do need to get a good night's rest before tomorrow. Would you mind — ?"

"I'd mind," he interrupted her. "I mind every second of this hell you've decided to put me through."

They walked into the sitting room and Greer stood awkwardly, just inside the door. Andrew went directly to a glass-fronted corner cabinet and took out a decanter and two glasses.

Greer's stomach seemed to flatten against her spine. "I don't want anything," she mumbled.

He set down the goblets and splashed each half-full with liquor. "Brandy," he said, ignoring her. "It'll warm us up. I'll start the fire."

"Please, Andrew," she insisted. "Don't bother for me. I have to leave."

"You don't have to do anything," he shouted, then ran a hand over his face. "I know what's happening here, but I won't let it. Do you hear me? I won't let it."

"Don't shout," she whispered. "You seem like a stranger when you sound that way."

"I'm sorry." He took a long, audible breath. "I feel like a stranger to myself. None of this makes any sense and I feel so helpless. There's nothing standing in our way now, Greer. Nothing."

If only he were right. But his vision was distorted by a dozen elements he wouldn't allow himself to face. "Andrew," she said quietly. "For a while I agreed with you — a future for us seemed possible. But that was only because I wanted to believe it. There *are* things standing in our way. I'm not the complacent, lady-of-the-manor type. I need the niche I've made for myself in Seattle and I can't recreate it here." Greer's voice faltered, but she was determined to go on. "In time you'll come to understand what I mean — about other things that wouldn't work, too. Let's simply accept that they exist and not try to hash each one through. It's too painful — for both of us. Go to bed and sleep. Tomorrow it'll all look different. I can find my own way back to Weymouth."

Andrew watched her intently, his face gradually darkening. He lifted a glass and swallowed without taking his eyes off her.

"So reasonable," he said as he came toward her. "Take two aspirins, drink plenty of fluids and go to bed. You'll feel better in the morning." The tone of his voice sent shivers of alarm down her spine. "Sounds like one of my lines. Only nothing is going to be better in the morning if you aren't with me."

"I can't be."

He caught her elbow as she turned away. "You can't? Or you won't stay with me? You're running away."

"No!"

His laugh cut into her heart. "Direct hit, my love? You *are* running away. And we both know the real reason. Don't you think it's time you admitted it — particularly to me?"

She walked a few paces from him and stood, staring blindly at the wall. "You don't know the real reason. You couldn't." Suddenly Greer knew she had no choice but to tell the truth. "I can't have another child," she said simply.

He didn't answer. Had she spoken too quietly? "I had a hysterectomy several months ago. I'm sterile."

Andrew's glass clattered on the coffee table. "I know," he answered. "I've known since we were in Guernsey."

The sound of her own thundering heart was deafening. "How?" she asked him. "You never said anything."

"It wasn't up to me to say anything," he told her. "You had to trust me enough to be honest. I knew when you did, you'd be ready to tell me about the surgery." Instead of the anger Greer had anticipated, Andrew's voice was filled with sadness. "I'd wondered about the second scar on your abdomen," he continued. "It all came together when I mentioned pregnancy. You went to pieces. And you were always edgy around Simonne. At first I thought I'd imagined that, but then I knew I hadn't. Being near children hurts you. I'm so sorry, Greer. I wish Colleen —"

"Shh." She swung sharply to face him. "I'm getting used to it," she assured him. "I already have. And it doesn't hurt me to be with Simonne — I enjoy her. There was nothing anyone could have done about Colleen. No one's to blame." Please, let him understand she didn't want him to feel guilty.

He pressed her hand. "Why didn't you tell me before?"

"You should have children of your own, Andrew. I never met a man more suited to being a father."

She saw the angles of his elbows as he put his hands on his hips. "Thank you. You didn't answer the question."

"I can't give you those children."

"You were an adopted child."

"Yes."

"Your parents loved you as if you were their own," he said, reasonably. "Why can't we do the same thing? I've loved dozens of children who passed through my life. I could certainly love a couple I was lucky enough to keep."

"You make it all sound so simple," she told him. "But it's not, Andrew. You deserve the best and I can't give it to you. We don't belong together."

"You're making excuses to escape, my love." His tone cut her to the quick. "What is it with you? The risk? Are you afraid to let go and risk another total commitment in case it doesn't last forever?"

"Stop it," Greer blurted. "It's not that. I'm over that." Suddenly she was desperate to make him understand. "All the things I set out to do, I've done," she said firmly. "I know I'm a complete woman in every way but one. And I've accepted it. Children don't make me curl up inside anymore. My family isn't the fairy-tale group I'd hoped for, but at least I found and faced them, and in time I'll reconcile myself to that, too. I'm not running away," she insisted.

"I don't believe you," Andrew said, grabbing her arm painfully. "What about the risk? Aren't you afraid to love in case you lose again? Isn't that why you're trying to walk out on me?" His angry face was inches from hers.

Greer twisted from his grip and slumped into a chair. "I *was* afraid to let go of my feelings again," she said heavily. "But that was a mistake and I realized it. Not to love is a loss in itself." In the silence that followed, Greer could hear Andrew's heavy breathing. "But sometimes we think we've found something perfect and it turns out to be all wrong," she went on. "We confuse what we want with love, what we need with love, and a dozen other physical responses with — love. And that's what we did. Leave it at that, Andrew — let me go without turning this into something ugly. We've had special times together and I want to remember them." She appealed to Andrew, but his back was turned toward her. She knew he was terribly hurt and angry.

"Not good enough," Andrew said, without turning around. "If you've achieved all your admirable goals — and you'd like to believe we could be together — why are you leaving?"

Greer reached for the second goblet. The mouthful of brandy she took was too large and she coughed while it burned her throat. "I've got to," she said. Tearing eyes distorted his image. "I've got a life in the States, a business. That's where I belong."

"Crap," he spat, spinning to face her. "There's nothing there to stop you being with me. You're running, Greer. You're terrified of something. For God's sake, tell me what it is." As their eyes met and held, the anger seemed to drain away. Greer dropped her head and rubbed her eyes wearily.

Andrew came to sit on the edge of the table and tried to hold her hand. "If it makes you feel better to think I'm scared — fine," she said. "But let's stop this. I can't take any more."

"I could go to the States, you know. I've been offered jobs. I even considered some of them," he admitted.

She looked at him sharply. "But you didn't take any of them. Why?"

"I was established here," he answered. "And there was no reason then to consider them for personal reasons, although I always thought the opportunities were good. I could consider them now."

"You're established here," Greer repeated slowly. "How long would it be before you regretted giving up what you've worked for — giving up the chance to have your own children — giving up all this?" She waved a hand around the room. "You're English, Andrew, to the core."

He raked his hair. "I'm a man to the core, and human. I want to be with you."

"But I don't want to see the day when you look at me and remember all I've caused you to give up. I couldn't stand it."

"Damn." With a jerk, he stood and went to the window seat. "My window on the world. Hah. I wish I had a glass ball and I could see ahead to a time when all this would be resolved — happily. What do I have to say to convince you?"

Greer joined him and placed a hand on his forearm. "That you'll continue the hearing against Coover," she said softly. "That you don't intend to do anything differently from the way you'd have done it if you'd never met me again."

"That's not possible," he answered. "Nothing remains the same and we have to make changes sometimes. Even if they hurt."

Cold wound around Greer's insides. And changes *do* hurt, she thought. For now what Andrew felt for her would be enough, but it would be wrong and ultimately destructive to allow what he suggested.

"Andrew," she said. "If you give up the hearing and then decide to take a job in the States, who'll keep an eye on Winston Coover? Not quite two years to retirement, isn't that what you said? You can't leave and I can't stay. That's it. I'll always — care about you." *Too much to ruin your life*.

Rain slashed the smoky windows of the terminal satellite at Seattle-Tacoma Airport. The Pan Am 747 made a slow arch and nosed toward the building. Greer peered at shadows moving beyond the tinted glass, but couldn't make out faces. Casey would be there — probably already crowding the passenger entry doors. For the first time since yesterday a small glow of happiness eased the stricture in her throat. She was home.

The solid thud of the loading arm against the plane's fuselage started passengers rummaging in overhead bins. Ahead, a shaft of light flooded in as the door opened, and Greer struggled to her feet, avoiding reaching elbows and crushing bodies. She straightened and joined the shuffling line. *Smile.* Casey had no idea what had happened since they were last together. Some of it Greer would explain — maybe all in time. For now she would hit only the high points. Andrew's face formed a clear picture in her mind, his amber eyes steady and questioning. Greer inched forward. Forget him, she'd told herself constantly since they parted. There would be no forgetting him — ever.

"Greer! Greer — here we are."

She looked up as she left customs and saw Casey's blond head bobbing above the crowd. "Hi," she mouthed, struggling to raise a hand weighted down by a plastic duty-free sack.

Josh Field, relaxed and younger looking than she remembered, hauled her hand baggage to a chair as soon as he could reach her. "We've missed you, Greer," he said. She didn't remember thinking of his smile as boyish, but it was now. "Let's have a look at you."

Casey swooped before Josh could stand back and assess her. Greer held her tall sister and blinked back tears of happiness — and gratitude. Close inspection might give away the misery she intended to hide. Masks took time to fix firmly in place and she hadn't had enough time, yet.

Makeup camouflaged shadows, but the pain her eyes would show if she wasn't careful.

"Oh, Case. It's so good to see you," she said sincerely. "I guess you'll finally let loose of this dark secret of yours. I've been aching to find out who the mystery man is."

"Let's get you home first," Casey hedged. "We're parked in the lot. I'll get the car while Josh helps with your luggage." Casey lifted Greer's carryon. "Aren't you going to ask if the shop's bankrupt yet?"

"Whoa," Greer demanded. "I can spot evasion tactics when I see them. *Who* is the guy — Jack the Ripper?"

Casey set the bag back on the chair and held out her left hand. A square emerald flanked by diamond baguettes glittered on her ring finger.

"It's gorgeous, Case," Greer enthused. "Whoever the guy is, he's got great taste and he knows nothing suits green eyes like oversize emeralds. If you get tendinitis from the weight we can always put your arm in a sling," she teased.

"Greer," Casey shushed her, turning bright red.

"What's the matter?" Greer widened her

eyes at Josh. "I'm glad because my sister finally stops dating deadbeats and finds herself a rich husband, and she doesn't want me to congratulate her."

Josh laughed. He put one arm around Casey's shoulders, the other around Greer's. "I don't think Casey likes you talking about her fiancé as if he weren't here," he joked.

Greer looked from her sister's pink face to Josh's amused gaze. "You two?" She opened and closed her mouth several times. "You stinkers. Why didn't you tell me? I always thought you'd make a fantastic pair, but I was afraid to hope."

"You don't mind?" Casey smiled slowly.

"Mind?" Greer nearly shouted. "It's the best piece of news I've had in — a long time."

They stood together, arms entwined, bodies held in a close triangle. Casey must have been afraid she would resent the engagement to Josh. Greer allowed tears to mingle with her laughter. There was only one man she'd ever want, one man she could never bear to see with another woman, and she'd had to give him up.

Chapter 21

In the distance a burst of red lights blossomed like a gaudy dandelion puff. Greer watched it mushroom and fade, then locked her car while another firework crackled.

Casey would have a fit if she knew she was out alone in the middle of the night, but jostling groups celebrating the New Year made her feel safe, anonymous.

New Year's Eve. Six weeks since she'd left England. Once it would have seemed impossible she'd be thinking of them as the longest weeks of her life. . . . She covered her ears and laughed when a couple stopped to blow a noisemaker at her.

Josh and Casey were at a party. They'd both urged her to go along, but she'd begged off, pleading a migraine. Her headache hadn't been quite that severe, but she'd needed an unshakable excuse to make them leave her alone tonight.

Greer crossed Pioneer Square, passing a

circle of revelers dressed in costume. They revolved, first one way, then the other, singing a discordant, but wildly enthusiastic chorus of "Auld Lang Syne." Detonators exploded on nearby railroad tracks and she broke into a run.

Past the laughing faces. Past grabbing hands that tried to pull her into the conga line they'd begun to form. She didn't stop until she'd stumbled headlong into Post Street and down the steps to Britmania's forecourt.

Breathing heavily, she dug in her purse for the keys and let herself in. For seconds she stood in the darkness, waiting for her racing heart to slow.

Why hadn't she gone with Casey and Josh instead of deliberately making an opportunity to wallow in self-pity? She tossed back her hair and marched around the store, switching on every light. In the storeroom she shed her jacket, started coffee brewing and flipped on a portable radio. Soft jazz — the kind she and Andrew liked. *Damn*. She took a deep, calming breath through her mouth. Tonight she wouldn't think about Andrew.

Bumping her toes with each backward shuffle, she dragged a box into the shop. It had arrived a week earlier, one of several from England she'd put off opening. This was postmarked Salisbury. It would contain the items she'd ordered from the city's Cathedral Guild.

Greer sat on her heels and fished a penknife from the pocket of her white slubbed silk pants. She shouldn't be working in this outfit. It had been outrageously expensive and designed to lift her spirits. An aqua shirt, worn blouson-style, was cinched at the waist by a wide metallic sash in shades of cerise, aqua and black. This evening she'd thought of Andrew while she dressed. He would have looked at her appreciatively and commented on the way her eyes picked up the color of the shirt. . . .

Should she call him? Greer stared at the phone, the palms of her hands instantly damp. Did she dare? It was New Year's Eve, a time for well-wishing, particularly to those you — love. Casey knew something of what had happened in England and had nagged Greer to contact Andrew. Love had turned her younger sister into a starry-eyed romantic. She attacked the box, slitting tape and peeling back flaps with feverish haste. To hear his voice would be so sweet, and such torture. It would only make her cry and achieve nothing for either of them. *If* he'd even speak to her after the way they parted. Anyway, it was after midnight in Seattle, Andrew would already have been in bed and asleep for hours. Soon he'd be waking up to that old alarm of his.

Andrew in bed — asleep. Greer sat on the floor. In sleep he looked abandoned, his arms thrown wide, hair tousled. He'd always tossed until all the covers were on her side of the bed. Several times she'd watched him covertly, feasted on his lithe body, the broad shoulders and narrow hips, the strongly muscled legs and arms. The mental picture made her insides flutter, but it wasn't sexual fulfillment she yearned for now, it was the sight and sound — the simple presence of the man who was constantly in her thoughts.

She reached into the box and removed several potbellied objects. At first she looked at them absentmindedly, then smiled, remembering their appeal. Church mice. Tiny pottery critters with bristle whiskers and overlarge ears, their pointed noses jutting upward. Inexpensive items a child might enjoy or anyone else come to that. Greer decided a cathedral mouse was exactly what she needed on her own kitchen counter.

Beneath the mice she found a layer of clock replicas. Salisbury Cathedral had boasted the earliest known clock. A thirteenth-century contraption with no face. She wasn't sure how it told time, but started to line up several of its miniature copies on a shelf. Later, she'd read the brochure that came with them.

From the storeroom came the distinctive wheeze the percolator made when it was ready. Greer hoisted herself up and went to pour a cup of coffee. When the street door slammed, she almost dropped both pot and cup.

She hadn't locked the door. *Good grief.*

For an instant she considered shutting herself inside the tiny stockroom. No good. There wasn't any way to stop someone from coming in after her. A crawling sensation made her skin tingle. How *could* she have been so careless?

"Greer — are you in here?"

She froze. Coffee sloshed from the mug as she set it down slowly on the packing crate and pushed open the door.

"Greer Beckett!"

No one else had a voice like that. She stepped into the shop, threading and unthreading her fingers. "I'm here, Andrew," she whispered.

He carried a suitcase in one hand and an overnighter slung across his shoulder. Greer took another step and stopped. His tan raincoat was creased and hung open over a navy turtleneck and gray slacks. Shadow darkened his beard area, accenting high cheekbones and the clear lines of his mouth. He looked marvelous and only the field of silent appraisal between them stopped her from rushing to hold him.

"What are you doing here?" she managed at last.

He grinned broadly. "You never sent the decals for my car, so I decided I'd better come and get them."

A laugh caught in her throat. "Funny man. Everyone loves a clown." She blushed. "But what did bring you six thousand miles?"

His tired golden eyes flickered over her. "Needing to look at you," he answered. "To make up for six lousy weeks of not being able to look at you." Without glancing away he jerked a thumb over his shoulder. "That door should have been locked, Greer. Some maniac could wander in here."

"I forgot." *Because all I can concentrate on anymore is you.* Greer brushed dust from her pants before shaking back her hair and

417

meeting his eyes again. "There must have been something else you wanted, Andrew," she said, determined to remain calm.

He dropped the bag from his shoulder and covered the space between them before she could react. His embrace crushed the air from her lungs and her senses immediately registered the familiar scent of his sweater against her cheek.

Cupping her face, he tipped it up toward his. "I came for my wife," he said tenderly.

Everything inside Greer fell away. "I'm not your wife," she whispered.

"But you will be, won't you? You do love me?"

Greer's heart plunged. "I . . . yes, I love you," she told him. "But what I said in England hasn't changed. I can't be responsible for your dropping everything you believe in. And I don't want to make you anxious or ashamed — ever."

Andrew smiled and shrugged out of his coat. "I want to kiss you, sweetheart. But I'd better cool off a bit or I'm likely to ravish you right here on your shop floor." He backed into the only chair in the room and pulled her onto his lap.

Greer studied his finely chiseled mouth, the grooves beside it, and let her eyes wander over his features slowly, too slowly.

This couldn't be happening. Any second he'd say something that would shatter this beautiful bubble in time.

"You look so wonderful," he said.

So do you, Greer thought. She touched silver strands in the blue-black hair at his temple and moaned when he brought their mouths violently together. He turned her, cradling her body with his elbows and forearms, locking her to him until the heavy heat of desire invaded her very soul. Lips grazed. Tongues reached, softened to tease, then thrust their hard, demanding message. Fingers threaded through hair in tender desperation. And their bodies pressed together with a primitive force neither could control.

When they drew back, still holding each other's trembling shoulders, Greer's mouth felt swollen and the pulsing in her breasts swept downward between her legs. She tugged free and stood, turning her back. The chemistry would always be there, but it wasn't enough. After a lengthy pause, Andrew cleared his throat and spoke.

"I couldn't get a direct flight to Seattle," he said. "Had to come via New York or I'd have gotten in this afternoon. I found your home number but there was no reply. Coming here was a last ditch effort to reach you tonight. I really thought you'd be at a party."

"Why would I be at — oh, New Year's Eve." She felt disoriented, foolish.

"Greer," Andrew said softly. "There are things I've got to tell you."

"You're tired, Andrew. You should sleep first." It was too soon. She needed time to regroup.

"Sleep?" he echoed. "Oh, I don't think so, my love. I don't intend to sleep again until I've said everything I came to say."

My love — my love. Greer spun to face him. "I just made coffee. And I need some if you don't."

She went to pour a second cup, pausing in the doorway before rejoining him. His eyes were closed, his head resting against the chair back. An invisible hand twisted her heart. "*My* love," she mouthed silently.

"Drink this," she said, sinking to the floor in front of him. She held up a mug.

"Thanks." Andrew sat straighter. "I'm going to get out all I have to say fast," he warned her. "The strain of keeping it in and feeling totally alone is more than I can stand any longer. And I'm not very proud of some of it," he added.

Greer raised her brow, but said nothing.

"Remember how I accused you of not trusting me?"

She nodded.

"Well. After you left I realized I'd done my own share of holding things back," he admitted. "If I'd trusted you enough and told you the whole story that night we parted, I could have saved us both a lot of heartache." Steam from the mug veiled his face briefly when he drank. "The hearing did go on in the end."

They both heard her intake of breath. Greer smiled up at him. "You decided to do it after all. Andrew, I'm so glad."

"It wasn't me," he told her. "It was Michael Drake's family who insisted on it. Isn't that something? You think decisions are in your hands — that you're in control — but it doesn't always work out that way. After what I'd said to Michael's parents, they decided to demand the case be heard. And Coover's negligence came out, his steady loss of interest in his work. They took away his license — not that it'll hurt anything but his inflated ego. The guy's filthy rich. The surgeon and pathologist got suspensions and an operating-room nurse was reprimanded — all for concealing evidence."

Greer dropped her forehead to her

knees. "Thank God. But I don't see what that has to do with trust between us."

Andrew's fingers parted the hair at her nape and he rubbed slowly back and forth beneath her collar. "That's because I'm still skirting it." Pausing briefly, to kiss her neck, he went on. "I didn't want to go on with the hearing because of Bob. Or maybe more because of Lauren and Simonne." When she lifted her head, he smoothed the side of her face and hooked a knuckle beneath her chin. "The man who took you away was Bob's — friend, Neil Jones. It was Bob who was determined to stop that hearing."

"But why?" Greer frowned. "I don't understand. It always puzzled me that he didn't back you up, but I began to believe it was out of concern for you. He came to me, Andrew," she admitted. "He looked awful and begged me to stop you from ruining your career. Only I knew how much getting at the truth meant to you, and I couldn't bring myself to interfere."

Andrew gnawed his bottom lip and touched his forehead briefly to hers. "I should have told you."

"Told me what? Don't drag this out, Andrew," she said, moving away to see his face more clearly.

"Bob's bisexual," he said bluntly. When Greer tried to interrupt him with questions, he stopped her. "Please don't stop me until I get through all this." Taking a deep breath, he continued. "He confessed it to me after Jones took you from Ringstead. Neil and Bob were — damn it, I hate this. They were lovers at Cambridge. Bob straightened out and married, and everything went just fine until he ran into Neil again a couple of years ago. They've been seeing each other whenever Bob had an excuse to go to London. I never knew anything about it, but I did share a house with both of them while we were in college." Greer squeezed Andrew's hand in encouragement, and he raised it to his lips for a brief kiss.

"When Coover was looking for mud to sling at me — hoping to get me off his back — one of his henchmen stumbled across Neil and made a connection with me. I'd even seen Neil myself — in a restaurant a few months ago. They were going to make something out of that — or so Bob said. But what really had Bob running scared was the possibility that the truth about his private life would come out and ruin both him and his family. Neil played on that, threatened to incriminate Bob at the hearing if he didn't pay him off. Bob paid, but the hearing was still a threat and he tried to get at me through you, to stop the thing. That's it. I was afraid if the hearing took place and Neil was brought into it, Bob would be destroyed professionally, and Lauren and Simonne with him — and the baby they're expecting."

A pall of silence thickened in the tiny shop.

Tears sprang suddenly to Greer's eyes. "Lauren loves him," she said, thinking of her friend. "I don't understand how a man could do that to his family. And Simonne. Good Lord, Andrew — what will it do to them?"

He stood and hauled her to her feet. "They'll be all right," he assured her. "Bob's name never came up when the case was heard. Too many other people were scrambling to save themselves. It all sounds impossible when you first hear it, but Bob's a strong man."

She shook her head.

"He is, Greer. He's had a rough time, but he knows what he wants now."

"I don't see how they can work it out," she said miserably. "Hold me, please."

Andrew folded her close, rocking gently. "Bob's taken a leave of absence," he explained. "He's going to get counseling. All they know at the hospital is that he's exhausted and needs a complete rest."

"Lauren knows the truth?"

His fingertips traced her spine. "Yes. Bob told her. She's got guts, that lady. A lot of women would have been blown away, but not Lauren. As long as I've known her she's been Bob's shadow. Now she's the strong one. It'll work," he said with conviction.

"You didn't want me to go to the police about that man in case they found him and he told them about Bob," she said as she sought the rough skin along his jaw with her lips.

"Can you forgive me for not telling you at the time? I was so afraid of a slip and I'd promised Bob I'd make sure there wouldn't be one."

"I forgive you — I understand. It took me weeks to be open with you. Oh, Andrew." The insistent brushing of his thumbs on the sides of her breasts sent her against him, and she felt the slight rotation of his hips against her stomach.

Andrew's breathing quickened. "Leaving England and coming to you was the one way I could think of to prove how much I love you."

"Leaving England?" Greer leaned away. "What do you mean?"

"Just that, my darling. I told you I'd been offered jobs in the States before. When I contacted your children's hospital here they told me there was a position available if I wanted it. I said I did and started packing. My place in Dorchester has already been filled."

Greer stared at him. "You've given up everything you worked for?" she said, struggling to believe this was really happening. "It isn't fair. That's why I couldn't stay with you — you have too much to lose. And for what? I don't have enough to offer."

"Mmm." He inched the neck of her shirt aside and bent to kiss her softly swelling flesh. "You're wrong," he whispered. "*You* had too much to lose, and everything to offer: yourself. It wouldn't be easy for you to start again in England. It *will* be easy for me here — and exciting. Opportunities for research and really achieving something in my field exist here. They aren't so plentiful in England." Andrew continued to explore the front of her shirt, pushing the silken material aside as he went. "Can we talk about this more later?" he said thickly.

"You intend to live here?" His mouth

found her nipple and she shuddered.

"Only if you'll let me."

She slid a hand around his neck. "What about children?"

"One step at a time," Andrew said, fondling her hair. "We don't have to settle everything this instant."

"Darn," Greer laughed, then sniffed. "I'm going to cry."

"You're so beautiful when you cry, Greer," he said as he straightened. The muscles beside his mouth trembled. "For the second or third or who knows how many times — will you *please* be my wife?"

He closed his eyes and she stood on tiptoe to kiss each lid. "Yes," she said. "Yes."

"I began to wonder if we'd ever be alone." Andrew crossed the room and threw himself flat on the bed. "Come here, Mrs. Monthaven."

Greer poured champagne into two fluted glasses and handed one to Andrew, evading his reaching fingers. "Not until I at least get to put on the confection my sister bought me to wear on my wedding night," she said.

"Do it then," Andrew ordered, grinning wickedly. "But it's a waste of time."

In the bathroom she unpinned the corsage of baby Hawaiian orchids from her mohair lace jacket. Carefully, she filled a water glass and propped the flowers inside. The short jacket and floating chiffon dress were of palest ivory, and the only jewelry she wore was a single strand of pearls and matching earrings — a gift from Josh.

The three weeks they'd spent clearing away formalities for this day had seemed endless while they lasted. Tonight Greer hardly remembered them. Finally she and Andrew were where they belonged. Together. She was glad they had chosen to remain in Seattle for their honeymoon. Andrew wanted to learn as much as possible about the area and there was still a lot he hadn't seen.

While she undressed she relived the simple wedding ceremony in a small church near the condominium she and Casey had shared. Andrew's face came to her clearly, the tender, almost tremulous expression in his eyes when he slid the ring on her finger and the tears of happiness he'd made no attempt to hide while she placed his.

Casey's gift was made of shimmering amethyst satin. Greer slid the gown over her head and let it fall sensuously over her body. Spaghetti straps, no thicker than threads, held the classically cut bodice in place — just. The fabric scintillated over every curve and indent, outlining her erect nipples, the dip at her navel, the mound between her legs. She ran her hands over the sleek surface and colored slightly. She wanted to excite him, to draw them both closer and higher than they'd ever been.

Andrew was no longer on the bed when she emerged. Sheer curtains billowed inward from the Edgewater hotel room's open windows. She picked up her glass and went out onto the veranda. He stood with his elbows on the railing, staring toward Elliott Bay.

"Hi," she said. "You'll freeze out here."

He turned to look at her. "Not with you looking like that. But you will." Quickly he draped his jacket around her shoulders and clinked his glass to hers. "To the moontide."

Greer pressed close and shuddered as his hand surrounded her breast beneath the gown. She couldn't think. He kissed her mouth while his fingers avidly caressed her yearning flesh.

"Drink," he ordered at last.

She took a sip and tried to remember his toast. "What are we drinking to?"

He moved behind her, wrapping an arm around her ribs. "See the way the moon makes a vivid blue path on the incoming tide," he whispered into her hair. "I've always thought of it as the moontide. I told you how I used to watch it do that on Ringstead Bay. The first time I saw you your eyes reminded me of my moontide."

"I'm glad we can go to your house whenever we want to," she said. "It wouldn't seem right if you'd given it up completely."

Andrew rested his chin atop her head. "Gibbs will keep the home fires burning. We'll go there regularly — if you want to."

"I'll want to." She smiled and wriggled to face him. "Let's go to bed."

"Anything you say." He led her inside and within seconds the ethereal gown was an iridescent puddle at Greer's feet. He shed his own clothes and settled her on the bed, stretching his length beside her while he stroked every inch of her waiting body.

Their lovemaking was languorous at first, then frenzied, its explosive climax leaving them spent and clinging, damp limbs entwined.

"Sweetheart," Andrew said when their hearts and breathing calmed. "When you left after Colleen died, there was no light in your eyes, only pain. I used to dream over and over again of finding a way to awaken the moontide in them."

"You found the way, darling — loving me."

About the Author

C

Stella Cameron is the bestselling author of more than forty books, and possesses the unique talent of being able to switch effortlessly from historical to contemporary fiction. In a one-year period, her titles appeared more than eight times on the *USA Today* bestseller list. This British-born author was working as an editor in London when she met her husband, an officer in the American air force, at a party. They now make their home in Seattle, are the parents of three grown children and have recently become grandparents.